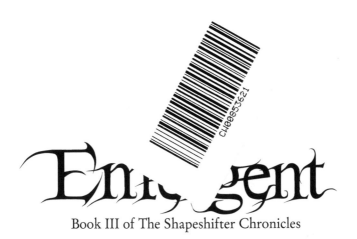

Emergent

Book III of The Shapeshifter Chronicles

Natasha Brown

Copyright © 2014 Natasha Brown
All rights reserved.
Edited by Scott Andrews
No part of this book may be reproduced or transmitted in any form or by any means, electronic or mechanical, including photocopying, recording, or by any information storage and retrieval system, without permission in writing from the author.
This is a work of fiction. All names, characters, places, and events are the work of the author's imagination. Any resemblance to real persons, places, or events is coincidental.
www.theshapeshifterchronicles.com

ACKNOWLEDGMENTS

I would like to thank my fans for being patient and my family, who supported me over the last nine months while I focused on writing this book in my free time. I would not have been able to write a story centered around true love if it weren't for my husband and children.

TABLE OF CONTENTS

CHAPTER 1

Ana stared at the cream-colored wall through the murky light and felt every second pass like pebbles dropped onto her back. The mattress beneath her was hard and uncomfortable. It caused her to toss and turn all night long. Or maybe it was the memories of yesterday that kept her up. How could she even think to dream at night when Chance, the person her heart beat for, was gone? Had left. Dreams were for people with hope.

Ana readjusted under the sheets for the millionth time that morning, turned over to see that Lifen, her new mentor, wasn't in the neighboring bed. She hadn't heard her leave, but Ana supposed that wasn't very surprising, especially for a woman who was both a shapeshifter and a healer. Stealth clearly wasn't an issue for Lifen, considering she'd been checking in on Ana over the last four months without her knowledge.

"Are you awake, Ana?"

A beam of light poured into the room and Ana looked over at the sliding glass door that led to their hotel balcony. Lifen peered at her from between the thick curtains. Her long black hair was twisted into a bun on top of her head and she blinked her narrow, dark eyes in Ana's direction.

"Yeah." Ana's dry throat made her voice scratchy.

"You did not sleep, did you? I hoped you would get some rest..."

Ana shook her head, pulled out the overstuffed pillow she was lying on and pressed it against her face to muffle her weeping. Tears soaked into the fabric and cooled her swollen eyes. She thought she had cried herself dry, but the pain wouldn't go away.

"Maybe if you talk about it, it will make you feel better." Lifen's fingers touched her shoulder. The torrential emotion dwindled away so she could breathe again.

Ana threw the pillow aside and rubbed her temples. When Lifen joined her on the edge of the bed, she rested her hand on Ana's back. The skin under her nightshirt tingled and the heaviness she had just experienced lifted momentarily.

"I keep seeing Balam's death." Nothing could stop Ana's tears from pouring out again as the words formed at her lips and hung in the air. She could still envision Markus, Chance's cousin, poised on top of the man who'd taught them both so much over the last two months, and the last moments of his life. Balam, Chance's great-grandfather, had lived through the Spanish invasion, only to die a senseless death at the hands of a boy suffering from the shifter sickness.

Ana brushed away her tears and held her palms to her eyes. She wished the sickness didn't exist. It was the root of their problems. Too many had died because of it, and now Chance was infected, poisoned with the voices of unbalanced shifters.

"Are you sure Chance has the sickness?" Ana whispered, feeling foolish for asking the question. She avoided Lifen's eyes as she awaited the answer.

"You said Chance killed the boy who was stalking you, correct? That boy, Markus, had the sickness and ended the lives of many other shifters. If Chance was beside him as the energy wave was released, then he could not have avoided it. He is infected."

Ana nodded and her cheek quivered while she recalled the darkness that crept into his handsome face moments after the death of his cousin. His penetrating gaze had moved over her body with violent hunger and his icy stare had chilled her heart. The softness behind the excited gleam in his eyes was gone. Just that lurid glare remained, and then he had vanished.

7

What if he was just upset about Balam's death and that's why he left? In her heart she knew the truth. His protective nature would never allow him to abandon her unless it was in her best interest. And being around her would be too great a temptation for a shifter who couldn't control his hunger for power.

Now that her abilities were awakened, she would be too enticing. Without their knowledge, when Chance saved her life so many months ago, he'd planted a seed of power within her, awakening both the ability to shapeshift and to heal. She'd only discovered that fact yesterday when she'd shifted into a horse on her way to help Chance.

"When I said I'd go with you, you promised to teach me how to save him so I can cure him of the sickness, but I *still* don't understand why we have to leave here." Ana sat up and her voice rose with every word. Her lip trembled as she thought about leaving Mexico and the last place she saw Chance.

"Calm yourself," Lifen said through pursed lips, but then her face softened and she continued. "I must return home to Canada to my other students—it isn't safe for me to leave them alone. I have already been away from them too long. There I can teach you what you need to know about healing. Sadly, you are not able to help Chance yet, since you truly just came into your powers yesterday. It is not something a beginner can do. It will take practice and time, but I sense so much potential in you. I see you becoming truly great."

"But what about Chance? It feels wrong abandoning him here. I can't leave him. I *won't*. What if he comes back looking for me?" Ana's throat tightened again.

Lifen adjusted on the bed to face her. "What if he does? He killed the power-hungry shifter. You tell me Chance was a kindhearted person. But even the most peaceful shifter would be poisoned by the voices and memories from just one unbalanced shapeshifter. If he comes back for you, he will not be the same person you grew to love. It would be safer if you remained hidden from him."

Ana stood up and brushed past Lifen. She stomped over to her bag and pulled out a set of clothes. A bra dangled from her hand as she pointed at Lifen. "Well, what about you then? If I'm not ready, why can't *you* help him?"

Lifen rose gracefully from the edge of the bed and pulled open the drapes, letting in the morning light. "When trying to free the mind of a shifter who's been imprinted with another's personality and memories, that shifter must be willing to let the healer in. It is not as simple as healing a wound or soothing an achy belly. It involves the psyche and removing foreign energy. You must be careful because many things can go wrong. Chance does not know me. He will naturally be distrustful, which will make it a challenge. If he resists me, then I cannot help him, because it will only cause harm."

"But what if he *wants* to be healed? I know he would, if I could just find him and talk to him." Ana's throat tightened again and she took a deep breath, trying to force her airway open. She was desperate for the opportunity to put things right. Her fear of leaving the area without at least trying to find him and help him was overwhelming.

It was all because of his instinct to protect her. Although she'd threatened never to forgive Chance if he sacrificed himself for her again, it wasn't anger that poisoned her heart, it was guilt. If it weren't for her, he may not have been forced to make a choice that put his life in danger again. Maybe she could have done something differently. When she ran into the jungle to find Chance, she'd intended to help him, but in the end she'd been his downfall.

Lifen waited in silence as Ana remained trapped in her tortured thoughts. Finally, her mentor spoke. "Even though I do not think this will yield the result you seek, I will help you track him so you may try to convince him. But I do not wish to see you hurt. I did not wait patiently by only to lose you now."

"Oh, thank you, Lifen! He wouldn't hurt me, I'm sure of it. He'll listen to me and you'll be able to help him so we can all go back to your place together. It'll work out, I know it will." But she didn't know it. Ana's confidence went only as far as her words.

Lifen gave Ana a sympathetic smile. Ana wasn't the only one who knew her words were empty. "Alright, young one. We must collect our things so that we may revisit the last place you saw him. The longer we take, the harder it will be to catch his scent."

Ana darted around the room and crammed her things into her travel backpack. It was hard for her not to fold everything neatly and do a proper job of it, but she didn't care if her clothes got wrinkled. It didn't matter. All that mattered was finding Chance as quickly as possible.

"What about your stuff?" Ana asked Lifen after she accounted for all of her things.

Lifen tucked a stray hair into her bun and slipped an elegant silk purse over her shoulder. "I have all of my belongings on me. Shifters must learn to travel light." She paused, glanced at Ana with her lips upturned. "You may be going a little lighter than I recommend, Ana."

Ana frowned and looked down. She only had on her sleeping shirt and underwear. "Right."

Lifen wandered gracefully to the door, her pale blue sarong curled out behind her as she moved. Ana unzipped her bag and pulled out a pair of jean shorts and a fresh T-shirt. She shoved her jammies back into her pack and pulled her hair into a ponytail. She hadn't even seen herself in a mirror yet, but it would have to do.

Morning light poured in through the open door and Ana rushed to catch up to her mentor. While they wandered through the hotel hallway, Ana thought of something and cursed under her breath. She wasn't sure which would be more challenging—catching up with Chance, or telling her mom she wasn't coming home just yet.

CHAPTER 2

"Mom? Are you there?" Silence met Ana's ears while she pressed the phone against her head.

"I'm here, I'm just speechless. I don't know what to say to you. Clearly you're choosing to do whatever you want now that you're an adult. I don't know why you're even checking with me anymore."

"Mom, c'mon, don't be that way. You should know what it's like when life has its own plans for you. Things change." Ana couldn't help but start tearing up again. Her mom was going to get a front row seat to the waterworks show.

"Ana—are you crying? Is everything alright?" Her mother's bitter tone turned to concern.

She couldn't respond without breaking down entirely and she didn't want to do that. She couldn't tell her mom what was really happening because she didn't really know herself. Ana had no idea if Chance was going home or had contacted his parents. She knew nothing. It was best to pretend everything was fine with him, right? Confused and unsure of herself, she went with that choice, hoping it was the best route for now.

"Baby, I can tell you're upset. It's just that Eva and I miss you. It's been almost two months since I saw your shining green eyes. Ever since your heart healed, you haven't looked back and I admire that in you, but I just worry that you're not thinking things through."

Ana breathed out slowly and prepared to speak. "I know you worry about me, Mom. I'll be okay. I'm just wrapping up here and then I want to head up north."

"Where are you going?"

"Just Alberta, Canada—not far from home. Heard there are some really remote, beautiful places to visit and get away. Maybe I can stop by on the way up." Ana looked at Lifen sitting next to her in the taxi car. She winced, hoping she wasn't pushing her mentor by suggesting another delay. She was, after all, insisting they search for Chance. The strained expression on Lifen's face made Ana stare out the window. "I don't want to regret my life. I need to see the world before I settle for the daily grind of working and paying bills."

"What about money? Do you have any left? Can you even afford to go off like a gypsy?"

Melissa's voice rose higher and higher with every word spoken. Ana didn't have the energy to try to smooth things out. She would have to later. "I still have money. And if I need any more then I can just get a job or something. Listen, I really didn't mean for this to turn into a fight." The connection started getting scratchy and Ana simply didn't have the strength to continue with the conversation. "Hey Mom? You're cutting out—why don't I check in with you in the next couple of days and let you know where I'm at, 'kay?"

"Okay baby, but this discussion isn't over yet. Love you and travel safe, you hear me?"

"Of course, Mom. Love you."

"Love you too, baby."

Ana ended the call and held the phone in her hand for a minute before slipping it into her backpack. The call hadn't gone as horribly as she'd thought it would, but it left her feeling even emptier than before. Her old life was a distant memory. For a brief period over the summer everything had been perfect. Her heart had no longer prevented her from doing the things she wanted to do. They'd been safe and in love.

"Making plans?" Lifen's voice snapped her back to the present.

Ana sighed and threw her hands in the air. "She's my mom. It was hard enough leaving to come here with Chance. I know you need to get back soon—I'm sorry, but convincing her to let me go to Canada is a hard sell if I don't work it a little."

Lifen sat quietly next to her and didn't respond.

Ana was on edge and she knew it. She was snapping at her mentor and she barely knew her. It probably wasn't a good idea getting too irritable with her. "Sorry. I just—"

"I am trying to remember back to my youth, which was a very long time ago. I am confident I never treated my teachers in this way, but do not worry, I surround myself with younglings. I am familiar with emotional outbursts."

The taxi driver spoke over his shoulder, letting them know they were getting close. Ana stared out her window and recognized the area. They were approaching Ek Balam's entrance, the place in Mexico where Chance and Ana had begun their search for his great-grandfather.

"You don't want to go by Sanchia's house?" Ana said, "I could ask her if Chance has been there. I know how to get to the creek leaving from her home."

Lifen pulled some cash out from her pouch and handed it up to the driver, who pulled into the ruins' parking lot. "I know my way around the area very well, Ana. I have been keeping an eye on you without your knowledge."

She guessed Lifen was right.

When the car stopped, Ana thanked the driver and they got out. There were only a few other vehicles in the lot. Memories flooded her thoughts, and she recalled coming here with Chance on their quest to find Balam. She relived his hopelessness, his hand clutching hers, and his sad hazel eyes. Ana would give anything to smell his spicy scent today and feel him rushing up behind her in their playful game.

"Ana?" Lifen held her hand out to her as she waited in the shade of a Ceiba tree. Its massive spiky trunk rose high above the jungle and its dense, green foliage was shaped like a leafy umbrella.

Right. Time to find him. They both wanted to do this quickly. Granted, for different reasons, but it was a shared cause.

She jogged to catch up with Lifen and followed her to the edge of the lot. Her teacher looped her decorative pouch from her shoulder and handed it to Ana.

"It is best that I take my travel form, and the form that best suits tracking. Will you carry my belongings for me?"

Ana nodded and slipped it around her neck. "Are you sure you want to shift right here?"

Lifen gave a polite nod and led Ana into the trees and off the road. They wound through some narrow saplings and her mentor's lithe body moved ahead like a shadow touching the earth. She disappeared behind a tree. A moment later, a scruffy dog darted out with her ice-blue sarong in its mouth. The creature jogged up to Ana, yipped, and dropped the cloth at her feet.

Ana leaned down and picked it up. She couldn't help but give the canine a scratch along its spine, and she felt its muscles twitch and contract at her touch. She had to admit, she liked Lifen most when she was a dog.

"Okay, lead on—just don't lose me out here."

Lifen barked and wagged her tail. Her shaggy form trotted away. Ana adjusted the strap of her backpack and set off after her. She was used to trekking through the jungle with Balam and Chance, so she had no issue keeping up with her mentor. However, she had no idea where she was.

"You know where you're taking us?" Ana called out to the dog while it wound its way between the narrow tree trunks.

Without slowing, Lifen turned her snout to the side and yipped again, but this time she was a bit gruffer. Ana figured it was dog for *stop your complaining and keep up*, so she dug her feet in and picked up the pace. Droplets of water absorbed into her clothing as she brushed past hanging leaves. The downpour from the day before left the ground moist and it smelled of clay. It was slippery in spots, but her balance had improved over the last few months, which helped her navigate through the mud.

Her blood pounded in her ears, nearly covering the sound of the birds above as they squawked at the intruders. Exercise felt good. The pinch in her lungs and the strain on her muscles forced her worries away, if only briefly. After a while, the surroundings grew familiar and they slowed.

Water coursed down from the hillside and into a muddy valley. A downed tree trunk stretched across the creek and Ana had to fight the urge to turn around, to close her eyes and force the memories of yesterday away. The engorged waterway had shrunken down and was no longer an angry torrent, but a peaceful stream again. It almost seemed like a different place.

Lifen scurried down the embankment to the log and ran across. Ana thought of Chance, trying to remind herself why she was there, and forced herself to follow her mentor. When she reached the other side, she watched as Lifen pressed her snout into the earth throughout the clearing.

"This is where it all happened, but it looks like you already figured that out." Ana scuffed her shoe in the dirt. "This is where Chance killed Markus in yaguar form. Sanchia came here with me and helped me push his body into the river. Well, it was more of a river yesterday. This is the last place I saw Chance. After the energy burst, he just looked at me and flew away."

Ana swallowed the lump in her throat and pointed in the direction he had disappeared. Lifen lifted her nose in the air and whined.

"Now what? Do you smell anything?"

The dog trotted up to her and pulled the blue sarong from her grasp. Ana turned away. Moments later, Lifen's voice answered her question.

"I can still smell a trace of all four of you here. If you had the ability to shift and fly with me we could go search for him quickly, but you only just awakened your abilities. It will take too long if we keep moving like this."

Ana spun around to face her mentor. Wrapped in the fabric, Lifen frowned at the skies. Ana grew worried. Lifen wasn't suggesting they abandon the plan, was she?

"Well, I can try to shift," Ana said. "Just give me a chance—I don't want to be the reason we can't catch up to him."

Lifen stopped and stared at Ana. It reminded her of Balam when he studied her the first time they met. She had no idea what Lifen was thinking, but she wasn't about to take no for an answer, so she dropped to the ground and crossed her legs in the same way she had seen Chance prepare countless times before.

"I can see you are determined. I admire that. I will allow you to try—but if you are unable to transform, then I will need to scout ahead and come back for you. Most younglings struggle to shift into a new form. You only just came into your power yesterday, so do not be hard on yourself if you cannot do it." Lifen settled across from Ana and touched the center of her chest. "Close your eyes and take long slow breaths."

Ana did as she said and let her lids slide shut. She slipped into a steady breathing rhythm and focused on the rise and fall of her chest. Her muscles relaxed. It was almost as if her body sank into the hard, clay soil.

"Very good. Every human has energy within themselves, but shifters and healers contain much, much more. It is the difference between a battery and a power plant. We have the ability to absorb energy around us. Every beginner needs to be able to sense their own energy, so that when you call to it, you know where to find it. Focus inward and let yourself feel it, see it in your mind."

Ana's heart raced with excitement. She realized suddenly that this was the moment she'd been daydreaming about since she found out Chance was a shapeshifter. Well, if she was honest, it had been longer. For as long as she could remember, she'd longed to fly free like a bird, allowing air currents to carry her through the skies. Becoming another creature had its appeal. She only wished Chance was here to share her moment.

Ana pinched her eyes shut and steadied her breathing. He would see it soon enough, she told herself. They would be back together—today even.

Just two days ago, Balam had helped her realize her power. She recalled the warmth that radiated from her and the butter-yellow glow. At the time, she'd had no idea where to find it until it snuck up on her. She hoped it was like riding a bike.

Her attention focused inward and she called out to her power. She knew it was there, somewhere. Just knowing that it was inside her gave her confidence. Slowly, a rising tide of energy built up in her chest and she felt it pull into a ball, like the sun.

"Have you found your power?" Lifen whispered from somewhere nearby.

Ana nodded with her eyes shut, frightened anything could break her connection.

"Very good. What animals have you mapped?"

Ana had heard Chance, Niyol and Balam discuss animal mapping on many occasions before, but had never experienced it herself. Even yesterday, it had taken her by surprise when she'd shifted into a horse while she was desperately trying to get to Chance. She'd had no idea she had the power to do that. The faint image of the horse, traced with blue iridescent lines skirted her thoughts. One moment she was freaking out about reaching Chance, and the next she was stumbling around on four legs.

The more Lifen spoke to her, the more her energy eased away. "I haven't mapped anything myself. I shifted into a horse yesterday out of nowhere."

"A horse?" Even though her eyes were closed, Ana could hear the excitement in Lifen's voice. "I understand you do not have any experience shapeshifting, but you do have another's memories of it. You must try to access those memories of the animals Chance shifted into if you want to shift yourself."

She would have to resurrect one of Chance's memories to be able to shift into an animal. Either that or she'd have to try to map one herself, and she got the feeling Lifen didn't want to spend the time teaching her that skill just now.

The only problem was she didn't know how to summon one of his memories. Chirping birds echoed all around her, and she grew frustrated. It felt like they were chiding her, teasing her. Another sound, much closer, met her ears and she was startled to realize it was her. She was crying.

Lifen's hand touched her shoulder and she reluctantly opened her eyes. "It is okay. Let me go track him and I will come back to you soon. Do not be hard on yourself. You only just came into your impressive power yesterday."

"No, but I want to come with you," Ana whispered through tear-stained lips.

Lifen rose to her feet. "It will take too long if we go together. I will track him down and come back soon. Stay here."

In one motion, she reached for the fastening point of her sarong, opened it and took to the skies as a blue bird. She hovered above Ana, squawked and darted off through the wiry growth.

Ana's hands knotted into fists and she pounded the ground. A roar escaped her mouth, so loud that she felt it reverberate in her lungs. Chatter from the surrounding wildlife quieted for a moment, and Ana almost expected to see a cougar emerge from the bushes. Her fingers stung from the blow to the solid, clay earth and one knuckle started to bleed.

Her heart raced and all she could think about was Chance. All the times he had come to her rescue and she couldn't even do the same for him. If only she could have shifted into a bird, or something worthwhile. If only Balam were still alive and Chance were himself again. If only.

***

Chance pushed through the underbrush, lifted his muzzle and sniffed the air. His paw snagged on a branch, so he lifted it higher and forced his way past. He had lost track of time. He'd been traveling all morning as a bear and he'd been moving since yesterday without sleep. He didn't want to shift back to his human shape. Being in his *nagual* form seemed to help buffer the voices in his head. There was no other animal that he'd rather be than the grizzly. His needs were limited only to his primal instincts. Survival. That was all he allowed himself to focus on.

Memories clamored to barge into his consciousness. Like a closet filled with too many things, waiting for someone to come along and open the door and let everything tumble free. He was frightened of them, and he hid himself in the only way he knew how. If he focused on one paw at a time, lumbering wherever his feet took him, it helped. Helped keep him from the pain.

Chance had no idea where he was going, but he knew he was heading north. What he really needed was a place to hide, to tuck himself away. He needed to try to clear his mind and think things out. He didn't want to, but he knew it was necessary.

Turn around, go back.

Chance stopped and grunted. His backpack, which he'd hung around his dense neck by tying the end straps together to make one large loop, pinched at his flesh. The urge to go back where he had come from made him feverish. To go back to Ana. That was where his compass and internal voice were telling him to go. But Chance couldn't trust his instincts. Not while all of the fragmented souls' imprints were pushing around inside his mind. The soft, friendly whisper of his grandfather, Niyol, was buried by a powerful essence that was unfamiliar to him. He knew it wasn't his great-grandfather, Balam, because he felt him too, fighting against the dominant voice.

An argument raged in his mind from too many sides. It wasn't the first time this had happened. He shouldn't have allowed himself to think. He had let them back in. Chance could hardly move, so he stumbled over to a large Ceiba tree and sat at its base.

Go back to her. Her power is rare. If you consume her, you cannot be stopped. The acerbic voice compelled him to stand up, but he fought the urge and remained sitting.

The only way to protect Ana from yourself is to stay away. You must fight it, Chance. Chance found strength from Balam. No matter how much it hurt walking away from the love of his life, he knew it was for her own good. It was to protect her. Always her protector. He would have saved her from Markus again if given the choice. He may have damned himself and his soul for eternity, but it was all for her, all for Ana.

Too much had happened yesterday. He didn't want to dwell on it. It wouldn't change anything. It wouldn't change the fact that his power-crazy cousin Markus had come looking for him and killed his great-grandfather instead, ripping his power from him. While he was still reeling from this exchange, he'd gone for Ana. The only way Chance could protect her was to stop Markus in his tracks. Chance had plunged a stake into the base of his cousin's skull, ending his torment for good. But in so doing, he'd been forced to absorb his cousin's massive power and, along with it, the fragmented memories and voices from all the shapeshifters that he had killed and anyone they had killed in their lifetimes. It would confuse even a sane and stable mind.

The whole experience was very different from the time his grandfather, Niyol, had saved his life by starting a healing connection, emptying all of his power into Chance before he expired in death. Since that point, the imprint of Niyol had guided him through memories when he needed them most in a gentle, unobtrusive way. That was very different from what was happening now.

Balam had warned Chance that killing another shifter was very different than what he had experienced with his grandfather. When you die while funneling your power into another shapeshifter in a healing connection, it is a peaceful transference, without fragmentation. When a shifter is killed, their energy is unleashed from their body. Splintered pieces are absorbed by any nearby shapeshifters, leaving an incomplete and unbalanced impression.

Niyol's kindhearted soul was welcome to Chance, although the poisoned, power-crazy conscience that he could only guess was Markus, and the forceful, mysterious voice, were not. His willpower alone wasn't enough to push their influence from his mind.

If he was going to avoid reconnecting with Ana, then traveling home to Idaho was a very appealing second choice. But that plan had its own reasons why it wouldn't work. How could he go home without Ana? What if she were there to meet him?

Balam had mentioned the fact that healers could help a shifter that had been poisoned like Chance was, but he had also said that they were hard to find these days and kept themselves hidden from shapeshifters. It was hopeless.

Ana's face skirted through his thoughts, her green eyes and sweet smile. Would he see them ever again? He had to try for her.

Mmmm, yes, let's try. She is very special.

Chance's vision grew foggy. He had the sensation that he was looking through the bottom of a glass, the center focused and the edges blurry. A memory forced its way into his thoughts and he found himself in a dry, hot landscape. Every breath he took expanded in his lungs and burned. The hairs on his arms shone in the light and his dark skin drank up the sun. Black hair hung down around his shoulders as he stared out across the dusty landscape.

Chance had experienced plenty of his grandfather's memories before. It reminded him of some he'd had about Niyol when his grandfather was young, but somehow, he sensed that this one was different.

He stood in tall, golden grass that rolled in waves along the hills. A noise alerted him and he turned around. Chance recognized the man. It was Niyol's father. The creases around his mouth deepened as he spoke. "Nastas, my son. I know you are to meet Mai, but you need to help your brother bring in the sheep from the outer pasture."

"Can I do it when I get back?" Nastas said. "I promised to meet her at midday, but it has already passed. She will think I will not meet her and go home."

"If you are not hunting, you are getting distracted by Mai."

"I am the best hunter in the valley. Aren't you proud of my skills?" Nastas stuck out his chest and Chance felt the pinch of a bowstring across his almond skin.

"Yes, my boy, there is no one as clever as you, but I wish your cleverness didn't get you out of helping with the sheep. Very well, since you never miss, then I would like to see the blessings of your skill at dinner tonight. Do not forget to help your brother, Ahiga, on your way back and be aware of yourself. I hear rumor of a howler moving through the land."

His father walked away toward a mud and stick home. Chance recognized it from one of Niyol's memories he'd experienced a few months ago.

Nastas leaned down and picked up a rock, adjusting the bow out of the way that hung across his chest. Without looking, he tossed it into the tall grass ahead of him. A loud groan sounded and a tall lanky teen stood up. Chance swallowed and his heart pinched in his chest. He knew that face. The boy's skin may have been smooth and his hair black as onyx, but his eyes were the same, exactly the same. He was staring at his grandfather.

"Good try Niyol, but you'll have to be trickier than that to sneak up on me. I'm leaving to meet Mai and if I'm lucky, I will bring dinner home."

Niyol laughed. "You are always lucky, Nastas."

"Go see if Father needs any help. I need him in a better mood when I get home later. You are his favorite." Nastas snickered. "What am I saying, you're everyone's favorite."

"Even you? Even when I follow you on the trail and scare the game away?" Niyol crossed his arms and arched his brow.

"Well, maybe not then, but..."—Nastas strode over to the lanky teen and put his arm around him—"you're still my favorite little brother. I'll always look after you. So, how about helping your big brother out?"

Niyol's thin, wide lips split into a grin and he stepped away from Nastas. He jogged back home, calling out, "Father! I can go help Ahiga with the sheep..."

The memory was definitely from Niyol's brother's point of view. Nastas. But he wasn't the psychopath Chance was expecting. He seemed to truly love his brother, which was not at all what Chance had seen from Niyol's previous memories. This was unanticipated.

Nastas waved to his brother and started off. He moved swiftly, his body crouched as he cut through the fields. Soon he came to a rocky bluff and made his way down a narrow trail that led to a stream. All the way he was alert and aware of his surroundings. Nastas lifted the bow over his head. He plucked an arrow from his leather quiver and pressed its end to the bowstring as he settled behind a large rock.

Maybe Mai will forgive my lateness if I offer something for her table.

Nastas lay still for so long Chance started wondering why he was still experiencing the memory. They were usually short and to the point.

He stared intently at a few trees that grew in a cluster near a curve of the stream and pulled the end of his arrow back, the string stretched tight against his fingertips. His hawk-like eyesight focused on movement. Brown speckled feathers blended with their surroundings, but not well enough. Nastas let go and watched his arrow fly into its intended target.

A squawk sounded and his heart grew light with pleasure. *I will get another on the way home to make Father happy.*

He jumped to his feet and retrieved his kill, flinging the limp quail over his shoulder. Nastas took notice of the sun in the sky and hurried away. He followed the curve of the stream and continued for some time before he stopped again to stare at a piece of tan leather on the ground.

Chance had been growing weary of the memory, but he snapped to attention when Nastas sniffed the air. He stared at the earth and spotted a few dark mahogany flecks. A familiar human scent and the sweet, metallic whiff of blood hung on the air.

Mai was here. But where is she?

Chance was eager to see what happened next, but the memory faded and he found himself staring at a spiky, green agave plant. His heart raced from feeling Nastas's anxiety. It was something he could closely relate to. Months ago, when Markus had called him from Ana's phone, he'd flown into a panic and tried to save her. The fear that had gripped his heart was exactly what Nastas had experienced in that memory.

He stared down at his thick, furry legs and moaned. He was still in bear form. Chance shifted back, and slipped his pack to the ground. He grabbed a rock from the dirt and flung it through the trees. "Rah!!"

While his pulse slowed and he calmed himself, his thoughts raced. He didn't understand the meaning of the memory. How could Nastas become so evil? No one had been able to explain to him how shapeshifters just changed after they contracted the sickness. It didn't make any sense.

Does it need to make sense?

He supposed it didn't. Not really. It didn't matter how it happened because he didn't need to worry about it now. He was safe and protected. No one would be able to hurt him because he was powerful.

Chance's consciousness twisted away from him and he slipped some clothes on before flipping his backpack over his shoulder. One footstep after another led him forward on his trail north, closer to home, but after too many hours of stumbling ahead, he was exhausted. He considered tucking up under some brush and taking a nap. He wasn't confident he was doing the right thing, so maybe sleep was the answer.

No, do not stop. Keep moving. I know you're tired, but it will all be worth it.

He knew the voices of Balam, Niyol, Markus and Nastas in his head, but the loudest one, the one that pushed him the hardest, he'd never heard before. Almost as soon as the thought occurred to him, it was gone. Chance moved on without considering a rest.

CHAPTER 3

Chance, he yelled at himself, *don't let yourself get pushed around by some dead psycho, whoever it is. Take control.* His fists clenched and his muscles tightened. He remained this way until his thoughts quieted and his heartbeat slowed.

It had barely been a day since he'd taken on the imprints and memories of Markus, Balam, Nastas (and who knew who else) and it was beginning to unravel his sanity. Markus had appeared to argue with himself the day before, and now it all made sense.

Chance couldn't allow himself to go mad like his cousin had. There was no way he'd ever make it back to Ana if he did. He'd have to find a way to overcome the madness. Until that point, he'd have to be smart. His foot caught on a rock and Chance realized just how exhausted he was. Instead of resting the night before, he'd stayed awake and kept on moving, but now his body was limp and his mind, mush.

He was at his weakest point right now, and he didn't want to open himself up to the influence of Markus, Nastas or whoever else was in there pushing him around. Time to find a safe place to rest. Maybe he'd feel clearer after a nap.

Again, a very loud, resounding *no* echoed through his thoughts. *You must keep moving. You are stronger than any average man. You can handle it. There could be other shifters tracking you. You are not safe.*

Chance stopped as he considered a terrifying thought. If shifters could follow him, then what about Ana? He wouldn't be there to protect her if she was discovered by a shifter with the sickness. By someone like him.

You had better go back and check on her. Just to make sure she's safe.

He grunted in agreement, forgetting the reasons why he should stay away from her, and turned around. For at least an hour, he ran through the wilderness, retracing his steps back toward Balam's house with Ana's face clear in his mind.

It wasn't until the faint echo of a familiar voice broke into his thoughts that he slowed to a stop so he could focus on it better.

You must stay in control of yourself and your actions. It is always you who will make the choice. The choice to let yourself be swayed is yours.

Balam. His voice was distant, but Chance understood every word that traced through his thoughts. He didn't understand any of this. It was all so different from the fusion of his grandfather's memories. So much more interactive.

Awesome. How was he going to know which voice to trust? Or if he was truly making choices for himself without being influenced by another, less trustworthy personality? He questioned his choice to find Ana. Maybe staying out in the middle of nowhere was the best option. Find a desolate island in the Pacific somewhere and protect the world from...himself. There was always one other choice. A choice that was so final, he dare not consider it yet.

A gentle breeze picked up. He stretched, letting the air current wrap around his sweaty body. Birds fluttered on nearby branches and he stopped. A familiar scent.

I'm surprised you've survived this long! Self-preservation is weak in this one.

Chance ignored the comments and sat bolt upright. He scanned the dry landscape for anything out of place. The hairs on his arms and legs stood on end. He couldn't explain it, but he felt a powerful source of energy nearby. He'd never experienced anything like it before.

"I know you're there," he shouted. "Show yourself." He scanned the landscape. Chance called to his power and his blue core of light reacted quickly, ready to respond at his will.

The abundance of energy gave him confidence and he puffed up his chest, almost eager for a fight.

A blue bird swooped down and hovered in front of Chance before disappearing behind a small grove of trees. He held still, anxious to see what would happen next.

I told you to be careful of being followed. You feel that power? Strike first, ask questions later.

A pale leg stepped out from behind the tree and Chance's eyes widened as a black-haired woman emerged. She was breathtaking, ageless. Her black hair curled down her chest like a sheet of silk. He swallowed hard, realized she was naked and forced his gaze away.

"Hello, Chance." Her voice was mesmerizing and her face familiar, somehow.

How did she know his name?

"I've been looking for you."

He was fairly confident he would have remembered her if they had met. But he couldn't shake the sense that he'd seen her, though he definitely would have noted meeting another shapeshifter. *Wait, she's a woman.* A woman shapeshifter. Like Ana. How was that possible?

She's tasty. Maybe you should keep her as your pet.

Chance looked at her again and felt a hunger growing within. Her power radiated out and it was all that he could do to restrain himself from shifting and attacking. He told himself that it may come to that, but his curiosity won out. He wanted to know how she knew his name . . .and how she'd come into existence.

"Who are you?" Chance asked.

"My name is Lifen and I have been following your mate's growth over the last few months. I have been tracking you and Ana."

Ana? Her face flashed in his thoughts and his chest squeezed so tightly it pained him. "Where is she? Is she safe?"

"Yes, she is safe. I had to leave her behind because she asked me to try to help you." Lifen stepped toward him. "I can help you Chance. I am a healer."

He didn't like this at all. How did he know he could trust what she said? His senses were telling him he was in danger. "Stop—don't come any closer. Stay away from me."

Don't trust her. All of the voices in his head seemed to be in agreement.

Lifen paused, mid-step. "Ana asked me to come. You're safe with me."

Anger roiled up in him. "I don't know that. For all I know you, killed Ana first and came after me, or you're lying now and you've never met her. I have no proof you are who you say you are. I have no reason to trust you."

Just hearing Ana's name put him on edge. His instinct to protect her fought against his memories of the insatiable hunger he'd experienced when he last saw her. The internal argument went on until he thought he'd go insane.

"I can help quiet the voices in your mind. I can see that you are wrestling with them now." Lifen spoke quietly, as though she were speaking to a deer that was ready to bolt.

She wants your power. Pay attention to your energy levels—feel them slipping?

Chance focused inward and did, indeed, feel his blue core begin to crackle and dim.

"I bet. And that wouldn't involve killing me? I'm not stupid."

"I only want to help you. You have to let me—if you fight against it then it will only harm you."

"So you *do* mean to hurt me. Stay away unless you want a fight." Chance rose to his feet and the muscles in his arms flexed.

She is special, very special, but too old. If you can't tame her, then take her.

Chance completely agreed. He pushed past his sapped energy and fur rippled across his body. His shorts tore and fell to the ground as he relished the size of his favorite form. A growl reverberated in his chest and poured from his maw.

Lifen didn't seem surprised or threatened at all by his display. Her lips curled up, almost in sympathy, which only confused and angered him.

"You are quite powerful indeed. Very impressive. You may be more powerful than myself—you may not be, but I did not come here to end you. I came here as a favor to my new student. If you were not poisoned with the shifter sickness, you would be of some value. You're damaged goods."

Any small modicum of doubt in his mind vanished after her speech. He wasn't damaged—he was empowered, and ready to give her a good show. How dare she judge him.

Instead of using bear form, he decided it wasn't impressive enough. He gathered up his energy, concentrated on the thunderbird mapping in his mind and let the transformation take over. Cinnamon feathers rippled down his arms and legs, and his beady eyes settled on the thin-framed woman before him. He snapped his beak and lifted his talons to display the length of his weapons. This would frighten anyone.

"Ah, the thunderbird," Lifen said. "You are not the first to show me this form. It had its place with your ancestors. If only they had spent more time perfecting it . . . It is really only a large eagle with a lightning rod for a beak. Directing lightning is only useful if there is enough electricity in the air."

This woman was infuriating him. Did she think she could just toy with him? Belittle him? All she'd displayed was the ability to shift into a small finch. She claimed to be a healer but hadn't shown any amount of power. He could feel her energy from where he stood, but that didn't mean she was any kind of threat.

"I know what you're thinking," she said. "I'm just a weak woman. Well, youngster, I don't feel the need to show off like a fool. I don't need to. I know I am the one in control of this situation. Take your human form and just walk away. I do not need you. I do not want you. I only wish to keep my promise to my newest, most talented student." Lifen blinked and stared at him with such intensity he wondered how many fights she'd been in and won.

We are unified and strong together. Take her. She belongs to us.

Chance stepped forward and Lifen's arm shot up. Before he could take another step, his heart began to squeeze in his chest and his breath caught in his throat. Pain radiated through his abdomen and he stumbled back. Air hissed from the holes in his beak and he grew faint. Unable to stand any longer, he tipped over, his wings spread haphazardly.

As his consciousness failed and he fell into darkness, he heard Lifen's voice beside him. "You are not good enough for her. I told you Chance—you should have just accepted my help. You are on your own now."

CHAPTER 4

Ana paced frantically along the bank of the stream and stared up at the sun through the trees. She had impatiently watched it arc across the sky and now knew it was mid-afternoon. She was completely powerless and hated being left behind. How would Chance react without her there to gain his trust?

It was an odd sensation, but it almost felt like he was there with her, which was both soothing and agitating. She was done waiting. Ana didn't really care if she got herself lost in the jungle, she wasn't scared. Balam had taught her about the fauna and wildlife. She was confident.

Ana snatched up her backpack and Lifen's belongings. She adjusted the talisman Balam had given her along with Chance's necklaces so they wouldn't pinch her neck under the straps and then set off in the direction Lifen had flown.

Before long a bird swooped down and squawked at her. She stopped. "Lifen? Is that you?"

The bird scurried forward across the leafy ground and lifted to peck at the edges of the blue fabric she was carrying. Ana took that as a yes. She spread out the cloth before her and Lifen's head rose above the top.

"Thank you, Ana." Lifen wrapped it around her body as if she had done it thousands of times before.

"Where's Chance?" Ana asked and tried to swallow the lump that had formed in her throat.

Lifen reached out and held her hands, which made her fingers tingle. Her face grew serious.

Ana couldn't read her expression, but she was confident her mentor didn't have good news for her.

"I found him, Ana."

Her heart skipped a beat, but then she acknowledged the obvious. "Is he okay? Is he hurt? Why didn't he come back with you?"

"He was safe and from what I could tell, unharmed."

Ana was filled with anxiety and could have burst. She was starting to question if Lifen had any experience giving bad news. *Rip the Band-Aid off already!*

As if she could hear Ana's thoughts, Lifen pulled her into a gentle hug and whispered, "I am sorry. I was not able to convince him I was there to help. He is too sick to know what is good for him."

Ana pinched her eyes shut and tried to accept the news. Things were falling apart and only getting worse. If she had only been able to shift and gone to see Chance, she was sure things would have turned out differently. Her pain began to turn into anger. No amount of crying, sobbing and feeling sorry for herself was going to change things. Chance had saved her life twice. Had given all of himself for her and it was her turn to save him. Now that things were getting rough, it wasn't time to fall apart. She pulled away from Lifen and wiped away the last of her tears. She was tired of feeling powerless and it was going to end now. Chance had given her life when her body had given up. Now, she was going to use her amazing powers to save him.

"Well then, let's get to work. If anyone's going to help him, it'll be me and if I need to be more powerful and more experienced, then I need to get started. We've gotta get out of here immediately. I have to stop home on the way, or otherwise there'll only be more problems. C'mon."

Ana handed Lifen her pouch, jogged back to the stream and carefully stepped across the fallen tree trunk. Lifen stayed close behind in human form, even when Ana ran along the trail. Branches slapped against her skin and she pulled vines loose while she sped past. She had a singular focus, and there wasn't time to waste. Even if it killed her, she would save Chance.

***

Thankful to fly home to Idaho, Ana didn't care if it used up the rest of her savings. She just wanted to get moving. She put the golden snake hairpin that Balam had given her into the front pouch of her bag so she could keep it close. Ana wasn't about to let anything happen to it.

After they were waved through U.S. customs at Spokane International Airport, Lifen pulled her aside near the women's bathrooms. "Ana, I think it is best if I do not go to your home in human form. There will be too many questions and I admit I do not socialize with people without powers anymore. I would be more comfortable in canine form, if you do not mind. I think it would be easiest."

Ana was relieved that she'd said something. She had been worrying about how to introduce her to her mother. She hadn't said anything to Melissa about traveling with Lifen, only that she was coming home.

"Yeah, I think you're right. If you don't mind being a dog for a couple days, then that works for me."

"Just remember, Ana, we need to leave as soon as possible. If we are going to drive north, it will take us even longer to get back and I need to get home to my other students. I cannot ensure their safety while I am gone."

"I understand. I want to start training too—maybe we could fit in a little along the way?" Ana asked hopefully.

Lifen's lips upturned. "That may be possible."

"Fantastic!" Ana's excitement died as she thought of Chance. "What do I do about Chance? What do I tell my mom?"

"It may be painful for you to do, but what if you tell her you broke up? It is not that far from the truth. You are not together." Lifen said it factually. Ana knew she was only being helpful, but her words stung.

"Yeah, I guess that's the easiest thing to say. Mom asked if Chance was coming home with me and I changed the subject. I think she knows something's up, so she didn't push it." Ana adjusted her backpack and sighed. "Well, you ready to get going? Mom'll be waiting outside. Where do you want to change?"

Ana found it amusing, saying it like she just needed to change her clothes or something.

Lifen started into a nearby women's room. "Here is fine."

Ana followed her inside and was relieved to see there were only a couple of women fixing their makeup at the mirrors. They walked over to an empty section and entered two neighboring stalls. Lifen handed Ana her pouch from under the stall and then a moment later, her scruffy nose poked underneath too. She crawled onto Ana's side and wagged her tail happily.

Ana chuckled and slipped Lifen's purse over her neck. "Oh! What about a leash? No offense, but you kinda look like a stray."

In response, her mentor dropped her snout to the ground and lifted the blue sarong in her mouth. Ana shrugged. "That'll work."

She looped one end around the dog's neck and tied it off in a loose knot. Lifen looked up at Ana with her dark eyes and gave a soft yip. It was time to go. Ana stepped out of the stall with her new pet and into the airport hallway. They wandered toward the exit and passenger pickup.

"Mom should be out here if she left on time," Ana muttered to Lifen. "She said she'd have to leave early from work and since it was late notice she wasn't sure if her boss would give her a hard time or not." A man in a business suit brushed by them and gave Ana a funny look. When the automatic doors opened for them, a burst of humid air brushed past her and Ana's favorite smell met her nose. Rain. The gray Northwestern skies made her feel justified in her depressed mood.

"Not a surprise—it's raining." Ana sighed.

"Ana! Over here, baby!"

She turned and saw her mother calling out the passenger window of her sedan. Melissa pulled up to the curb and came to a stop. In a rush of movement, she wrenched open her door and hurried over to Ana, wrapping her in a tight embrace. Ana tried tucking away the tears that threatened to spill out. She'd successfully hidden her emotions during her travels and now they took her by surprise. Her mother's loving touch made her feel safe, if only temporarily.

"Hi, Mom." Her throat tightened while she spoke, and she attempted to sound normal.

"Oh, I'm so glad you're safe and sound! And finally home." Melissa's voice broke as she stroked Ana's hair.

"Of course I'm safe. I missed you too, Mom."

Melissa pulled away and stared wistfully at her daughter. "My, this is the most tan I've ever seen you. And look how muscular and fit you are. You look so healthy."

It was Ana's turn to study her mother. She seemed different somehow. Clearly Ana wasn't the only one who'd changed while she was gone. For some reason, it bothered her. She wanted to think of her mom in a timeless way. She'd always depended on her to be her anchor and strength. Ana looked at her again and realized how vibrant and happy she seemed and regretted her selfishness. "You let your hair grow out. Looks good."

Her mom blushed, tucked a strand of hair behind her ear and mumbled, "Well, I've been trying some new things out."

"Where's Eva?" Ana craned her neck to look in the windows of her mother's sedan.

"School. Which reminds me, we've gotta move if we're going to make it back in time to pick her up. I don't normally get the chance to pick her up from school—she's been taking the bus home. She is excited to see you. Don't want to make her wait." Melissa walked over to the passenger door and did a double-take. "When did you get a dog?"

Ana looked at Lifen. She had temporarily forgotten about her. The dog's dark, intelligent eyes peered up at Ana from under her shaggy, gray fur. Her mentor sat patiently on the sidewalk as though she were waiting for an introduction. "Oh, right. Sorry. There's so many strays in Mexico. This one kinda wormed her way into my heart. Couldn't leave her behind."

"Has it had its shots? Don't want Eva's dog to get sick. Don't ask me how much I had to spend on that rescued lab from the pound."

"Don't worry—she's completely healthy. She's the best behaved dog ever. She's potty trained and it's almost like she understands English. You'll love her." Ana chuckled to herself while she led Lifen over to the car. Melissa leaned over to scratch Lifen's head.

"She's got long hair. You know how I feel about long-haired dogs. Oh well, load her into the back."

Ana opened the back door and Lifen jumped onto the backseat, turned in place twice and sat with her tail wrapped around her feet. The straps of Ana's backpack were digging into her shoulders, so she was relieved to slip it off and stow it on the floor behind the passenger seat. She couldn't help but give the dog's chin a scratch before shutting the door.

"The rain's so much colder here," Ana said as she buckled up and wiped a water droplet from her face.

"Well, we can't all live in Mexico."

Melissa pulled into the throng of cars weaving their way out of the airport. The repetitive thumping of the window wipers dulled Ana's senses and she sat in silence, unsure how to make conversation. Everything she could talk about was connected to Chance.

"So, when are we going to address the elephant in the room?"

"Huh?"

Melissa switched off the radio and gave her daughter a sympathetic grin. "You and Chance. When I spoke to Aiyana the other day, she didn't know anything about Chance coming home. She said she hadn't heard from him, and in fact, she sounded worried. You know you can talk to me, right baby?"

Well, thanks to her mother, she didn't need to avoid it any longer. Time to get it over with. She swallowed and stared out her side window so she wouldn't have to see her mother's eyes when she fumbled with the truth. "It's complicated."

"I understand. Love's complicated."

Just get it over with. "We're not together right now. I don't know where he is and I don't know when I'll see him again. But I don't want to talk about it."

Silence.

Ana pinched her eyes shut and forced her memories of the last few days from her thoughts. They were only clouding her emotions right now. She needed to focus on what she had to accomplish. She needed to smooth things out at home and get on the road so she could begin training with her mentor.

"I'm sorry, Ana. I won't push you. I'm here if you need to talk about it."

"Thanks."

Ana was grateful that Melissa changed the subject and kept the conversation on things that had nothing to do with Chance. She learned more about the construction project at the center of town than she cared to know, and all about Eva's classes at school, which Melissa wasn't very subtle about. Ana knew Melissa's standpoint on school over travel, but thankfully, she let it drop without another word.

"How're Aunt Tera and Uncle Jace?"

Melissa pinched her lips together, as though suppressing a smile.

"What? Nothing bad I hope?" Ana asked, her curiosity piqued.

"Well, Tera's not too happy about it, but Jace has opened a bait shop with a friend of his."

"Is that a bad thing?"

"No, certainly not. I keep trying to remind her that now he's getting paid to do what he loves. He doesn't have as much time to go fishing himself and the shop's doing pretty good since it's the only one on this side of the lake."

"Well, what's the problem?" Ana liked her uncle a lot. He might be like a grown teenager, but he was sweet and always ready with a joke. She always thought Aunt Tera was hard on him.

"Guess he's been keeping all the excess night crawlers in their fridge. You'd think he'd started World War Three. What I think Tera needs is her own hobby to focus on."

"I thought razzing Uncle Jace *was* her hobby."

Melissa laughed. "Poor man."

They made their way through town, and Ana tried not to dwell on the high school as they passed by the lot. It felt like so long ago when she had met Chance and they had stood awkwardly by their cars making plans for the first time.

"Here we go," Melissa said in a singsong voice and drove up to the middle school.

Eva would make her feel better. There was nothing like her exuberant little sister to distract her from her problems. When Eva saw the car, she said something to her friends and sauntered slowly to the curb.

Ana rolled down her window and called out, "Hey sweetie! Surprise, I'm back!"

"Hey."

That wasn't what she'd been expecting from Eva. Anything short of jumping up and down and screaming was out of character for her.

"You've grown like crazy since I was gone. Not in high school yet?"

"Ha, ha."

Ana noticed that her little sister no longer looked like the young girl in her memories. Her hair was no longer in braids, but flowed free over her shoulders, and her lips had the trace of tinted lip gloss.

"What's up? No hug for me?" Ana started to open her door and Eva placed her hand on the frame to stop her.

"At home—not in front of my friends." Eva opened the back seat of the car and Lifen sat staring out at her. "You have a dog?"

Ana glanced in disbelief at their mom.

Melissa gave a knowing smirk back. "Remember when you stopped letting me give you displays of affection in public?"

But she was Eva's sister, not her mom. She couldn't help but feel hurt at being snubbed. Melissa drove away from the school and Ana rolled her window back up. The happiness at seeing her sister had morphed into something painful.

"Hey—where's Chance?" Eva asked from the back seat.

And it only got worse.

CHAPTER 5

"I see the van made it back safely."

Ana spotted the yellow VW parked next to the shed. It shone brightly through the gloom. It had been a gift from Uncle Jace when they moved to Idaho. She had needed something to drive her and her sister around in while their mom was at work. It had served its purpose. It had even helped get Chance and Ana to Denver, Colorado, on their travels down to Mexico, but he had surprised her with tickets to Cancun so they had left it at Melissa's friend's house.

"So, how was the visit at Beth's?" Ana asked her mom.

Melissa parked in the driveway and shook her head. "When isn't it an adventure? It was great seeing her. It's been almost a year since we left Denver and I thought I would have been happier visiting her there, but I just missed Clark Bend the whole time. Beth set me up on a blind date—like that was going to go anywhere—and kept me busy, but I had to leave with enough time to get back home. But I think Eva had fun at Aunt Tera's, right sweetie?"

"Yeah, we went to a cooking convention. It was fun."

"Thanks for driving the banana van back home for me, Mom." Ana knew it was a long drive and in such a loud vehicle too.

"Well, I was the one that wanted you to fly to Mexico and not drive. It worked out. I saw Beth and I got my way in the end."

They climbed out of the car and Ana pulled Eva into a hug before she could hurry up to the front stoop.

"Hey, I missed you. A lot."

Eva pulled away and her sad eyes looked into Ana's. "I missed you too, but you left. I'm not your baby sister anymore. Things are different now, Ana."

Since when had her sister become so mature? She supposed she'd always been that way. Not only had Melissa always protected her, but Ana even depended on her little sister for support. Families were supposed to do that for each other, right? So, why did she feel so alone then?

Ana nodded. "Yeah, I know."

"You guys coming in?" Melissa called from the house.

Ana dried her cheeks with the edge of her shirt.

While she walked up the path, Eva's fingers laced between hers. "Things may be different, but I still love you," Eva said.

Melissa held open the door to the little blue house and a blur of yellow shot out past them. The puppy's tongue licked Ana's free hand with so much fervor, she was thankful it was soft. She pulled her hand away and wiped it on her shirt.

"Daisy, meet Ana." Eva laughed.

Ana turned around and watched Lifen sitting patiently beside the car. When Daisy saw the scruffy canine, she immediately forgot about Ana and bolted toward her. As soon as the puppy reached Lifen, it sniffed her, sat back, and cocked its head. A soft whimper pierced the air.

"Well, that's strange," Melissa said as she held open the front door. "She loves other dogs—jumps all over them."

"C'mon, Lifen," Ana called. "Let's go inside." She figured there was no reason to call her anything different.

"That's a unique name," Eva said with a frown. "Where'd you get it from?"

"Dunno. Just remember hearing it once and thought it was a nice fit."

Lifen followed Ana into the house with Daisy on her tail.

"No dogs on the furniture," Melissa said as she hung her purse from a hook on the wall. "I just replaced Grandma's old couch and I don't want it to get stinky and hairy."

Ana admired the replacement sofa. It definitely improved the look of the living room and the smell too. She wandered over to it and plucked off a yellow hair. "Does Daisy know the rules yet?"

"She's a good girl," Eva said. "She's trying to learn all of Mom's rules, but there's so many." She squatted down to hug her dog, whose eyes popped from her head as she was squeezed tight.

"Really, I don't think I'm asking too much," Melissa said. "No using my house as a bathroom, don't eat my food from the table, tongues out of my coffee"—she winced—"and keep off the furniture."

"Mom loves you, don't let her fool you." Eva kissed Daisy's head and jumped back up.

"So, I think I'm going to take my things up to my room and unpack." Ana started for the stairs and Lifen followed behind her.

"Okay, go ahead and settle in," Melissa said. "What's for dinner tonight, Eva?"

"Burritos in celebration of Ana coming home."

"Sounds good. Now get that homework done—I know you have some and I'll be back down in a while."

Some things don't change, Ana thought to herself as she dragged her belongings up to her room. She was exhausted. It felt almost like it used to, except her heart wasn't thundering in her chest.

She unlatched her door and dropped her things to the floor. When she flipped the light switch, a multitude of tiny points illuminated her ceiling. How could she forget? A gift from Chance. She pinched her eyes shut and almost felt his hand in hers, guiding her into her room, and his breath on her neck the night he revealed his present. The night he asked her to prom.

Ana, don't do this to yourself. She forced her sadness aside and sat on her bed. Lifen's muzzle appeared on her lap and she rubbed between her mentor's ears. "It just brings back so many memories being here without Chance. But it only makes me want to get moving that much faster. I've got to help him."

Lifen turned and looked at the pile on the floor.

"Right, well I'd better get moving then. I don't know the last time I used a washer to do my laundry. Oh, and a hot shower."

Ana unzipped her backpack and emptied it onto the floor. The last two months of her life lay crumpled and wrinkled in a mess, something that went against her cleanly nature. She picked out her valuables—the golden snake hairpin from Balam and a few knick-knacks she had picked up along the way—and threw the rest into a laundry basket. She grasped the cluster of necklaces around her neck. Chance's bear heartline pendant, as well as his Mayan jade jaguar, twisted together with the protective obsidian necklace that Balam had given her. *You will see him again soon.*

Once her dirty clothes were deposited into the wash with a healthy dose of soap, she returned to her room. She needed to plan for her trip. Although it was soothing being back with her mother and sister, she wasn't home. It was different this time. Home had an altogether different meaning now. Like the old adage, "Home is where the heart is," Ana's heart was roaming around in the wilderness of Mexico.

She knew it wouldn't be easy convincing her mother she was safe heading out on her own, but she'd do her best. In the end, she'd go anyway, although she hoped it wouldn't cause a rift between them.

This trip would be different. She didn't have to pack light. Lifen had told her they would be able to drive all the way in, weather permitting, which was one of the reasons they needed to get moving. Canada during the winter would be extremely different from fall in the Yucatán. No more shorts and T-shirts. Ana pulled out a large suitcase from her closet and laid it on the floor.

"Now what will I really need?"

She sighed and stared at the clothes in her closet. Lifen trotted over, lifted up on her haunches and tugged on a thick, winter coat. Then, she pulled out a pair of hiking boots from a row of organized shoes. If a dog could give a, *duh, use your head,* sort of expression, Lifen nailed it.

"Of course, sorry. Okay, so it'll be kinda like winters in Colorado, except more snow probably."

Satisfied, Lifen leapt onto Ana's bed and curled into a ball for a nap. Ana figured that was all she was getting from her mentor at present and focused on her wardrobe. She pulled out her warmest clothing, then folded, tucked and sorted everything in the neatest way possible. Even the most experienced traveler would have been impressed with her pack job.

"Ana?" Eva's face emerged from around the edge of the door. When the rest of her followed, she crossed her arms and pointed at the filled suitcase on the floor. "You're not leaving *again*, are you?"

"Oh, sweetie. Come here." Ana opened her arms up to her little sister, who reluctantly moved into her embrace. "It's something I've got to do for myself. You know how proud you were when you had the lead in your dance recital a couple years back?"

Eva shrugged and Ana pulled away so she could tuck some stray hairs behind her sister's ear. "I've never been able to take the lead in anything. I've always had Mom, you and Chance there to protect me. And I feel like I have to go explore on my own so I can feel proud of myself. Does that make sense?"

"I guess so. I kinda know what you mean. With you gone, I've had more attention from Mom, but that's not always such a good thing."

Ana caught Eva's eye and they laughed. Ana wrapped her arm around her sister's shoulders. "See, it's different when you've got other people telling you what to do and being there if you fall. I mean, that's a good thing sometimes, but I want to pick myself up if I screw up and know that I can do it myself. I wouldn't leave if I didn't know you were able to take care of things here at home. I mean, look at you cooking the meals like a professional chef—you have talent, Eva. Mom's lucky to have you around helping out. I always took you for granted before, but you act like my older sister half the time."

Eva's cheeks flushed with pride and her shoulders lifted. She still seemed disappointed and sad, but Ana could tell she'd saved the situation from going nuclear. Although there was still time for Melissa to take it to that level...

"C'mon, I want to see how you do Mexican food. Think you can fit in with the natives? Can you fool my senses? I've been eating the real deal for months. Oh, and I've got a recipe for you—Mayan hot chocolate. How about I make some for dessert?"

Her sister's eyes widened as she spoke with enthusiasm, "Did you know chocolate came from Mexico?"

"Somebody's been watching too much Food Network in her spare time." Ana squeezed her sister's shoulder and they started out of the room.

Food was laid out on the dining table and Daisy patrolled with her nose in the air. Melissa sat waiting at the table and gave a warning glare at the dog. "I'm not the only one who thinks it smells good. It's been a while since we all sat at the table together. This is nice."

Eva sat down next to Ana and reached for the bowl of rice. "Too bad it won't last for long."

Ana pinched her eyes shut and swore to herself.

"Oh, really? Is that so?"

When Ana opened them back up, her mother was staring at her with a hardened expression. "Is it too much to ask to have my daughter *want* to be with her family?"

"Mom..."

"I thought you'd go down to Mexico, see something new and come home ready to hit the books. You're smart, Ana—straight A's your whole life. You want to just throw that away?"

"No, Mom. It doesn't mean I'm throwing my life away if I take a break from school."

"This time I'm putting my foot down! You can't go. You've been gone for two months—it's time to take a break. Give yourself a rest."

Ana stood up and shouted. "No! I'm eighteen now and you can't make me do anything! You're not being *fair*."

Melissa dropped her fork to her plate and pointed at Ana. "No, what's not fair is being left on your own without someone to help take care of you and your kids. Without an education, how will you get a high paying job to support yourself? Don't make the mistakes I did, Ana."

She couldn't hear anything past life being unfair. Memories played out in her mind and anger boiled up like a volatile mixture of vinegar and baking soda. Ana let loose. "I know all about life being unfair. My whole life I've been told that I can't do anything! Your heart can't take it, Ana. Even when my heart healed, you *still* told me I shouldn't leave home." She waved wildly in the air. "Newsflash, I made it. I'm alive and I want to live. Bad things happen all the time, but that's no reason to hide away in fear. It's reason to go out into the world and experience it. I've got to get out of here and figure out what I was put on this Earth to do. How am I supposed to move forward without direction?"

Melissa stared at Ana like she was seeing her for the first time. Then she did something completely unexpected. She cracked a smile.

"What?" Ana said, baffled. "You think my pain's funny?"

Wide-eyed and confused, Eva turned to look at her mother, and then her sister. Her frown grew until she scratched her head and muttered to herself, "You guys are nuts."

"Why, I think you're right, Eva," Melissa said. "But isn't it comforting to know it runs in the family?" She stuck her finger in the refried beans, leaned over and wiped it on both girls' cheeks. "Listen up—I don't know when I grew into a control freak, but it happened. Can you forgive me for loving you more than myself and forgetting what it's like to be a passionate teenager?"

Ana sputtered in confusion and answered, "Yeah?"

"I can't promise I'll stop worrying and hounding you. But I will try to let you make your own mistakes and remember that you're an amazing person who's capable of troubleshooting her own life." Melissa dropped her napkin into her lap and pointed at Ana's cheek. "You want me to take you seriously with food all over you? I'd wipe that off."

Eva was the first to start laughing. Ana couldn't help but join in. She'd missed this. A house full of estrogen had always supplied plenty of emotional turns, but through it all, there were laughs too.

"What is up with you, Mom? Not that you aren't normally funny, but Eva and I usually just laugh about you *behind* your back." Ana used her napkin to clean off her cheek and shook her head.

Eva sat up straighter and said behind her hand, "Mom's been dating."

Melissa blushed and placed her hands on her hips. "Eva!"

"Really? You've been dating? Anyone special?" Ana wasn't sure how to feel about the news. Her mother had been alone for so long, she was used to it. Not that she cared about her dad, it was just, weren't they enough for her?

"Eva's making it sound like I'm seeing all sorts of men. I'm not. It's just one man and his name is John. He works a couple doors down from the bank—he's a veterinarian."

"I like him." Eva announced factually, as though that settled the discussion.

"You do?" Ana was surprised. She expected her sister to be on her side.

"He likes my cooking," Eva said with a shrug, "and he's nice to Mom."

Melissa's cheeks were rosy and her eyes bright. Ana noted there was something softer about her. She had let her hair grow down to her shoulders. Normally dark and lifeless, new stylish highlights helped bring out the color of her skin. Ana couldn't remember the last time her mother seemed so happy.

"You like him?" Ana asked, holding Melissa's gaze.

"Yeah, I do."

Ana grabbed her burrito from her plate and took a bite, ready to move past her mother's news. "Well, the only thing we didn't cover is Eva's love life—you don't have any surprises for me do you?" She stared at her sister.

Eva stuttered. "No, you know Mom doesn't allow dating until high school."

"That doesn't mean you can't like anyone."

"Well, I'm not about to talk about my crush at the dinner table with burrito hanging out of your mouth!" Eva said in all seriousness. Then she dipped her finger into her beans and wiped it on the other cheek so she looked like a football player that took a detour through a kitchen. "*Now* I can take you seriously."

For the next hour, while they ate and laughed at the table, it was like it used to be. Ana forgot about her troubles, or the fact that there was a dog curled up on her bed who was really a shapeshifter. It was like traveling back in time, when it was just the three of them and that was enough for her. Before she fell in love with a boy who stole her heart.

***

Ana filled a bowl of dog food for Lifen. When she straightened up, the dog's dark eyes remained on her and she sat completely still. Daisy inhaled her food as soon as it touched her dish. When she was done, she couldn't take her eyes off of Lifen's untouched dinner.

Ana leaned down and pet her mentor's head. "Sorry, I'll grab you some leftovers when they go to bed, okay?"

In response, Lifen licked her hand and her eyes drooped even more.

"Fine. I'll get something out now. Good thing Mom and Eva are in the living room watching television." Ana went to the fridge and pulled out the container of beans and rice that she had just deposited there minutes before. She opened it and held it out for Lifen, who dipped her muzzle into the food. Daisy was only momentarily distracted with the fact that she wasn't getting a special treat, because she helped herself to Lifen's dog food instead.

"Hey, Mom?" Ana called, "I'm going to head out back to look at the stars for a little bit. Then I'm going to bed—tired from all the traveling."

Her mother answered from the living room. "'Kay, baby. Love you."

Ana threw the empty Tupperware into the sink and muttered to Lifen. "I'm just going outside for a bit and will be back soon. You can come with me if you want or stay inside."

She grabbed a jacket from the backdoor hat hook and stepped onto the deck. Lifen licked her muzzle clean and stepped outside with Ana. Rain-covered pine needles and lichen mixed to create Ana's favorite scent.

Excited to be back at her stargazing stone, she hurried over the lawn to the pathway. Her sweats got wet as she rushed through the darkness to her special spot. Water dripped off the evergreens, making soft tapping noises. The trail opened up to reveal the place that, only months earlier, she had grown to need on a nightly basis.

A large slab of granite stone jutted out over a field that was barely visible in the dark. The trees opened up enough to expose a clear view of the sky. The rain clouds began to dissipate and reveal the twinkling lights above. Ana sat cross-legged on her gazing rock. Rainwater soaked into the seat of her pants, but she didn't care. Lifen's shaggy body slid up beside her, and she wrapped her arm around her, something she wouldn't have dreamt of doing when her mentor was in human form. There was something so disarming and comforting about spending time with a dog, even if it was really a person. Ana considered that it could have been the reason Lifen chose the form.

"I used to come out and look at the stars every night."

Lifen's muzzle lifted and she stared up at the sky.

"You have a good view at your place?"

Her mentor turned her head and looked at Ana. A flash of a beautiful, crystal-clear lake with clouds reflecting on its glassy surface emerged in Ana's thoughts. Snowcapped mountains ringed the blue water, as well as tall spindly evergreens. It was the same place she had dreamt of for the last couple months.

Ana recoiled in surprise. "Did you just push your thoughts into my head?" She wasn't sure she liked that.

Lifen blinked then stood up and walked back down the trail to the house. Clearly she didn't feel like talking. Maybe there was more than one reason her mentor preferred staying in animal form around people. Ana made a mental note to ask again later.

She wasn't ready to go back inside yet and rested her head on her arm. With a deep sigh, her eyes traced the branches nearby and Ana longed to hear the soft hooting from an owl. Before she knew about Chance's shapeshifting abilities, without her knowledge, he would join her at night in his feathery form.

A strange sensation came over her. Ana whipped her head to the side, searching for Tifen in the forest, but she couldn't see anything. A vision formed in her thoughts, fuzzy around the edges, and sharp at the center.

The perspective made her dizzy at first. She was high up, staring down at the ground below. It was night, she guessed, but it almost seemed like she was wearing night vision goggles. She saw everything very clearly, but it looked strange, different.

She's so beautiful.

Ana's heart skipped a beat at the sound of Chance's voice. Was he there? She rose to her feet, and swayed uneasily while she stared into the dark.

She could never love someone like you.

A tear fell from her eye as she realized his voice was only in her head. Her thoughts blurred and she saw herself laying on her stargazing rock. Ana suddenly realized what was happening. It had to be one of Chance's memories. It made sense. When a shifter died, their powers were released from their body and went into any others nearby. Chance had died trying to heal Ana, and all of his power had gone into her. His grandfather, Niyol, had given himself to save his grandson from death. Ana recalled Chance describing the memories he'd received from his grandfather's energy transfer.

Ana steadied herself. This strange sensation wasn't unfamiliar to her. This wasn't the first time she'd experienced it. Only days earlier, she'd felt Chance's despair when he had tried to save her after Ana's heart had failed on the mountaintop. He'd shifted into a horse to carry her home. At the time she'd experienced this memory, she'd been sharing the same feelings. Desperation had gripped her as she stood helplessly in the jungle, needing to save Chance from Markus.

That's when everything had changed and she'd shapeshifted for the first time.

Ana stood on her gazing stone, her heart racing in excitement. Chance was far away from her, but now she knew he was with her. Her hands drifted to her chest and she cupped them over her heart.

She felt him with her when she lay down in bed that night, pulled the covers up to her chin and nestled in. As she closed her eyes and drifted off to sleep, thoughts of Chance spun through her mind. His spicy scent touched her senses and she breathed deeply.

A bulky form stormed through the jungle, its dark fur brushing past vines and spiky foliage. Grunting and panting noises rumbled from its chest. The bear was hungry for something. Ana clutched her pillow tightly, filled with anxiety.

The beast paused behind some trees as it focused on its target: a young woman hanging wet clothing on a line.

CHAPTER 6

Chance lifted his paw, midstep and grunted. Saliva washed his mouth as he felt her energy. It was minimal, but she had more than the average person. It was something.

The young woman stood no more than fifty yards away from him, doing her chores. They weren't in a metropolis—the tiny house was in the outskirts of a nearby town. He wouldn't risk going so near in bear form, although he was hungry. Hungry for more than just food, he wanted more power. It was a thirst that needed quenching.

You will feel like new if you take her. Never mind sleeping. Consume her. She's yours.

He stood poised behind the scrub brush and trees, which were few and far between. As he had moved farther north and out of the Yucatán, the landscape grew drier and sparser. It would be harder to remain in such a large animal form without drawing attention, which was something he didn't want, and all the voices in his head were in agreement. At least on this subject.

Chance sniffed the air and could smell the woman's floral scent, but it was the aroma of food pouring from the house that made his stomach rumble. Before he could move, his thoughts clouded and were no longer his own. From the dark recesses of his mind, a memory surfaced. He was flying over the jungle. From his perspective, warped ripples radiated out from the earth and into the air. Wind currents carried him over the green wilderness and his attention was caught by a ballooning of the magnetic fields.

That's interesting. I wonder what's down there.

Nastas's internal voice echoed in Chance's head. It sounded like Nastas, but there was something very different about his tone. It was cold and hungry, and nothing like Chance's last memory with him. He had changed.

Nastas's curiosity piqued as the magnetic warping guided the bird's form down through the trees and beneath the canopy. Chance observed the scene in his head, and leaned against a tree for support.

He knew where Nastas was and it scared him. After weeks of living and training there, he would recognize the outlying area of Balam's home anywhere.

Nastas perched on a tree as he studied the impressive home Chance's great-grandfather had built among the Ceibas. A melodious song came from the high openings of the stone building. It was a woman's voice and she was singing words he couldn't understand. Possibly Mayan. It didn't matter, it was beautiful.

I feel stronger here. There is much power. I wonder if there's a hidden treasure inside.

Chance couldn't take it. He fell over onto the hard, clay ground and started groaning, clawing at his own furry face. He had to stop it. Turn it off. But the memory wouldn't stop. It kept on going, like he was chained to a chair and forced to watch.

Nastas flew up to one of the large openings in the living room and settled on the ledge. He centered on the pretty song, which was coming from a woman working in the kitchen. Her long onyx hair was loosely braided and hung down her back. As she moved around, it swung across her white blouse, almost like a metronome keeping rhythm.

She turned and saw the bird perched on the sill. She continued to sing, but she reached for a blanket and leaned down. When she reemerged, she no longer had the blanket. The words of her song turned into humming as she moved into the living room and approached Nastas.

"May I help you in some way?" She addressed the bird, knowingly. "Do you need sustenance, or are you passing through?"

Chance looked into the face of his great-grandmother, a woman he had never met and saw Itzel, his grandmother. She shared her mother's soft features and kind eyes. He knew why Balam fell for the lovely creature that stood before him and felt sadness for his loss.

While he experienced his own emotions at seeing his great-grandmother for the first time, he also felt Nastas's hunger grow. He felt him stare at her and appraise her power, deciding if it was worth his energy to absorb her.

Chance knew the answer before he acted. He pinched his eyes shut futilely. He knew it wouldn't help. He couldn't stop the horror from playing out in his head.

Something that meant nothing to Nastas, but caught Chance's eye, was a leather cord strung around his great-grandmother's neck. It disappeared beneath her thin blouse and seemed innocent enough. Upon closer inspection, he realized what he misinterpreted as a naïve air seemed to be an act instead. So good, in fact, Nastas didn't think anything of her slipping her necklace off and clutching it discretely in her grasp.

Interesting, she knows I'm a shifter. Don't come across many like her. She's alone and too weak to stop me. When I'm finished with her, I'll have my fill. Nastas noticed fresh fruit laid out on the table as well as a fresh batch of corn cakes. They smelled delicious, and it only reminded Chance of the mornings spent with Balam at that very table.

Nastas spread his wings, glided down to the floor and shifted into a cougar, eager to consume her energy. His guttural growl echoed off the stone walls and he looked at her, expecting a frightened reaction. It was part of the game he had developed. It pleased him.

Instead, this strange woman, his prey, braced herself with her arms up, ready for a fight. Although he was surprised by her fire, it amused him as well. She knew what he was, and she was going to try to protect herself. He stared at her athletic frame. It might help her last a few more seconds, but he was confident that she wouldn't be able to defend herself against his power.

His ears lay down against his head and he prowled toward her in an evil dance to pluck her life thread. Something dark gleamed from her closed fist. He didn't know what it was, and he didn't care. Chance observed everything in reticence. Was this what it was like being brainwashed? He resisted against Nastas's urges, but it would be so much easier to simply give in. The sensations that coursed through his body were intoxicating.

Why wait? I'm hungry for breakfast.

Nastas launched forward and Balam's wife held her arms out in front of her. As he moved through the air, her hands flipped him over her, and they both rolled backwards. He watched his tail curl out above him as he crashed into the wall. As soon as he landed, he flipped onto his paws, filled with rage. He pounced on top of her, wrapping his jaws around her neck and squeezed. Chance's great-grandmother flung her arm up and sank something sharp into his thigh right before she went limp. A soft burst of light radiated out and seeped into him. Nastas rolled his head back as he absorbed it completely.

It was a pleasurable sensation, like an endorphin rush. It took a few minutes for Nastas to take a deep breath and move off his prey. When he looked down at his leg, Chance recognized the hemlock pendant implanted in Nastas's flesh. He gently eased it out with his teeth and dropped it to the floor. Its point shone red with blood and gleamed in the light.

What a witch. She was worth the sting though. And she left me food, how nice of her.

Nastas strutted to the table and leapt atop it mid-stride. Cups of hot chocolate tipped over and bathed his paws in warmth. He licked them off and ventured over to the plate of corn cakes. Loud purring reverberated from his mouth while he devoured the food.

The memory faded away, and Chance was left with the distinct feeling that nothing could threaten his power. He was strong and in control. Nothing could stop him from what he wanted most.

Balam's home dimmed in his thoughts and he remembered where he was. On his back and in bear form, he groaned while he rolled over. He slowly rose to his feet and shook the disorientation away, like dust off a hat. Where was he?

Humming met his ears, not unlike Nastas's memory. He turned to spy the young woman who was hanging her last pieces of laundry out to dry. She wasn't particularly pretty, but Chance didn't care about that. He was drawn to the energy that flickered beneath the surface of her skin. She was transmitting to him like a shortwave radio.

Chance stood up on his back legs to crane over the landscape, scanning for people. He couldn't hear anything but the sound of the girl's song and the soft trilling from birds in nearby bushes. Tall lanky trees surrounded him and kept him hidden, but the modest home was in the middle of an open, grassy field. Definitely not the place to stomp around as a bear on the off chance a farmer with a shotgun saw him.

He considered shapeshifting into yaguar form, and the only reason he didn't was because of his promise to Balam that he would protect it. He needed to take a sleeker, smaller shape anyway, to approach the home unseen. If a bear could smirk, he would have as he thought about Nastas.

Good choice.

His dark fur rippled golden, and he shrank into a large feline. A tingling sensation trailed along from the tip of his snout to his whiskers. He rubbed his face against his leg to sooth the itch. Already in position, he arched his back, feeling every vertebra stretch. Chance lowered his body so the hairs on his stomach brushed the ground and he prowled across the grassy field. The young woman moved to another clothesline and pulled a set of sheets off. Her back was turned to the predator watching her as she meticulously paired the corners together and folded the bedding.

The closer he got, the stronger his need for power grew. It was nothing like he'd experienced before. Primal urges pushed him forward, compelled his fangs to lift, ready to cut off her blood flow and to release her reservoir of energy from her body. She was close enough for him to surge on top of her. He lowered his hindquarters and prepared to pounce.

Something sturdy collided into his ribs, sending him tumbling into the side of the house. The woman turned and let out a high-pitched scream, threw the sheet she was folding onto Chance, and moments later he heard the door slam shut. His claws tore at the striped yellow fabric as he tried to see what had barreled into him, but a weight pressed into his side and neck, and he grew dizzy.

A man's voice said something he couldn't understand.

He needed to get out of there, protect himself, but he couldn't. His body wouldn't respond. Stars and bright light swirled in his vision before everything went black.

CHAPTER 7

"It was like it was real and not just a dream."

While Ana made her bed, she spoke to the dog lying on her floor. It was really starting to get annoying that Lifen wouldn't shift into human form to talk with her. For that reason alone, she wanted to get on the road. Enough waiting.

"Fine, we're going to leave today so I can get some answers from you."

When she opened her door, a folded note fell onto her foot. She opened it and found Eva's explicit threat that if she left without saying goodbye her little sister would never forgive her. Ana wouldn't dream of sneaking out while Eva was at school, or while her mother was at work for that matter.

Even though she slept in, she didn't sleep soundly. The whole night her dreams were filled with images of Chance and she worried that he wasn't safe. She didn't like not knowing. It killed her not being with him. Not being able to help.

Ana rushed downstairs eager to get breakfast. Lifen seemed to have the same idea while she loitered next to the fridge, waiting for Ana.

"You know, no one's home right now. You can shift back so we can talk." Ana reached for the cupboard door. Lifen just sat and stared at her while she prepared a cup of coffee. "Guess you're giving me the silent treatment until we leave. Okay, I've got to run out to grab a couple things at the store so I can finish packing while Mom and Eva are gone. We can leave early this evening, if I play my cards right. Don't know how long it'll take to get to your place, but we'll probably have to stop at a hotel along the way. Hope you're not planning on staying a dog the whole time..."

Ana got them both breakfast and took another long shower. Even though she took one the night before, she took another just because she could. After throwing on a pair of jeans and a sweatshirt, she grabbed her keys and prepared to leave. Ana sighed and thought about what she needed to do to get ready for her trip. If the tables were turned, she knew that her love would stop at nothing to save her. She hoped she'd live up to the model he'd set.

***

"Already?" Eva's knuckles settled on her hips and she rolled her eyes. "One more night? *Please*, Ana?"

They were standing in the living room and Melissa had only been home for half an hour before Ana chose to spring it on them.

"I'm sorry, sweetie. I've got to get moving. I have a job opportunity at a ski lodge up north and they're expecting their first big snow dump any time. Do you think that banana on wheels can make it up an icy hill without any trouble?"

"Oh, speaking of which. I spoke to Tera today and I mentioned your plans to head to Canada, so Jace swung by the bank and dropped these off." Melissa tapped a hard plastic case that was leaning up against the wall with the toe of her pumps. "Chains. Have you ever put them on before? Do you know how?"

Her mother frowned and leaned down to read the label. The large sticker that contained the instructions crinkled at her touch, and the edges fluttered to the floor. Ana momentarily shared Melissa's concern, since she'd never had to do anything to her car except put gas in it. She pinched her lips together and noticed Lifen lying under the kitchen table, her chin resting on her paws. The dog was staring at her mother out of the corner of her eyes in such a way it made Ana laugh. "Nope. I have no idea, but I'm sure I can follow the how-to. If all else fails, I'll try to flag down a cop or highway patrolman or something. I'm not worried. There isn't supposed to be snow for another couple days, but that's why I've got to get moving."

"You know how much I hate this, right? But I like knowing you're not so far away from me. A couple hours' drive is better than you being halfway across the world."

"I wasn't halfway across the world, Mom. I was in Mexico."

"Same thing. You sure you've got everything you need? Your good winter jacket, heavy socks, thermal underwear, hats, gloves, boots, sweaters..."

"Yes—I've got it all. I swear. I was very careful packing—you know me. "

"Yes, I do, and I don't know what I'm worried about. We're going to miss you sweetie, but I'm going to expect you for Christmas." Her mother held her tight in an embrace and she sniffled before letting Ana go.

Eva walked up to her and gave her a hug. Her sweet face lifted and she announced, "I don't like you going, but I agree with Mom—it's better knowing you won't be far away. You'd better call me."

"I will, I swear. You keep up the good work at school and keep an eye on Mom for me." Ana leaned down and whispered in Eva's ear, "Tell me if things get serious with her boyfriend. Remember, you can call me too."

She kissed the top of her sister's head and pulled on her coat. With her keys in hand, she went outside with her family to the van. It sat in the twilight, pointed down the driveway with all of her baggage loaded and ready to go. Lifen waited inside with her head out the driver's window.

"You call when you get there." Melissa hollered while Ana climbed into the car.

"I will, Mom."

Ana fired up the engine and rolled up her window. She gave one last wave before pulling away. It would only be harder to leave the longer she spent saying goodbye. Sadness pitted in her stomach while she thought about leaving home without Chance.

She sniffed and wiped her eyes. Lifen sat on the seat beside her and cocked her head. "It's Chance. I just miss him so much and I'm worried about him. Who knew being in love was so painful." Ana gripped the steering wheel. "How long are you going to make me suffer? You aren't really going to stay a dog the whole trip are you?"

The dog leaned over, licked her hand and wandered into the back of the VW van. A minute later, Lifen climbed into the passenger seat, wrapped in her blue sarong and buckled up. Her long, black hair appeared to need a good brushing after her stint as a canine over the last day. She stared out her window in silence and Ana wondered if she would ever speak.

"It was interesting staying with your family. When you are hidden in plain sight, it is fascinating what is revealed. Your mother and sister love you very much. That is obvious. It was nice being a part of your family for a day. Mine passed away so long ago. Their memory is only a whisper in my thoughts."

Ana put her foot down on the accelerator and sped up on the highway while they made their way out of town. She had so many questions for Lifen, but it was clear her mentor didn't like revealing much about herself, and she didn't want to ruin the moment by pushing her for more. She was rewarded with her silence when Lifen continued. "I have pieced together my own family. I look forward to introducing you to them. They are like my children. After seeing you with your mother and sister, I have no doubt you will fit in well. Like any close family, it is built on trust."

"You can trust me," Ana volunteered, hoping to get more information.

"I would not have brought you this far if I didn't. My home is a safe place for younglings who need it. Who need guidance, training and a place to call home. In the new world, our kind have struggled to fit in. When people discover our special talents, young ones can be cast out or even hunted down. It is no longer safe to reveal oneself to normal humans. In my time, when there was still a sense of magic and wonder, you had a better chance, but now there's only fear."

Ana couldn't stand it—she was dying of curiosity. "How old are you, Lifen?"

Lifen brushed her hands on her arms. Ana reached back for a sweater she had left out and handed it to her mentor. "Thank you. I have lived through much upheaval and have seen the destruction of man. I left China so long ago, it is hard to remember when, and traveled the world. No matter where you go, it is the same."

She guessed she wasn't going to get a straight answer. "Why'd you pick Canada?"

"It is quiet there. Not as many shifters seeking you out as in the cities."

"Pretty too, I imagine." Ana thought of the shining lake and the snowcapped mountains she had seen in her dreams. It reminded her of the question that was left unanswered from the other night. "I think I've dreamt about your home. Last night when we were looking at the stars, I saw it in my mind. Did you do that? Is that like a special power?"

Lifen pulled on the sweater and swept her hair to the side. She adjusted in her seat and avoided looking at Ana. "It is hard to explain. Healers can have simple psychic abilities. While healing, it is helpful to link with the subject's psyche to soothe them, but this is only something you may do at close range. Months ago, one evening while I was meditating I sensed you. I knew you were different and special because it is not normal to be able to reach your consciousness from so far away."

"Wait, what do you mean?" Ana asked. "I reached out to *you*?" What did that even mean?

"Yes, while you were sleeping, your mind took a trip and visited me. I offered images to you of my home and did so many times, but only while you were at rest and when you freed yourself from your body."

"Well, what about last night, when I saw the lake in my mind while we were looking at the stars?"

"I did not put that image in your head. You took it from mine."

Ana stared at Lifen, completely stunned. "I don't understand..."

"You are very talented, Ana. A natural."

She thought about her vivid dreams of Chance and a lump formed in her throat. It tightened when she spoke, like a noose pulling closed. "What about my dream last night of Chance? It seemed so real... Was it?"

The implications of that frightened her. If it were real, then did that mean he'd killed an innocent woman? A chill laced down her spine and goose bumps rose on her arms.

"Most likely, yes. When you're deep in sleep, you appear to be able to drift away from yourself."

"Can you do it?" Ana held her breath while she waited for an answer.

"Only in close proximity." Lifen stared out the window and changed the subject. "We want to take highway 95 north into Canada. We can look for a hotel once we cross the lines. I think I recall hearing you say you brought your passport?"

Ana pointed to her backpack which was sitting on the floorboards between the seats. "Yeah, I've got my passport and your bag is in the back. Should have everything. How long will it take to get there?"

"I think we should get there tomorrow midday. I will let my family know we are coming and they will be prepared to welcome us properly."

"How many people live with you?" Anxiety crept into Ana's thoughts. She didn't have much experience making friends. In school, she typically kept to herself to avoid drawing attention.

"It's ever-changing, but right now, there are three younglings. Many others I have helped visit from time to time. They will all eventually leave, but only when they have mastered control of themselves. I will not be responsible for more poisoned shifters running free."

Lifen began to sing a song that was very familiar to Ana. It had been the musical backdrop to her dreams of Lifen's home in Canada. It was clear Lifen wasn't prepared to reveal anything more about herself. Ana knew it was in her best interest to drop the questions for now until Lifen was ready to share some more.

She had plenty to think about anyway. Ever since she met Lifen, she'd assumed her mentor had placed the visions of the crystal blue lake in her dreams. That she had been responsible for pushing thoughts of that place into her mind last night. The news that it was Ana's own abilities completely surprised her. She hadn't expected it.

Lifen said she was special. Unique. A natural.

Ana had so many questions that she wanted answered all at once, but it was obvious that her new teacher wasn't going to divulge anything more right now. She would have to work for it. She thought back to the countless times she'd soothed Chance's agitation when answers didn't come quick enough. *Patience, Chance,* she'd said to him. Where was he now that she needed him to calm her own nerves? They were vibrating so palpably she was practically humming with energy.

There was one way she might see him again, and see where he was. Through her dreams. If she could somehow visit him again while she slept, then she'd know if he were safe. The memories from last night were still fresh in her mind. He wasn't himself, dangerous even. But she had to know, even if the truth was too painful.

She gripped the gear shift tight as she turned north on the highway. Bright lights from oncoming traffic shone through the windshield and she flipped the visor down. Twilight had faded into tar-black night and she said a silent prayer.

CHAPTER 8

Chance woke with a start. He was in a dingy room with an earthen floor. It was empty of furniture, lights, or anything that made it livable. He sat upright too fast and became dizzy, so he leaned his back against the cement wall. While his blood pressure settled, he scanned the space and let his senses open up.

It was dark, although his sharp eyesight was able to discern everything he needed to. He was covered with the sheet that had been tossed onto him, that had hidden his attacker from view. Its yellow stripes were murky gray in the twilight. His backpack lay on the floor beside him. The ground buzzed with sounds from insects and the crackly beat from a radio came and went. A road must be nearby.

He smelled food. His empty stomach gurgled, demanding, while he lifted his nose to the air. Like Balam had taught him, he shifted the inner contours of his nasal cavity without changing his outward appearance. The aroma of meat, spices and cornmeal overpowered him and a flush of saliva washed his mouth. From outside the front door of the abandoned shack he could also detect the odor of human sweat.

He needed to leave, to get out of there. Whatever or whoever put him here could be dangerous, or could be after his power.

Hold on, I sense energy. A lot of energy. Don't let yourself get taken by surprise. Know your enemy.

The voice in his head swayed Chance to stay for a peak. He adjusted in place, closed his eyes and concentrated on the mapping that came to him first. A wood mouse. It was a form he'd never taken before. However, Nastas had. Energy coursed through his body and the hairs on his skin multiplied, turning into a thick blanket of gray fur. He shrank into the tiny mammal, leaving behind the sheet and his belongings. His tiny feet scurried forward, inching toward the open door. Long whiskers brushed against the floor, gathering dust as he went, and with every step, the long wispy sensors helped him feel movement in the air.

Chance stretched out his pink, wet nose around the doorframe and breathed in deeply. More of that delicious smell. It was making it hard for him to focus on much else. High above him, the body of a man rose like an enormous redwood. He was giant, at least to a tiny mouse. The man was eating something wrapped in shiny tinfoil. Outside of the aroma that poured from the meal, Chance detected a massive amount of power radiating from the man, and it was clear he was no ordinary human. That meant trouble.

Was he dangerous? And why had he grabbed Chance? He couldn't have intended to kill him because Chance would be dead otherwise. Although that didn't mean he couldn't try to steal his power when he changed his mind.

Chance was extremely curious as to why this man kidnapped him, but that in no way outweighed his growing hunger for power. As soon as he sensed the man's aura dripping with energy, a switch was flipped. The young woman from earlier was no comparison to this man. She was a fleck of dust next to him.

Can you imagine the power you'd have after stealing his energy? You'd be unstoppable. You can't just kill this one— he's too old. It's best to learn more, and be patient.

"Instead of sitting there staring, would you rather join me? I brought food for you."

The man dropped his gaze to Chance, who froze in the doorway, unsure what to do. So much for stealth. How long had this guy known he was there? Taking him by surprise was out, and he began to doubt he'd have a chance bringing him down anyway. The man's steely eyes had a frightening edge to them, and Chance didn't doubt he knew how to protect himself.

"I know what you are thinking, and no, it is not worth your effort to try to kill me. It will only end badly for you. Instead of letting your primal hunger take over, feed your body. I can see you are neglecting yourself. You are unwell. Let me help." He pointed to something the size of a brick wrapped in tinfoil that lay beside him. From Chance's perspective it was huge. "I have no interest in harming you, and believe me—I could if I wanted to."

Chance considered what the man said and decided it made sense. He was desperately hungry and so very tired, tired of listening to the voices in his head that pulled him every direction so he never knew which he should listen to. He needed a break. Maybe he was making a mistake, but he didn't really care right then. Maybe it was best to be put out of his misery. If this guy killed him, at least he wouldn't hear the voices any longer.

He scurried back into the dingy shack and to his belongings. Within moments, he was standing naked in his human form. His eyes adjusted to the low light and it took him a second to decipher the shapes around him. He pulled out a pair of shorts and a T-shirt from his pack, and threw them on quickly. There was no point waiting any longer. He strode out the open door to meet the man sitting outside.

Now that the man wasn't looming over Chance like a giant, Chance was able to make out his features much better. Stick straight, onyx hair hung down to his dark narrow eyes. He appeared to be middle aged, probably older than Chance's parents. He wore a pair of shorts and a button-down shirt. His skin color was similar to Chance's but his build was much sturdier. Chance stood there studying him.

The man held his hand out to a dirty patch across from where he sat cross-legged. "Please, join me," he said.

Chance hesitated, then walked over and sat down.

71

The man held out the foil-wrapped food. "Eat."

He didn't need coaxing. Chance tore open the aluminum and began wolfing down the tamales. As the food settled in his stomach it made him notice just how starved he had been. Cramps pinched his abdomen with every mouthful and he had to remind himself to chew instead of swallowing bites whole. *Slow down.*

"You do not need to speak now, just eat. My name is Batukhan and I am pleased to meet you, young shapeshifter."

Chance nodded and was able to say, "Chance," between bites.

"Hello, Chance. You probably have many questions, and I will do my best to answer the ones I can while you feed yourself. I too, am a shapeshifter, which is how I know what you are. I can see you have much power, power that does not appear to be stable within you. It was I who stopped you from attacking that young woman, which is something you may have already surmised, something I hope you will have the conscience to thank me for later." Batukhan sat very still and it appeared like the top of his head was hung from a hook because he sat so straight. "I imagine there is a battle waging inside of you, young man, and that you struggle with finding your way. I know the situation you are in and have decided to help you."

Chance finished chewing his last bite of food and experienced the rush of nutrients entering his cells. He crushed the foil in his hands. "How could you possibly know what I'm dealing with?"

"I can see it in your eyes and I've seen it before. That, and I've been following you."

The serious expression on Batukhan's face gave Chance pause. This guy had been following him? He hadn't sensed anything out of the ordinary since he'd had that strange run-in with the stunning Asian woman, Lifen, who had claimed she wanted to help him. The woman who had said she'd seen Ana.

Chance's heart squeezed in his chest as he thought about the look on Ana's face when he'd flown away. He missed her so much it hurt, which was why he'd been avoiding dwelling on her memory. He couldn't trust himself right now to make any decisions. Especially when it came to Ana. His instinct was to run to her side and protect her. But what if those innocent feelings turned into hunger, like in his last moments with her? She wasn't an average human any longer. She was a shifter and she was the last person he ever wanted to hurt.

"Chance, can you stay present with me? I know it is hard."

Chance met Batukhan's eyes and nodded. His voice came out gravely. "You've been following me?"

"I had a dream the other night of an old friend. I hadn't seen him in some time so I decided to come visit to see if he was okay, but it appears he is not."

He couldn't possibly be speaking of Balam, or could he?

"Who? A shifter?"

"A man by the name of Balam. I met him on my travels. I guess it would have been about a hundred and fifty years ago. Sadly, he seems to have passed from this Earth."

Chance cupped his hands around his eyes and his blood pressure spiked. Thoughts of his great-grandfather were painful and he grew frightened, unsure what to do. What would Balam suggest right now?

"Did you know Balam?"

Through gasps, Chance said, "He was family."

"I see. Calm yourself, youngling. Take deep, slow breaths and think about something that is peaceful . . .the ocean or the sunset."

He did as Batukhan said, and imagined the repetitive waves lapping at the sand. His breathing steadied and his anxiety subsided. Chance lowered his hands to his sides and avoided eye contact.

"Very good. Well, now I know why I dreamt of him, and I am glad I decided not to follow Lifen's scent trail. I smelled so many people around Balam's home, but I was surprised to recognize hers, so I decided to track it and found you instead. I was curious to see why she didn't bother."

Chance inhaled sharply and tensed. *Didn't bother with what?*

"No, I don't mean it the way you think. Can you tell me about yourself?"

The food in his belly had improved his clarity of mind, but Chance was still extremely confused and unsure which instincts to trust. Batukhan was more aware of what was going on than he was, and he didn't like that. He constantly felt like he was in the middle of a game of pin the tail on the donkey. He'd been blindfolded and spun senseless and didn't know what direction to go. Was Batukhan someone to trust? It was far too early to tell, but he said he knew Balam and he'd just given him food. Dog catchers throw scraps out to capture strays too, and it did not mean he was a friend.

"No. I won't share anything about myself until you tell me more about who you are and why you're helping me." Chance scoffed at the word *help*, but he wanted to see Batukhan's reaction. "You can start off with telling me how long I've been asleep."

"I understand." Batukhan placed his hands on his knees and allowed his shoulders to roll back into an even straighter posture. "You have been getting much-needed rest. Your eyes are hollow and sunken, but not as bad now that you have slept for a day."

"A day?" Now that he thought about it, he didn't feel as battered and mentally exhausted as he had been. Since he'd left Ana's side, he hadn't had a night's sleep.

"Yes, you very much needed it."

"Right. So, give me the rundown on who you are, Batukhan." Chance enunciated his name carefully.

"I was born around eight hundred years ago in Mongolia. Shapeshifters held much power, but common men were not aware of that. We kept our existence secret, as we were far more powerful this way. The Mongols believed in omens, luck and magic and that was how we shaped the future. In my youth, I was full of excitement and was eager to change the world . . . and I did."

Batukhan grew quiet and his eyes turned down to the ground. "I met a girl and we were both changed forever. Ever since, I've been trying to make things right. To create balance, but it is slow work."

Chance couldn't quite understand what he was talking about. But he felt the emotion that churned below Batukhan's restrained exterior and knew he spoke the truth. "Why does love make things so complicated?" Chance grumbled.

The edge of Batukhan's lips turned up slightly and he answered, "Love itself is calm. Turbulence comes from individuals."

"I guess." Chance stared at Batukhan, trying to decide what to do next. "So, what do you want with me?"

"I would like to help you. I am not a healer, but I know someone who can teach you ways to quiet the voices in your head. He helped me."

"How do you know about the voices? Did you have the sickness?"

"Yes, when I was young I killed another shifter and absorbed his power. Plus I have developed my own unique problems. For the longest time, I thought it was my punishment and didn't seek a way to correct it, but I grew to change my mind. Chance, I can see the confusion in your eyes, and feel the unbalanced energy radiating from you—you are losing the battle. I have met others like you who need help to rise above it all. The longer you wait, the harder it is to clear the voices, and if you don't rest it will only make things worse. The more souls you consume, the harder it is to hold on to who you were. It is hard, but you need to hurry if you wish to hold onto your soul."

Don't listen to him. He's only trying to disorient you. You can't trust him.

The voices pulled on his thoughts like children fighting over a toy. He knew there was no way he could truly trust Batukhan, but with Ana fresh in his mind, he knew he had to fight for her.

"Fine. What do I do next?"

CHAPTER 9

Ana woke disappointed the next morning. She didn't remember any of her dreams, but was confident she hadn't visited Chance. Besides that, it felt like the first day of school all over again, but worse. Her mother and sister weren't there to give her a reassuring hug.

She barely spoke to Lifen while they checked out of their hotel room and loaded up the van.

Lifen buckled up in the passenger seat. "Are you ready to meet your new family?"

Ana nodded, but kept quiet. They drove back onto the one-lane highway and continued north. They were surrounded by evergreens and mountains. Snow had been falling through the early morning hours, and a few inches already clung to the trees and the side of the road.

"Thank you for leaving last night," Lifen said. "We should get to my home before the roads get bad." She looked at Ana. "You are very quiet this morning. What is wrong?"

Ana turned the wipers on high and glared out the window. "I didn't dream about Chance last night. I'm worried about him."

"I see. When it is time for you to start training, you will need to allow yourself to focus entirely on yourself. You cannot let him distract you from learning. I know you care for him, but you will need to let go of those feelings if you wish to help him."

"I love him. I can't just *let go* of those feelings."

"I understand, Ana. But how can you learn if you are thinking about him? Your abilities are impressive. You show so much potential. I would hate to see you slow your learning because of Chance. Would he want that?"

What would he want? She knew that he'd be supportive of her developing her powers, and if he were free of the sickness, he'd be with her now. But he wasn't, and she had to help him. The only way to do that was to listen to Lifen. Time was not on her side. Anything could happen to Chance. If she believed her dreams and what she'd been told, then he was like Markus reincarnated. A power-hungry shifter without a conscience. It turned her stomach to think of him in that way. He was her soul mate. The one who'd saved her life on multiple occasions. He was kindhearted, compassionate, and maybe a little impulsive, but she loved that about him.

"I'll try."

"What else is wrong?"

She really didn't want to talk about it. Not with Lifen. She knew she was her mentor, but they hadn't bonded that much over the last couple days. Ana didn't feel like opening up about all of her anxieties. Lifen stared at her and she was pressed to say something.

"I'm not good at making friends," Ana said.

Lifen blinked at her and then continued gazing out the window. Thankfully, she didn't respond and Ana was allowed to continue to worry in silence.

The highway got slick by the time Lifen instructed her to turn off onto a paved road that stated clearly it was private property. Ana floored the accelerator to get enough speed to make it up the initial ascent. When she made it to the top of the hill, she expected to see a home, but instead, the road kept on going. They curved through a mountain pass for some time before they came around a turn and a cerulean lake shone through the trees.

"Is that the lake?" Ana asked nervously.

"Yes, that is our lake. Bluer than the Mediterranean and clear as glass." Lifen balanced gracefully in her seat as the van bumped over the drive. "We are nearly there."

Now that they were so close, Ana's stomach twisted in knots. She didn't know what to expect, but she did know it wouldn't be anything like high school. She wouldn't go unnoticed amongst crowds of people. Her heartbeat thundered away and she gripped the wheel tight.

The road widened and a large gate blocked their way. A sign mounted at the center read, *Animal Rehabilitation Center.* Ana looked at Lifen questioningly.

"It is a mission that falls hand in hand with our purpose," Lifen said, "and it is the perfect cover. Go ahead and pull up to the box and enter star nine five."

Ana pulled up to a black security box ten feet away from the gate and punched in the code. The mechanism that controlled it slowly pulled the large, wooden gate aside until she had room to drive through. The van crested a hill which then sloped down into an enormous driveway. A four-door garage was straight ahead, and a huge galvanized outbuilding was to their right.

"Why don't you park right here and I'll have one of the boys park it in the garage." Lifen pointed to a loop in the drive beside the garage where handrails disappeared down the slope of the mountain. She presumed the stairs led to the home, but she couldn't see it from where she sat.

"Okay." Ana pulled up and shut off the van. After listening to the thunderous Volkswagen engine all morning, the silence was deafening. Snowflakes clung to the window wipers now that they were still.

Lifen got out, and Ana followed suit. A tinny, creaking groan broke the silence. Ana opened the side doors of the van, handed Lifen her pouch, and began to pull her own baggage out.

"Oh, no," Lifen said. "The boys can do that for you."

Ana shrugged and grabbed her backpack. It had her personal effects in it and she preferred to keep it close by. She shut the van doors and followed Lifen to flagstone stairs and a matching walkway. It zigzagged down the mountainside and led to an amazing home built onto the ridge below them. It looked like a resort or something that would be featured in Sunset magazine. The picturesque lake sat at the base of the mountain. Even through the snow falling, it glimmered bright like a precious jewel.

When they got to the large wooden front door, Ana tried calming her nervous heartbeat and took a deep breath. Lifen walked in and called out, "We're home. Hello?"

Ana closed the door behind them and was stunned by the museum-like interior. Track lighting laced the vaulted ceilings and detailed paintings hung on the walls. The entry opened up into a large living room with floor-to-ceiling windows.

Lifen took her shoes off and set them on the grass matt she and Ana were standing on. She put on a pair of silken slippers and offered a pair to Ana, who did like her mentor.

"Lifen!" A voice echoed through the house.

A lanky young man sauntered into the entryway and held his hand out to her. "Welcome home."

"Thank you, Jordan. It is good to be home. Anything out of the ordinary while I've been gone?"

"No, there have been no visitors. We have been caring for the animals and continuing our studies as you instructed us to do." The young man eyed Ana curiously as he answered.

"Let me introduce you to Ana Hughes. She is my newest student."

Jordan's brown eyes flickered with confusion, but he turned to Ana and shook her hand politely. She felt an electric charge when he touched her and laughed nervously to cover her surprise. He brushed his brown hair out of his eyes. "Welcome, Ana. I have made some lunch for your arrival."

"Thank you, Jordan." Lifen stepped ahead of him and he gestured for Ana to go first. They went down a hallway and turned right into another open room. A long wooden table reflected the light coming in from the windows. Rice, beef with steamed vegetables and a covered bowl sat at its center.

"The others know you're here. They'll be here in a minute."

Jordan reminded Ana of a boy she used to know in sixth grade. He was the teacher's pet and always had a holier than thou attitude, which got under her skin. She hadn't liked him and she wasn't sure if she liked Jordan either. Ana hoped the other boys didn't have an elitist attitude, because it would make it that much harder to fit in.

Lifen sat down at the table and beckoned Ana to sit beside her. Jordan craned his neck to look down the hallway and muttered, "I'll go see where they are. Be right back..."

He ducked out of the room and Ana took a closer look at the food on the table. She was hungry after a long morning of driving through the snow. Lifen placed a small bowl in front of her and uncovered the pot. A curl of steam rose above the brown broth.

"Miso soup," Lifen said. "Have you ever had it?"

"No, I haven't, but it smells good."

After Lifen put a small bowl at each of the other seats, she used a large serving spoon to dish out soup into each one. Dark leafy greens, white cubes and green onions floated in the broth. Ana hadn't eaten anything like it before, but she was hungry enough to try anything. She was tempted to pick up her spoon and begin eating, but she didn't want to be rude, so she waited patiently and hoped the others would get there soon.

Voices echoed down the hallway. "Finally," Lifen said. "It will be nice having another woman here for a change. Males can be so self-centered."

Laughter boomed in the doorway, and a group of guys wandered in. They quieted immediately when Lifen turned to them, her serene face hardened.

"Sorry, Lifen," they said. "Welcome home." Each of them stepped forward to shake her hand. They moved to the table and paused when they saw Ana. She tucked her hair behind her ear and awkwardly stood up, unsure what to do.

"Hi, I'm Ana."

"Finally," a twenty-something guy said. "You hired a maid. Thank you, Lifen. But where's the new student you were bringing back?" He turned around. If it weren't for his condescending comment, Ana would have thought his blue eyes and handsome smirk were ruggedly charming. Heat radiated across her cheeks and she wasn't sure if it was her embarrassment or anger that prompted it.

"Ryan, she *is* the new student," Jordan muttered under his breath.

Ryan's eyes widened and then he laughed with a little too much amusement. His long blond hair gave him a laid-back skateboarder's appearance, but once he opened his mouth, that preconception was broken. "Wow, I apologize. Just didn't think..."

A third boy with tight, black curls brushed past the others and held his hand out to Ana. "Hey, my name's Derek. It's nice to meet you, Ana. Don't mind Ryan–he's a jerk to everyone."

Ana shook Derek's outstretched hand, happy to concentrate on something other than Ryan and Jordan, and experienced a gentle shock of energy when they touched, similar to when she shook Jordan's hand. He lowered his eyes and his umber cheeks pulled up to reveal a set of dimples. Ana decided he was the most likeable out of the lot.

"Give her a proper welcome, Ryan," Lifen said in a serious tone.

The smirk on Ryan's face was replaced with an apologetic frown that she didn't buy. "I'm sorry, Ana. I'm sure you'll like it here."

"Thanks," Ana muttered before sitting down in her chair.

Derek strode around the table and took the seat beside Ana, while Ryan and Jordan sat across from her. She really didn't want to dwell on the awkward introduction, so she moved on to small talk and hoped she'd grow to like her new "classmates," although they weren't off to a good start. "The food looks great."

Jordan placed a napkin on his lap. "I wanted to have something warm for Lifen when she arrived. I know how much she likes my cooking."

Somehow, Ana wasn't surprised.

"Thank you, Jordan," Lifen said. "Your thoughtfulness is appreciated."

Ana breathed in the aroma from the soup and her stomach gurgled.

"Here, let me get that for you." Derek stood and served her a portion of rice, steamed vegetables and meat.

"Thanks, Derek." She watched the others serve themselves.

"If I had a pair of breasts, would you help me too?" Ryan flicked his hair back while batting his eyelashes.

Ana wasn't sure if the insult was aimed at her or Derek, but his reaction startled her. He grabbed his knife off the table. The softened expression that had made her so comfortable a moment ago had transformed into an angry grimace. "Don't push me, Ryan."

Maybe Derek wasn't as sweet as he appeared. She tried to brush away her fears, but every minute that passed made her worry she'd made a terrible mistake coming here.

"Boys, is this how you make someone feel welcome?" Lifen said with a cutting tone. She waited for them to settle before she closed her eyes and said, "Let this food nourish our bodies so we may channel our energy in positive ways."

They all closed their eyes and remained quiet for a moment. Ana was unsure what to do. Should she copy them or simply wait for them to finish?

"We focus inward to connect with our energy, and remind ourselves of our purpose—to be a positive force in the world." Lifen's soft voice drifted through the room.

Ana lowered her eyes and nodded. "I'll try it next time."

Jordan cleared his throat. "How was your trip, Lifen?"

"I don't often travel so far or for so long. I do not like being away from my students. I like knowing you are safe, but even though I missed being home, it was worth it. I brought back someone very gifted."

The guy's faces turned to stare at Ana, who was taking a large bite of rice and vegetables. She hastily chewed and swallowed, not enjoying being the center of attention, especially while she was eating.

"Where're you from?" Ryan took a sip of his soup.

It seemed like an innocent enough question, so she decided it was safe to answer. "Oh, well that's kind of a long story, but I'm originally from Colorado and this last spring I moved to northern Idaho. Not too far from here."

"Lifen, I thought you said you were down in Mexico?" Derek asked.

"Yes," Lifen said. "I had to go a long way to find our Ana. She was far from home when I sensed she was ready for instruction."

Ana lifted the strange spoon that was resting in her bowl. It was wide and seemed perfectly designed to scoop up a large mouthful of soup. She hoped no one would engage her in conversation while she tried her next bite. The warm, salty broth washed down her throat and coated her stomach. It was delicious and perfect after a long day of driving through the snow.

"Ana?" Lifen's voice startled her.

She swallowed another mouthful of soup and was disappointed to see she was everyone's focus again. "I'm sorry, what?"

"They want to know if you're like me," Lifen said. "If you're a shapeshifter as well." Then she added, "I thought it was best for you to answer."

As Ana's eyes combed past each of the boys, she saw they all seemed to be holding their breath, waiting for her answer. Even Ryan, who only minutes earlier had been smirking, was now staring seriously at her.

"Oh, right." She didn't really want to talk about it with people she'd just met. Plus, she hadn't actually told anyone yet. It didn't even make much sense to her, so how was she supposed to explain it?

"Hey, Ana," Derek said. "It's weird talking about it at first. No worries, I get it. If you want, I can tell you about when I discovered I was a shifter. That cool?" He gripped his spoon in his hand and pressed his lips together.

"Yeah." Ana took a shuddering breath, thankful that he'd helped her avoid talking before she was ready.

Derek pushed back from the table and crossed his legs. "I was almost seventeen when I first shifted. I definitely wasn't expecting it, neither. I was hanging in the backyard . . ." He gave a smirk. "Actually, I was blowing off steam, 'cause my girlfriend and I got into a fight. The little yappy dog next door, a Chihuahua or something, was letting loose at the fence. All I wanted was to get away and escape from my problems—you know?"

Ana nodded and rested her hand beside her plate, more interested in Derek's story than eating. From her periphery, she could see Ryan and Jordan finishing their food and staring out the large windows behind her. She guessed this wasn't the first time they'd heard the story.

"While I was staring at the little rat dog," Derek said, "it turned all blue with glowing lines—trippiest thing ever the first time. Thought it was getting sick at first, or was a freaky alien or something. But then my skin started tingling and next thing I knew, I was shorter than the weeds in the yard. Wasn't sure if I'd wished myself that way or what had happened. When mama got home I was scratching at the back door, shivering in the cold. She thought I was the neighbor's dog at first, but when she heard it barking ten feet away and saw my pile of clothes on the ground, she got a funny look in her eye and let me in, like she knew it was me. She gave me some food and water and told me to think about my human body and a feeling like 'going home.' Before I knew it, I was naked on the floor at my mama's feet." Derek's cheeks darkened and he rubbed the curls on top of his head.

"Don't remember you mentioning that juicy detail before, Derek," Ryan said and raised an eyebrow.

"You ready to tell your story then?" Derek fired across the table, adopting his fiery expression again.

Ryan put his hands up, feigning innocence.

"Didn't think so."

Lifen shot them both a glare. They quieted and focused on their food instead.

Ana was curious to learn more and eager to diffuse the tension. "So, your mom wasn't surprised you were a shifter?"

"After I ran to my room and got some clothes on, Mama said that her family always told stories about when her great-great-grandpapa was brought to America. He was no ordinary slave, and I guess he frightened his share of landowners as some big cat." Derek's white teeth flashed and he laughed in amusement. "I had plenty of questions for her, questions she couldn't really answer. But she said that before her grandpapa died, he'd told her that his dad had told him that it wasn't no story, and to keep an eye on any boys born into the family. That when they got close to being a man, they might just come scratching at the door in the form of a wild animal."

"That would've been a manlier choice," Ryan muttered under his breath. When Derek stared him down, he raised his hands in the air and rolled his eyes. "What, a Chihuahua? You can't really be proud of that one."

"Better than your city rat," Derek answered with a cold sneer.

"I think my gopher was a good, solid starting point," Jordan interjected.

"What about her? She more useful than her pretty face?" Ryan raised his voice. "I don't know why I'm defending my first shift in front of someone I know nothing about . . ."

They all quieted and faced Ana, awaiting her response.

Her cheeks flushed again and she tucked a stray hair behind her ear. "Um, I shifted for the first time a couple days ago."

"No kidding," Jordan said. "Don't see many shifters around, let alone a girl. That's pretty rare. So what was your first shift? A mouse, a squirrel . . .?" He raised his eyebrow.

Ana had nearly forgotten about Lifen, who was staring out the floor-to-ceiling windows. "I have never understood why everything must be a competition for men. It is their downfall." She nodded at Ana, as if to tell her to continue, and she thought she saw the corners of her mentor's mouth curl up.

"A horse," Ana said softly.

"What do you mean?" Ryan frowned. "You were born the year of the horse?"

"No, I shifted into a horse. That was my first form." *And only one so far*, Ana thought.

The wait was worth it, she decided. After hearing the boys banter about who was less of a man, she couldn't help but enjoy the expressions on their faces.

"I told you it was your downfall," Lifen said. "After you are done eating crow, please go up to Ana's van and bring her belongings down to the spare room beside mine, and please park her van in the garage before it becomes an ornament in my driveway. Whoever is remaining, please show Ana around the house and then we will meet in the meditation room in half an hour." Lifen rose from the table and the others stood

87

as well. Ana finished chewing and grasped her napkin in her hand while she pushed her chair back.

"Would you like me to prepare the afternoon tea as well?" Jordan asked.

"Please do." Lifen looked levelly at her student. "If you will excuse me, Ana, I need to tend to a few things before we begin. I hope you find yourself at home here. I know we will become a close family. We are all part of a special group. Remember, loyalty above all else. If you need anything, just ask. I am so pleased you are here with us."

Their teacher breezed from the room and after she left Ana took one last bite of food. She didn't have much experience being around men, outside of Chance and Balam. She stared out at the snow and said the first thing that came to mind. "So, is there Internet here?"

Ryan laughed. "You can kiss technology goodbye while you're living here. Lifen says it's to keep our focus pure, but I think it's just another way to punish us."

"Punish you for what?" Ana said.

"For being men, I don't know," Ryan said. "We're not allowed to date, leave the house or surf the Internet. At least she hasn't taken away my music—that'd be the last straw." Ryan combed his shaggy blond hair away from his face.

"Right, like you have somewhere else to go," Derek fired at him. "You know why she does what she does. It's to help and protect us. Why don't you go park Ana's van and bring her stuff down?"

Jordan piped up with, "I'll clean up and make the tea."

Ryan's eyes narrowed and he spun out of the room dropping words like, "God's gift" and "teacher's pet."

Jordan started stacking the dirty plates and avoided looking at Ana. "Right, well. You know what you need to do then, right Derek?" Outside of Lifen, it seemed like Derek was the only person pleased she was there. Hopefully, the others would warm up to her. Even though she didn't really like them much on introduction, it would be hard to live in a house if she had to walk on eggshells. She didn't bicker often with her mother and sister and when they did, it didn't involve yelling as much as crying and silent glares, but just being around her aunt and uncle too much gave her a headache. Aunt Tera liked riding Uncle Jace over the littlest thing. Ana hoped it wouldn't be this loud the whole time.

Derek patted her shoulder. "Don't worry. Now that Lifen's back, things will chill. Without her around we're all more on edge. How 'bout I show you around? And I wouldn't listen to Ryan. No matter what he says, we've got it good here."

"Yeah, I've never been in a house like this. Looks like it belongs in a magazine." Ana stared out of the windows at the sapphire blue lake that shimmered at the base of the mountain.

"Nothing like Chicago. I mean, it's got its nice points, but it's so quiet here. That was hard for me to adjust to." Derek led her out of the dining room and went straight across the hall to the kitchen, a long space with more vaulted ceilings. Travertine tiles covered the floors and pale bamboo cabinets hung on the walls.

All Ana could think was how envious Eva would be if she could see her now. "Wow."

Jordan brushed past her with an armload of dishes. He placed them in a large sink and said to Derek, "Make sure you tell her the rules."

Derek rolled his eyes. "Right. This is Jordan's territory. Don't mess with his food or move anything or he'll go bat on you."

"That was one time, Derek," Jordan said. "Don't know why you can't let it rest."

"Jordan's usually in charge of dinner," Derek said. "There's food in the fridge and cupboards for breakfast and lunch—food gets delivered weekly, so we get everything that we need. Lifen likes starting practice early in the morning at sunup since that's when your energy's fresh. Then we care for the animals, and if we do that quick, we have free time until the afternoon when we go at it again."

"If Jordan usually makes dinner," Ana said, "then what do you and Ryan do? Are there chores?" She thought about Ryan's comment about her being a maid and presumed she knew the answer.

"Well, Ryan and I rotate with cleaning and dishes," Derek said. "We do our own laundry and we all care for the animals, which means feeding, cleaning stalls, bathing and grooming."

"That reminds me," Jordan said. "It's your turn to do the dishes, Derek. I'm going to see if Ryan took care of her car and luggage." He adjusted his striped polo shirt, gave Ana a sour look and turned out of the kitchen.

"Hopefully you don't get any new scratches." Derek sneered at the pile of plates and bowls in the sink and muttered, "I'll do it later. C'mon, bet you want to see the rest of the place."

They walked back down the hallway, toward the entrance of the home. The large formal living room opened up across from the front door.

"Lifen serves tea here. Sometimes her old students drop by for a visit and to have some of her special blend."

Ana frowned.

"She mixes her own tea that increases the flow of energy. It smells like lawn clippings, but with some sugar it'll grow on you." Derek's umber cheek creased, revealing a dimple.

He led her to the other end of the house, which was the larger half. Derek pointed out the bathrooms, closets and some really interesting rice paper doors that slid open to reveal the meditation room, a space that was filled with big puffy pillows laid in a semicircle on the floor. Back in the hallway, a flight of stairs went down to a lower level and

Derek explained, "That's where us guys stay. We all have our own rooms, but we have to share a bathroom."

Ana hoped that meant she wouldn't have to share one with them. It was high on her list of things she'd rather not do. As if to answer her concerns, he added, "Don't worry. You're up here with Lifen, and you have your own bathroom too. This way . . ."

He took her to the end of the hallway and opened a door to his right. "Here you go. Lifen is just next door to you." He pointed to the door across from hers. "It's got a dresser in the closet and there should be hangers 'n stuff in there for you."

Ana clasped her hands together and stepped into her new room. The walls were painted crème, and a Chinese watercolor of mountains hung above the bed. Narrow windows let light in far above her where the walls met the vaulted ceiling. It was airy and bright here and nothing like her room at home.

"Like it?"

Ana sauntered to the bathroom door, which was next to her closet and pushed it open. Equipped with a toilet, shower and sink, it had everything she'd need. She had no complaints. "Yeah, this is great."

She sat on the edge of the bed and didn't know what else to say. Emptiness consumed her and she had no words left. So much had changed in the last week, she struggled to maintain composure. Even though she was surrounded with people, she felt alone.

Ryan's voice echoed down the hallway. "Got your things, Ana. You sure you brought enough? I thought chicks liked traveling heavy, with like ten bags." His laughter and the clacking wheels of her suitcase got closer.

Ana didn't turn around, but heard Derek say, "Hey, man, leave her be. Ana, take some time and meet us in the meditation room in half an hour. Just shout if you need anything."

The door shut and she flopped backwards on the bed; the fluffy, white comforter melded to her body. As beautiful as the house was, it seemed more like a museum instead of a home. It was sterile and clean, but not snug and comforting. Nothing like the little, blue house hidden amongst the pines back in Idaho. The narrow windows above her were too small to see the sky out of, making her feel like a gerbil in a cage.

She tried to remember why she had left her family for this place and closed her eyes and imagined Chance lying beside her, his spicy scent in the air, his dark hair hanging across his hazel eyes, and a smile playing at his lips. Ana reached her hand out to touch him, but he wasn't there.

***

"Try to clear your mind. Let your thoughts and worries fall away. With every deep breath, bring in energy from the space around you."

Outside of Lifen's voice, the room was silent. Ana inhaled and let air stir in her lungs before breathing out slowly, trying to do as her mentor instructed. She opened her eyes and saw white flakes blowing just outside. The floor-to-ceiling windows let in bright light and a crisp chill. The guys sat cross-legged beside her, facing the windows as well, spaced out a foot from each other. Ana's inner thighs burned as she let her knees droop toward the floor. She hadn't often sat this way, although she guessed she'd have to get used to it now.

"It may be more helpful," Lifen said, "if you keep your eyes closed to begin with, Ana. I find it is best to get familiar with sensing your energy within and the energy around you. These are the building blocks to being a shapeshifter and a healer."

Ana nodded and tried not to notice the faces that had turned to stare at her. Her cheeks flushed and she closed her eyes, happy to hide from the attention.

"Very good," Lifen said. "Boys, were you doing your daily energy practice while I was gone?"

Jordan answered, "I made sure to do it *twice* daily, but I can't speak for the others."

Ryan sighed beside her.

"Does that mean no, Ryan? How about you Derek?"

"Well, we really tried to." Derek's deep voice bounced off the walls.

Ana wasn't sure if Lifen would be mad. She didn't know her well enough yet to guess how she'd respond. Maybe it was because Ana was new, but Lifen didn't seem to be as hard on her as she was on the guys, although she couldn't really blame her mentor—for the most part, they behaved like prepubescent boys.

"I knew the answer before I asked it," Lifen said. "When you are in your youth, you are most susceptible to becoming unbalanced, which is why it is imperative to remain at peace and important to meditate daily." She quieted for a moment and then said softly, "And I suppose you left the property as well. It is for your own good that I ask these things of you."

Ana would have liked to open her eyes to see the guys' reactions, but she heard it in their voices. Ryan and Derek chorused, "Sorry."

"I expect you to demonstrate what I require from my students to Ana," Lifen said. "Self-control, always. Very well, it is time to quiet our tongues and minds. Meditation is how we keep ourselves at peace, and our energy balanced."

The room went silent and Ana was able to focus on the rise and fall of her chest, nearly forgetting about the room she was sitting in.

"Excellent, Ana," Lifen said. "Now try to think back to the moment you unlocked the energy within yourself. You must have been very calm and felt safe. Let your breathing guide you."

Ana recalled the warm, humid jungle and Balam's deep voice wrapping around her. With every exhalation she relaxed into the round pillow she was sitting on. The soft thumping of her heartbeat led her like a trail of cookie crumbs to the safe place that had released her power only a week ago. Soothing butter-yellow energy coursed from her chest and into the rest of her body.

"Very impressive," Lifen said. "Now allow yourself to connect with the sun. Its light is touching your skin—drink it in."

She wondered how Lifen knew what she'd just experienced, but didn't dwell on her curiosity. Although the air was cool and her eyes were closed, she could sense the light pouring in from the windows. The ball of energy at her core began to crackle and spark while she opened herself up to pull in the power around her. At first it resisted, but then a swell rushed in, making her lightheaded.

Someone coughed and Lifen said, "That's enough Ana. Stop what you're doing."

Dizzy, but very alert, Ana opened her eyes. Derek was staring at her with his mouth agape. Had she done it wrong?

"You are just a little better at that than expected." Lifen's lips parted in surprise. "You were pulling in more than the power from the sun—you were pulling from us as well. Do not worry. It just means I need to teach you one-on-one a little more before you are around the others."

Ana's cheeks flushed and she tried to think past her exhilaration. Her excitement surrounding her new abilities ebbed as she considered the consequences of her inexperience. Was she really just like a kid wielding a blow torch? Dangerous to be around?

Her worry must have revealed itself on her face because Derek spoke up. "It didn't hurt, really."

But he appeared shaken, as did the others. What she just did must not have been normal. Her cheeks flushed and she dropped her chin to her chest while the breadth of her embarrassment washed over her.

"I apologize. It was my fault. I do not often get the chance to train a beginner healer with so much power. Although I am very aware of what we are capable of, I underestimated you. For that I am sorry. I will wake you early tomorrow and we will work together before joining the boys."

She wasn't even normal to other shapeshifters or healers. Fan-freaking-tastic. She wasn't meant to have these abilities. Maybe that was the difference between her and Chance. He was born into them and they were thrust upon her. How could she have thought she'd be able to learn how to save Chance? He'd taken years of training to get where he was. A realization struck her. What if it required years to learn how to save him?

What if she didn't have that kind of time?

CHAPTER 10

"Wake up, Ana."

Ana's eyes snapped open and her heart skipped a beat. The room was dark. Where was she? She gripped the blankets in her fists as a wave of endorphins rushed through her body. Lifen stood beside her bed and set a mug on the side table.

Her dreams of home and her own bed were ripped from her consciousness. She wasn't with her mother and sister, and Chance wasn't going to come by later to take her to the movies. It was time to train.

"Meet you in the hallway when you are done dressing. We will work in the meditation room, but alone this time." Lifen slipped out of the room, closing the door behind her and leaving the scent of lilies in her wake.

Ana was so tired. All she wanted was to go back to sleep and slip back into her dream. Her eyes snapped shut and a voice in her head said clearly, *Remember why you're here.* Chance.

Her arm lifted the covers off of herself and the cool air in the room brushed over her exposed skin, raising goose bumps. Ana jumped up and placed her hands on her chest, feeling his bear heartline and jade jaguar necklace cool to the touch. She lifted them over her head and gave them one last look before placing them into the top drawer of her dresser. She didn't want anything to happen to them and she had vowed to return them to him when they were reunited. Ana closed the drawer and rested her fingers against its face. She would do everything it took to keep that promise.

The cool air reminded her of the time, so she scurried to the bathroom before grabbing a pair of jeans and a sweatshirt. It wasn't really all that different from life in Colorado during the winter, except for the fact that she was never one for waking early.

Once she was dressed and had on her slippers, she swept her hair into a floppy bun and gave her teeth a quick brushing. Her reflection stared unenthusiastically back at her and she shrugged. "Better get used to it."

Lifen stood in the hallway, facing away from Ana. Her long black hair hung down her back and over a loose-fitting dress. When Ana closed her room door, her mentor turned and beckoned her down the hallway.

"I think the boys are happy to sleep in this morning. I imagine they did while I was gone too. That's okay. It will give us a chance to work alone."

They walked to the meditation room and let themselves in. The huge windows opened out to the lake at the bottom of the basin. It had stopped snowing overnight and a pristine carpet of white covered every ripple of the mountain. Even though the sun hadn't crested the horizon yet, the glistening snow illuminated the shadowy landscape. Ana could see why Lifen lived there. It was magical and still.

"Please sit down, Ana." Her mentor held her hand out to the ring of round cushions on the floor.

Ana chose a green one in the center of the room and lowered onto it. Lifen selected a pillow and placed it across from her. Fluid as water, she crossed her legs into a meditation pose, making it look easy and natural. Ana grabbed one of her ankles and lifted her foot onto her opposite thigh. It wasn't nearly as comfortable as her mentor made it seem.

"I know this pose takes some getting used to. Do not worry—it will soon be very easy. You should have heard the boys when they first tried it." She took a breath and a serene expression touched her face. "Imagine a string is attached to the top of your head, lifting your spine. Pull your shoulders back and do not allow them to curl forward. That's it. Try to breathe into the pose. While you do this, imagine yourself becoming one with the world around you."

Lifen's voice was melodic and mesmerizing. Ana's sleepiness hung from her eyes like weights, but it allowed her to be guided easily into a meditative state. If she had been alert and fully awake, she may have thought it through too much. Instead, she did as her teacher instructed without question. Her spine elongated and lifted while she let her shoulders fall back. With every exhalation, she eased into her cushion. If it were possible to feel like a particle floating in the air, Ana experienced it.

"You have not fallen asleep, I hope. I would like you to open your eyes."

Ana sighed and lifted her lids. Lifen's pale face was only a few feet away from hers and her dark eyes blinked as she stared at Ana. She had always appeared ageless, but now there was something different about her. Her skin was almost opalescent. It glowed softly in the twilight. In surprise, Ana sucked in a quick breath.

"Tell me, what do you see?"

"You're glowing."

"You are connecting to the energy around you. This is something that people like us—shapeshifter healers—are able to do. What else do you see?"

Ana turned her focus to the room around her. Flickering motes curled up from the floor and into the air. She dropped her head back to watch them disappear through the ceiling, but when Lifen snickered, she stared at her in confusion.

"What about outside?" Lifen asked.

Ana jumped to her feet. She went straight to the window and touched her fingers to the glass. Shafts of iridescent light swirled up from the earth and into the sky. Or maybe it was the other way around. It was stunning and similar to the pictures she'd seen of the Northern Lights.

"Wow. It's so pretty. Is that energy too?" Her breath fogged up the glass and she wiped it away, eager to see more, but the glimmering light dimmed until there was nothing. "It's gone . . ."

"Come sit back down."

She listened to Lifen and settled onto her round pillow again, ready for answers.

"It didn't go anywhere. It's still there, but you fell out of your meditative state. The more awake you are to your physical body, the less connected you are to what you can't touch—the energy, or chi around you."

"Do you see it too?"

"Yes, I see it. But the boys cannot. Shapeshifters are able to see the energy mapping in other living creatures and mimic them by changing their own. Healers are able to see energy patterns of animals as well, but they are able to change that same energy pattern to return it to how it should be if there's an injury or sickness. This is how they heal. They are brother and sister to each other and require the same amount of energy."

"What about healers though? Can healers see the light too?" Ana asked, completely enthralled.

"No, they cannot. The more potent the shapeshifter and healer, the more sensitive they are to the energies. But it is nothing like what we see. If we allow ourselves, we are more connected to the life force around us."

"Well, what about yesterday? What did I do? Did I hurt anyone?" She held her breath as her heart pinched in her chest. Guilt rose up as she awaited the answer.

Lifen grew serious and she took a moment before responding. "That was my fault. I should have taught you first how to control your power before I had you sit with the boys. I have never instructed another like myself. I hadn't realized your capabilities. I have taught countless shapeshifters, and even a few healers, but none like us."

Ana remembered the look on Derek's face. "What happened though? What did I do?"

"You were pulling in the energy around you."

"And does that mean I was pulling in their energy too?" Lifen was falling back to short, choppy responses, and Ana worried she wouldn't get much in the way of answers from her.

"Yes, just a little."

Ana shook her head and clenched her fists. "That's not okay. I can't be around other people if I can't control that. I couldn't live with myself if I hurt anyone." She thought back to the time Chance was impaled with one of her traps and shivered.

"I am pleased that you care. You simply need to gain control of your power and that's done through meditation. I am not worried and you should not be either. The more familiar with it you become, the easier it will be. I think the saying is, it is like riding a bike."

Ana hoped Lifen was right. She couldn't bear it if she hurt anyone. She'd never thought about that before. When it came to daydreaming about Chance's abilities, she envied his ability to fly and see the world from a new perspective. His freedom.

If she needed to get a grip on her newfound talents, then she'd do what it took to be safe around others. "Well, let's keep going. I don't want to have to quarantine myself 'cause I'm a danger to be around."

"Very well. It may be best that once you connect with the energy at your core, you open your eyes so you can be watchful. Maybe then you can see how you affect the world around you."

Ana closed her eyes and took a deep breath. A familiar voice skimmed her thoughts. One she hadn't heard in a long time.

Focus, Chance. Let yourself relax. You have the power within you.

A memory that wasn't hers echoed in her mind. Chance's self-doubts and insecurities mingled with Niyol's voice. Her eyes watered and she clamped her jaw tight. Any concern she'd had evaporated when she thought about Chance. She wasn't alone in her struggles—he was with her.

A ball of electric energy lit up inside her. Her skin hummed with excitement and the hair on her arms and legs stood on end. She slid open her eyelids and stared at her hands, which were resting palm up on her knees. Similar to the glow of a distant planet, or the stars in the sky, she was luminous.

"Excellent, you connected with your power quicker that time. With your eyes open, I would like you to try to pull in the energy around you. Try to do this without touching mine." Lifen moved her cushion directly in front of Ana and sat back down.

Ana experienced a flicker of anxiety, but Lifen said softly, "You cannot hurt me."

Ana nodded and let herself relax again, focusing on the gentle waves of energy floating up from the floor. She attempted to pull it in. Swirls of light curled toward her and absorbed into her body. The glow surrounding Lifen rippled, like the air warping around a flame. Ana's intensity deepened while she made an effort not to touch her teacher's power. Her hands clenched tight and she grew faint.

"Don't forget to breathe."

Lifen's glow continued to ripple as Ana attempted to draw in the energy around them. She didn't want to give up, but couldn't take it any longer. She shuddered and a rush of blood flooded her head.

"You did very good, but it will require some more practice."

Ana braced her hand against her forehead and waited for the pounding headache to pass. When she had recovered enough, she asked, "So, why is it Chance never had to worry about this? Can shapeshifters or healers pull in energy from other people?"

Lifen's face darkened and Ana wasn't sure if she'd answer. Finally, she said in a soft whisper, "Yes. It is possible. Both shapeshifters and healers can do this, although they need to make contact with the person to do it. It is a true evil. It is something only poisoned souls resort to."

Ana immediately thought of Chance and her heart squeezed in her chest. Lifen noticed her grow silent and added, "It is true, your Chance has been poisoned. This is why you must learn to protect yourself first before learning how to save him, if it is at all possible."

"But I thought you said that I'd be able to save him?" Ana's throat tightened.

"I saw him, and the dark chi that pours from his body. It will be hard, even for the most experienced healer. I do not wish for you to die trying to save him—you mean too much to sacrifice yourself for someone that's . . ." Lifen tucked the edge of her dress around her legs and sighed. "I will never again place my life in the hands of a man. Learn from my mistakes."

Ana's mind was reeling. She didn't know what to say, and even if she did, words would fall short of the emotion churning in her heart. Stars flickered before her eyes and she began to sway forward.

Lifen reached for her and caught Ana before she crashed into her. "Ana!"

Through the maelstrom of emotion, fear and pain were first and foremost. What if she'd never see Chance again? What if she never felt his warm embrace? Or hear the words, *I love you*?

Instead of being lost in an ethereal void, the pale wood beams that ran the length of the ceiling came into focus.

Lifen's face hovered above hers. "There you go. Follow my voice and come back to me. Take deep, slow breaths and listen to what I'm saying. I want you to know the truth and your odds before going out into the world. This is why I protect my students by keeping them safe at home until they're ready to face the evil that is out there, and to ensure they will not add to it. You have the most potential of any student I have ever taught. If anyone can save Chance, it will be you."

Ana wiped her tears away and whispered. "Really? Is there even the slightest possibility I can help him?"

"It will require a huge amount of dedication on your part. You will have to work twice as hard as everyone else. Do you think you can do that?"

"Yes, I'll do anything." Ana propped herself up on her elbows and ignored the wave of vertigo. "So, have you met any other shapeshifter healers?"

"I have only met one other like us. We are special, you and I. This is why I wanted to teach you. I only wish I'd had someone to help me when I was a youngling, but I had to figure it out on my own."

"How old are you?" She realized the rudeness of her question after she'd blurted it out, but it had only been out of pure curiosity and amazement.

Lifen helped her up the rest of the way and stared at her. Ana winced apologetically and hoped she hadn't just blown her chance at finding out more about her teacher.

"How are you feeling? You should go get yourself some breakfast. Drink plenty of water and rest a little. I want you to practice some more." Lifen went over to a small wooden hutch that was placed against the back wall and slid open a drawer. "Take this to practice with."

She held out a candle and matches to Ana, who accepted it curiously.

"What do I do with this?"

"The same thing you were doing with me. When you try to bring in the energy around the flame and you do not control yourself properly, you will see it grow small. Once you can do it without snuffing the candle out and keeping control, then you can start practicing with the boys and I will begin to teach you healing. I will check in with you later."

"Sure, great." Ana nodded and watched her teacher leave the meditation room.

There went an opportunity to learn more about Lifen. After Niyol, she wasn't sure who was more cryptic.

Ana stared out the window at the sun peering over the craggy horizon. Shafts of light made the pristine snow glimmer and sparkle. The amazing scenery helped soften the blow she'd received by only a little. The news that it would be near impossible to help Chance and that she'd have to work harder than she'd ever had to wasn't really news, but reality was just beginning to sink in. Maybe it was the exhaustion she felt from trying to control her powers and passing out, but she had a feeling Lifen wasn't lying. This was going to be the hardest thing she'd ever done.

CHAPTER 11

"How early did Lifen wake you up?"

Ana turned around and found Derek entering the kitchen. He was dressed in a pair of jeans, a long-sleeve shirt and appeared fully rested. She groaned and kept searching through the cabinets for something hot to drink. As long as it had caffeine, she'd be happy. "I don't know, at least an hour ago she started training me. What time is it now?"

Derek craned his neck and stared at the oven clock. "Looks like it's pushing seven. It was nice while she was gone—Ryan and I slept in. Not Jordan though, you can set a watch to his schedule. Now it's back to work."

"Is there anything in here that resembles coffee? I need a serious pick-me-up."

He gave her a sympathetic grin and laughed. "No coffee, but Lifen has a caffeinated tea blend that'll slap you across the face. No offense, but it looks like you need it. Didn't sleep well last night?"

While Derek took over and pulled out a glass jar filled with crushed herbs, Ana leaned over the counter, bracing her head up. "I slept, but it was just rough in there. This isn't going to be easy."

Derek filled an electric kettle with water and bent over to open another cupboard. "I'm not good at making fresh oatmeal like Jordan, so I can offer you some instant creamed wheat or microwave oatmeal."

"I'll try some creamed wheat, thanks." She tucked a strand of her brown hair behind her ear and ran her finger along a vein in the stone countertop.

"Listen. It takes some getting used to." He looked cautiously at the doorway and edged closer to her. "Lifen takes some getting used to. She's intense, but you'll be okay. I can tell you're tough—I can see it in your eyes."

Derek reached past her to pull out two pairs of mugs and bowls. She watched him work and in minutes he had her breakfast ready and her tea was steeping in hot water. Ana sniffed the vapor rising from her cup and wrinkled her nose. "There any sugar?"

"It smells worse than it tastes. Give it a try."

She sipped the steaming tea and had to admit he was right. She had expected it to taste like lawn clippings, but it had a light flavor that took her by surprise. "Not bad, but it's nothing like waking up to hot chocolate in the morning."

A loud groan echoed through the kitchen and she turned to see Ryan stretching his bare arms above his head next to the fridge. He cleared his throat and scratched at his scalp. "Hey."

"Um, hi," Ana answered a little distracted with all of his bare skin. Tattoos lined his chest and arms, and when he turned to open the refrigerator she saw his back was more ink than anything.

"We're living with a girl now. Why don't you get dressed in more than your boxers. . . " Derek balanced both of their bowls and his tea cup in his arms before nodding his head to the doorway.

Ryan reemerged from the fridge drinking orange juice from the container. "I don't care—she's free to reciprocate. S'pose Mr. Perfect is shoveling the walkway?"

"You know it." Derek led her into the dining room, which was bathed in morning light. "Ryan's harmless. Once you get to know him better you'll see he's more than just a pretty face and an attitude, he's also a punk. When Lifen found him, he was living on the streets. His parents did a number on him."

"That explains a lot." Ana settled at the table and took another sip of her tea. There was so much to get used to. It was all so overwhelming. There was no one there for her to lean on. She couldn't hide from her troubles, or the mean kids in her room. She'd have to deal with it herself.

Derek pushed her bowl in front of her and she accepted it without looking at him. Ana took a bite of the warm breakfast cereal and felt it heat her belly.

"So, I know you're from Idaho, but how old are you?"

"Eighteen. Graduated this last summer. How about you?"

"I'm nineteen, Jordan's eighteen like you and Ryan's the oldest out of the lot—he's twenty."

"What about Lifen? I made the mistake of asking her how old she was and she changed the subject and ended our training session, but it could have had to do with me fainting too."

Derek raised his brow as he spooned a huge mouthful of creamed wheat into his mouth. He swallowed before answering, "Yeah, none of us really know how old she is. You know what they say about asking a woman her age—she won't have it. Jordan's looked up a couple historical events she's mentioned and we're pretty confident she's at least seven hundred years old."

If Derek was right, then that meant she was even older than Balam when he died. "Wow, and I thought *I* knew an old shapeshifter. . ."

"Oh yeah? Who was he?"

"His name was Balam. He was Mayan. He'd lived through the Spanish invasion and he was a really great man." Ana swallowed a bite that was too large and almost choked. Anything she could do to avoid thinking about his lifeless body and carrying it to his burial chamber.

"Was?" Derek asked gently.

"Yeah, he was my boyfriend's great-grandfather and mentor and the reason I was in the Yucatán."

Ana stole a glance at his face and saw him struggle with what question to ask next. "So you have a boyfriend? Where's he at?"

Why couldn't he have quizzed her about something else? Something she knew the answer to. Something that didn't make her heart feel like a dying star.

"Sorry, you don't have to answer if you don't want to."

"No, I'd rather get it over with. I'll just tell you and move on." Ana sipped her tea. The refreshing liquid poured down her throat and made her feel just a little more human after such a rough morning. "I don't know where Chance is. When we were in Mexico, while he was being trained, his cousin, Markus, tracked us down and tried to kill him for his power. Only problem was, he killed Balam instead. And as usual, when my life's at risk, Chance did what he could to save me and he put a stake through Markus's neck. Not sure how much you know about all of this stuff, but that means—"

"That means your boyfriend's got the sickness? That's rough. Sorry, Ana." Derek's spoon clattered back into his bowl and his brown eyes stared at her.

"Yeah." She gritted her teeth and decided she wouldn't cry. Not again. "I'm here so I can learn how to save him. He'd do the same for me."

Derek continued to gaze at her, but his expression deepened and he seemed to look at her differently. "Wow. I didn't realize that was possible. But if it is, I bet you're the one to do it. There's something about you that makes me believe it."

For the second time that day, her hopes faltered and she swallowed the lump that had formed in her throat. She tried telling herself that Derek wouldn't necessarily know anything about shapeshifters being healed. He wasn't a healer, just a young shifter.

He seemed to read her thoughts and added in haste, "Hey, just because I don't know anything about it doesn't mean anything. Don't let it shake you."

Ryan wandered into the room carrying a bowl and a full glass of orange juice. "You use those lips to your advantage yet, Derek? She told you how she became a shifter?"

Ana ignored him as he sat down next to Derek, but her cheeks warmed at his comment despite her agitation. He was still in his boxers and it appeared he had no intention of getting dressed, or at least, not until he got the reaction he wanted. She decided to try to block him out.

"She was telling me about her boyfriend." Derek gave Ana an apologetic grimace.

"Boyfriend, eh? Where's he at, then?" Ryan curled over his steaming bowl of what looked like oatmeal, and began wolfing it down.

"Ryan—" Derek spat in warning.

"He got the sickness while trying to save my life and I'm here to learn how to save his." She hoped the guys would tell Jordan because she really didn't want to go over it again.

Ryan twisted one of his blond locks between his fingers and raised his blue eyes to study her face. He exchanged a glance with Derek, who shot him a glare. "That doesn't explain how you're a shifter. You weren't immaculately conceived—no girl just becomes a shifter, it's not possible. What's the story there?"

Where was the closest getaway route? Ana fought the urge to jump up and leave the room. Ryan may have asked the question, but Derek seemed just as curious about the answer. Ana wasn't in the mood to keep talking. Not to someone who had the tact of a water buffalo in a museum. It took all of her courage to retort, "I don't know anything about you, Ryan. I only know your name. Where're you from?"

"Everywhere." He smirked at her. Well, clearly two people could play that game.

"Right. Nice tats—Chance just got one, a bear across his back. It was sort of a big deal."

Ryan sat back in his seat and folded his arms, almost protectively. "Chance, eh? I got all of these years ago. Before I turned. I tried getting some new ink, but it didn't take."

"Chance had his *nagual* tattooed on his back by his great-grandfather. It was also kind of a test—to see if he could shift and keep it." Ana avoided eye contact and kept eating.

"And?" The way he asked she could tell he was trying to seem disinterested, but it was clear just how much he cared to hear the answer.

"He shifted into a bear while the tattoo was still fresh. It looked like it was hard for him to stop his body from healing when he shifted back—it went against all of his instincts, but he was able to do it."

Derek leaned forward. "What's a *nagual?*"

"Balam said it was like a spirit animal. That shifters have a primary animal they have a connection with, the form they prefer to take. You can have plenty of forms you like, but there's one that's..."

"Yours." Derek nodded.

"Whatever. Sounds like a nut to me." Ryan grabbed his bowl and cup and turned to leave the room.

"You're just mad because you're twenty and haven't made a connection with any animal yet," Derek called after him.

Even though at every turn Ryan tried to be hurtful, she didn't buy it. He reminded her of a cornered animal protecting himself. It didn't make her like him any more, or excuse his behavior, but she could understand his attitude.

Ana stood and picked up her dirty dishes. "So, Lifen asked me to go do some energy practice with a candle. See you later?"

"Of course. The guys'll be getting ready to meet her in the mediation room, but I'll find you when we're done." Derek waved and left the room.

She sighed and took the dirty dishes to the kitchen. While she rinsed them off and put them in the dishwasher she stared at the candle and matches on the counter. Well, at least this way she wouldn't hurt anyone and no one would be around to watch her fail. She dried her hands and snatched the items off the counter. Time to play with fire.

CHAPTER 12

"Are you ready to move?"

Chance eyed Batukhan and tightened his grip on his pack. They had eaten and rested. Well, Chance had tried to sleep, but woke with every noise or movement. In the minutes he slipped out of his dreams, familiar voices had skirted his mind. Niyol's calm whisper echoed caution to him. *Be careful. Do not trust until it is earned. Keep your hunger in control, stay calm and be patient.*

It was like receiving a distant radio signal and he didn't want to move in case he lost the connection. He pinched his eyes shut, savoring the comfort his grandfather provided, but it was short-lived. Batukhan had woken him at the break of day and told him they needed to move.

"Where are we going?" Chance asked.

"Well, my friend migrates north to Canada during the winter, so we can find him there. But first you need some meditation practice. You need to learn to control the voices in your head before they begin to control you. You said it was only days ago that you got the sickness?"

Chance nodded.

"When I had the sickness, the extra voice pushed me to behave in ways I never did before. Luckily, my new focus was on women and drink instead of reaping more power. Although in my lifetime I've killed many in the name of my people, I am fortunate I never sought other shifters to murder. I have known others though, that have battled those voices. It depends on the energy you absorb and the power behind them."

"What's that mean for me?"

"It means, we need to move. I stopped you from killing an innocent girl. I think it is very clear the kind of voice you have in your head and how persuasive it is."

"If it's as bad as that, do you really think there's a chance I can control my . . . urges?" He thought about Ana and seeing her again. If he could control the voices in his head, then maybe he could trust himself around her.

"My friend can help you keep the voices at bay. Without his help, it could take decades of work . . . if you don't lose yourself entirely."

Decades? Pain rippled out from his chest and radiated to his arms and neck. Could he stand not seeing his Ana for so long? He pinched his eyes shut and controlled his shaky breathing. If it meant he'd see her again and hold her in his arms without hungering for her like cells needing oxygen, he'd do anything it took.

"It sounds like a long time to a youth like yourself, but when you've lived for centuries upon centuries, it is but a short period. I am pleased to see you care to control yourself. Yesterday I wondered if the voices were too loud." Batukhan frowned.

"I have to if I ever want to see her again."

"Love has the potential to save souls and consume them." Batukhan sighed and gave Chance a sad glance. "What is her name?"

"Ana. Her name's Ana. And I left her—I had to, so I wouldn't hurt her." *Stop talking to him. You're giving him too much information. Information is power.*

"That makes more sense. But I still wonder why Lifen didn't bother with you . . ."

"Ana—" He spoke her name before he could stop himself.

"I see. She must have powers. I understand now. Lifen would pick her over a shifter."

The voices were beginning to bounce around Chance's mind and he was having a hard time keeping them straight. Was he suspicious, angry or confused?

"Chance? Look at me."

A hand rested on his shoulder and he reacted. He swiped it off his body and spun free. His heartbeat thundered in his ears. Coiled in a squat, he looked around franticly, the sense of danger smothering his senses.

"You're safe, Chance. Calm your breathing."

Batukhan sat down in front of him with his legs crossed and his spine tall. *We need him on our side if you want to see Ana again. Listen to him, Chance. Calm yourself.* He did as his thoughts urged him to do and eased back into a sitting position.

"Very good, Chance. Take long, slow breaths. Let your body relax by letting the tension in your muscles go. Put a wall up in your mind. Do not let any thoughts in. Stillness, and silence."

With every breath, Chance allowed his muscles to unwind. No thoughts or urges whispered in his head while he concentrated on his task. He wasn't sure how much time had passed, but his eyes must have slipped shut because at the sound of a calling bird he snapped awake with a start. Batukhan was still sitting cross-legged in front of him and staring unfocused at a point behind Chance.

Chance flexed his biceps and pressed his fists into the earth, lifting himself off the ground. He rolled his neck clockwise and stretched. Batukhan didn't move and Chance eyed him curiously. "Hello? Batukhan, you awake?"

"Yes, I am. You seemed to fall into a deep meditation. Do you feel yourself again?" Batukhan's voice came out deep and melodic. "Are you now ready to travel?"

Chance shrugged. "Think so. How're we traveling? Animal or human?"

Batukhan blinked and raised his arms straight above his head in a long stretch. In one fluid movement, he rose to his feet and brushed the dirt off of his clothes. "Well, youngling, you tell me. Do you know a form that is good to travel in? I would say a bird, but you have your belongings. What would you feel most comfortable in?"

I'm no youngling.

Chance adjusted his pack and sized it up. It was too awkward to carry as a bird, that was for sure. Even though his preferred form was the bear, it was probably not wise to continue traveling as a beast most people would want to shoot. "I dunno. We need to move fast, right? And I probably need to stay away from populated areas. I don't trust myself. Maybe we could travel as dogs? I see them all over the place around here."

"A dog . . ." A sad expression flickered across Batukhan's face. "Yes. We will stay away from the roadways and trouble. We will travel northwest. My friend keeps away from people and hides out in the wilderness of British Columbia and Alberta, Canada. He's a nomad, but he's so smelly, it's nothing a tracking nose can't handle."

"Fine. Let's get moving." With the prospect of controlling the voices in his head, he was ready to go. Every minute not spent working on getting back to Ana was wasted time. He stripped his clothes off, shoved them into his bag and put the straps over his shoulders.

Chance cleared his mind and concentrated on the form. It was one he'd never taken himself, but it seemed there weren't any animal mappings that he couldn't reference since absorbing so many shifters' memories. Thin blue lines crossed and intersected into a canine's shape in his thoughts and his immense energy reserve sparked at his command. Brown fur rippled across his body while he shrank onto all fours. He pinched his nose up to chase away the itch that traced along his snout.

Batukhan swiftly mimicked Chance's actions and soon two dogs stood side by side with backpacks strapped across their torsos. It was almost a relief being in animal form again and Chance was happy to set off behind Batukhan, but as they began to move he noticed something strange about his companion. One of his front legs was curled up to his body, malformed. It didn't seem to slow him in any way, and he ran ahead without any struggle. Chance couldn't figure it out. How could that happen to such an old, powerful shifter? Was this the condition he mentioned? He'd have to find out later.

Despite the fact that they were traveling close to winter, moving with a fur coat was a warm business. They were constantly on the lookout for water, and when they came across a garden spigot, Chance took human form to refill his water bottle. While he tightened the lid, liquid sloshed out onto his hands and his vision clouded.

A memory crept through his mind and took hold of him. A familiar voice echoed through his thoughts, "I'm heading over to Jon's. See you later, Mom!"

Markus. His hands clenched automatically and the tendons in his neck tightened.

He ran out the front door of an apartment and around a brick building to a bike that was chained to a tree. After unlocking it, he jumped on and sped down a busy street. Pedaling as hard as his legs could go, he went up a hill and zoomed off the sidewalk and onto a trail that led along a stream. The sound of traffic fell away and all he could hear was the water rushing over the rocks and earth.

A fox ran out from behind some nearby trees and landed in the middle of the path. Markus clamped on his brakes and skidded out on some loose gravel. He fell forward onto his hands and screamed in pain. A plume of dust surrounded him and he winced as he stared at his scraped palms.

"Ah!"

While Markus lifted himself up, a figure stood before him. A Native American of about thirty, if he had to guess. Markus recognized him.

"Nastas." Fear gripped him and made his heart flicker in pain. "How'd you find us?"

The dark haired man grinned in such a way you knew it wasn't from happiness, but twisted amusement. "Why don't you call me Grandfather?"

"I'm supposed to stay away from you."

"But we're family. I've just come to check in on you—see how you're coming along. I see you've grown—in more ways than one."

Markus looked all around for some way of escape. Thoughts of his mother flashed through his mind. He was afraid these were the last moments of his life.

"Do not worry. I'm not here to hurt you. I just wanted to see you for myself. Sorry about your hands. You know what can heal that right up?" Nastas smirked again.

"My mother will know what to do to take care of it."

He can't know I'm a shifter. He can't. I have to protect Mom. I can't let him hurt us, I can't.

"Chance . . .?"

Chance fell onto his side and stared up at the sky. The memory had ended as abruptly as it had arrived.

Batukhan's face came into view. "Are you alright, Chance? Are you feeling yourself, or do you need to meditate?"

"Yeah, fine. Just got a little dizzy s'all. Let's go."

He put his water bottle into his backpack, and brushed his hands off, still feeling the ghostly sting of Markus's scraped palms. He shifted into a dog before Batukhan could ask him any more questions. The memories were the worst part of his sickness. He had no control over them and he didn't like it at all, especially since they were purely about fear, death and destruction. It was enough to poison any soul.

Batukhan waited for Chance to start moving and shifted right behind him. They hurried away from the spigot and back onto their trail north. While they ran, Chance was left to his own thoughts.

Even though Markus's face and voice were enough to make his blood boil, he couldn't help but empathize with him. All he wanted to do was protect his mom and himself from Nastas. Only thing was, Markus clearly hadn't taken care of the issue—and now it was Chance's problem.

CHAPTER 13

Ana sat in the living room with her candle on the coffee table. It was only a foot or two away from her while she perched cross-legged on a pillow. Her legs were going numb and she'd have to stretch them out once again like she'd had to do three times already to regain blood flow.

She took a deep breath and rekindled the yellow energy at her core. While staring at the flickering golden flame, she attempted to draw in the energy around it. The small wisp shrank and nearly went out. In reaction, she reversed the flow and instead, pushed her power out. The flame grew in size, licking its orange-blue tongue at the air. She groaned and pinched her eyes shut as her frustration got the better of her. Why couldn't she get it? Ana was determined; she would practice day and night until she could control her powers.

"Wow. Didn't your mom tell you playing with fire's dangerous?"

Her concentration broke and she whipped around to see Derek standing behind her. It took her a minute to let her cranky attitude dissolve away. "Well, my teacher told me to."

He squatted beside her and asked, "So, how's it going? And what are you actually doing?"

"Well, you know yesterday when I accidentally pulled in your energy?"

"Yeah."

"This is Lifen's way of trying to teach me to control myself. So I don't hurt anyone. But it's crazy hard and I don't know if I'm gonna be able to get this!" She blew out the candle and folded her arms.

"It's okay. Calm down, Brooklyn wasn't built in a weekend . . . patience." Derek tried to console her and rubbed her shoulder, sending a shock of energy into her body.

Her vision blurred and images filtered into her thoughts. A ring of evergreens encircled the small field in which she was standing. Ana had been there before—it was the location Niyol had trained Chance.

"Patience, Chance. You cannot build the kind of power you need to heal Ana overnight. It takes time and hard work. Try it again . . ."

Niyol's peaceful face held her gaze. His gray hair was pulled back, and kind, brown eyes stared at her. A wave of emotion overcame her and her throat pinched shut. Love and fear intermixed, and images of her own face skirted her thoughts. *I have to save her. I have to.*

"Ana? You okay?" Derek's voice cut through the memory.

The evergreen forest faded away and Ana was left staring at the wall. How had Chance been able to stand it? Seeing such painful memories all the time? It was almost too much for her.

"It's nothing, don't worry about it. Never mind. I can't give up."

She looked down and discovered Derek's dark hand holding hers. "He really must mean a lot to you."

"I'd do anything for him, just like he's done for me." She gently let go of his hand, not wanting to hurt his feelings. Derek was a really nice guy, but as tired as she was, she wanted to keep working with the candle. She couldn't fail.

"That'd be nice meeting that person who accepts you and loves you no matter what." The tone of his voice drew Ana's attention. His expression, so solemn and serious.

"What happened?" His comment diverted her own thoughts from Chance and Niyol.

"Aw, it's nothing. Just a girl back home. I thought we were solid together, but . . ."

"Then she wasn't the one, Derek. If she couldn't accept you, then it was her loss. You'll meet her someday."

Derek nodded, although he didn't seem convinced. "Yeah, maybe. It's just that, if I find someone, then I have to watch them die from old age while I stay young. It's not really something I'm game for. Sounds like torture. Chance is lucky . . . at least you guys'll age at the same rate."

That was presuming she could heal Chance, so they could return to each other. Ana's heart went out to him. "Guess that means we'll have to find you a healer."

"That'll be hard. Lifen doesn't let us off the property."

"Seriously? For nothing? Not even to see your family?" She grew unsettled, thinking about Lifen's promises to let Ana visit her mom and sister.

"Nope. Says it's for our own good. That it's dangerous out there and until she's satisfied, we are safe on our own we can't leave. It's fine. I mean, I video conference with my mom on my phone and that's all I really care about, except the guys get on my nerves."

"I can imagine." Ana thought about Ryan's show that morning.

Derek laughed and got up. "C'mon, it's time for us to go meet up with them. Time to get your animal on." He offered her his hand and she was lifted to her feet. "It'll be better having you around, trust me. I mean, Ryan's the closest thing I have to a friend around here, and that's saying something."

Ana pinched up her face. "It really does."

Lifen emerged from the living room with some tan fabric over her arm. "It is time for your next lesson. The others are getting ready now. I need everyone in the stable in five minutes." She offered Ana what appeared to be a long, thick robe. "This is for you. I require my students to be clothed properly for shapeshifting lessons. Please get changed—you may wear your shoes to walk up for now, but when you're skilled enough you will not need them. You will be able to regulate your core temperature and the snow will not bother you. The boys can show you the way. Jordan shoveled the walkway this morning."

"Thank you, Lifen." Ana accepted the robe and watched her turn around and leave. Lifen opened the front door and shut it behind her and they were alone again.

"Better get moving. When Lifen says five minutes, she means four. I'll meet you at the front door." Derek escorted her to the hallway and jogged downstairs. She heard deep voices welcome him and the word, "Hurry!"

Ana rushed into her room, quickly kicked off her slippers and then proceeded to remove her clothing. A flash of Chance lounging around in his sarong at Balam's house surfaced and she thought it was better suited to men than women. The chill in the air gave her goose bumps and she wrapped herself in the robe, making sure to secure it tight. She figured she'd get used to it, but for the time being, just knowing how naked she was beneath her covering made her self-conscious. Ana had no way of knowing how Lifen ran things and her blood pressure rose just thinking about exposing herself to her classmates. She questioned staying in her room, but after taking a deep, shaky breath, she wandered into the hallway and made her way to the front door. Jordan, Ryan and Derek waited for her on the grass mats.

"There she is," Ryan said. "You wear the robe well." He winked.

Ana's cheeks warmed in embarrassment and she placed her hand over the small V of exposed skin at her chest. The very tip of her scar pressed against the edge of the seam. She hadn't thought about the puckered ridge that ran the length of her sternum in so long. The sadness from another time in her life was almost forgotten. Chance and Niyol had helped her put aside the painful memories of her heart surgeries. She felt accepted and loved unconditionally, but now that she was alone and standing in a robe, her confidence wavered.

"Do you want to wear your boots, or are you going to show off like Ryan?" Jordan asked with a roll of the eyes.

Ryan slipped his hands into the pockets of his robe and lifted his bare toes. "If Lifen'd let me, I'd go naked."

Ignoring Ryan, Ana grabbed her winter boots and leaned over to pull them on. She was thankful her covering was so long and went down to the bottom of her calves.

When she stood up the guys were smirking at her.

"What? No boots after Labor Day?"

"Ladies first." Jordan opened the thick wooden door and bright sunlight streamed into the house.

Puffy white snow covered the mountainside and sparkled like glitter. Blue skies stretched out above them, and a few dusty clouds gave it texture. The gray stone walkway led the way above the home.

Jordan waved to a snow shovel leaning against the side of the house. "I shoveled this morning."

Ana turned back in time to see Ryan and Derek laugh silently. "Yeah, I heard you did. Thanks."

While she climbed up the steep walkway, the freezing air licked at her ankles and she held the front flap closed to prevent a draft. When she reached the top where she'd parked her van yesterday, she stopped to take in the view. The lake at the base of the mountain glimmered like blue topaz.

Derek pointed behind her. "See that over there? That's where we're going."

She turned around and spotted a large building with a metallic roof and remembered seeing it when she arrived yesterday. The guys moved ahead through the snow and she followed. When she got to the door, Derek held it open for her.

Animal noises echoed through the darkened space. It took a minute for her eyes to adjust, going from the blinding light outside to the shadowy interior. Strewn hay softened her footfalls on the concrete floor.

"Bet you've never seen anything quite like this," Jordan said.

Stalls lined the length of the building. In one she identified a horse, and in another, a deer. The cubbies changed from stalls to cages the further they walked. There were foxes, rabbits, various birds and in a few terrariums there were even some reptiles.

"Wow. Your own zoo."

"Yes," Lifen said, waiting for them at the end of the room. "There is more to learning an animal's shape, but also their temperament and behavior. We have much to learn from them. Caring for the animals is part of your responsibility while living here. Many of these creatures were brought here because they were sick or injured. I heal them and my students feed and care for them."

Lifen pointed to a closed door at the end of the hallway. "That's the treatment room. The boys have no reason to go in there. Although, once I feel you are ready I will teach you new healing techniques on injured animals."

"Sounds good to me. I like animals."

"Today you will do some animal mapping. I realize that you inherited some animal shapes, but because you are so young and inexperienced, I find it's best to work one on one. It will be much easier for you to connect with the forms if you can study them in person."

Ana's excitement built into a crescendo until one thought brought it tumbling down. What if she couldn't shift again? She'd only done it once before and the last time she'd tried she'd been unsuccessful. It was one thing to try and fail in private, but she was with the guys. They seemed more than curious about her and her abilities.

"Jordan and Derek, I want you two to practice with the horse. You can go into the arena to stretch out and move around. Ryan, I want to see you continue your work with the iguana. I expect to see improvement since I left to bring back

Ana—I don't want to have to heal you like last time. Pay special attention to the different mapping of the reptile. It is not the same as a mammal no matter how similar you think it is. This time I want you to study it for fifteen minutes before even attempting anything. Do you understand?"

The cocky smirk Ryan normally sported around was nowhere in sight. He gave a dark nod and slunk diagonally away from them to a large glass enclosure. Derek gave Ana a wave before joining Jordan at the opposite end of the building.

Ana's heartbeat echoed in her ears and she returned her focus to Lifen, who had been staring at her the whole time. "Are you ready, Ana?"

The whole trip she'd wanted Lifen to help her shapeshift, but now they were down to it, she wasn't sure if she had it in her. She wasn't a natural born shapeshifter. This wasn't her. As much as she'd envied Chance, she never really thought she'd have his abilities.

"What are you thinking? You look concerned."

Was she that obvious?

"Are you sure about this? I haven't shifted since the first time, and remember when I tried in the jungle, I couldn't do it?" She twisted her hands together and stared at the floor. "I just don't know if I can do this. I wasn't meant to be a shifter . . . I mean . . ."

"Look at me." Lifen's voice was soft, yet commanding.

She reluctantly lifted her gaze to her teacher.

"You are fated for this. Just because you were not genetically selected doesn't mean anything. You are afraid. That is natural. It will help push you in your education, but do not let it consume you. I did not want you to try shifting again until we arrived here because I wanted you to practice connecting with your energy and I hoped you would gain confidence. How did it go with the candle?"

Ana's shoulders slumped and she said, "Not as well as I'd hoped. I'm still pulling in the energy around me and the flame almost went out."

"I do not want you to get discouraged so quickly. Shifters work on their skills over years—decades. Did you notice any improvement?"

"Yeah, I guess I got a little better. When I started, the flame went out, and then before I stopped I was able to keep it lit, barely."

"It sounds like you are getting more comfortable with your own energy core and how it works, which is the most important thing for you. It is the basis of how your abilities work. Being able to connect with and understand yourself is paramount."

"Okay, I guess I understand. I'm just in a hurry."

Lifen rested her hand on Ana's shoulder and a warm sensation flowed through her body. All tension released and her worries were pushed just out of reach. "I know you want to save your Chance, but the focus must be on learning. The pressure you're putting yourself under will only hinder the process. You must try to push him from your thoughts."

He never did that when her health was in question, so how could Ana do any less for him?

The rustles and animal sounds in the building hushed and the hairs on the back of her neck raised. Although they were supposed to be paying attention to their own studies, she felt the guys' eyes on her.

"Let us begin. I know you have the knowledge and animal mappings from Chance, but you are still a youngling and should start with basics. It is easiest for shifters to start with mammals because we have similar genetic makeups. This is why I would like you to start with the arctic hare." Lifen stood aside to reveal a vertically stacked enclosure with three cages. In the middle one, two pale rabbits hopped around on scattered hay. They sniffed gingerly at the twisted wire and their soft brown eyes stared out at her.

"When mapping an animal, you must clear your mind and allow yourself to focus entirely on the creature. Do not look at it with your eyes, but with your senses. Similar to earlier when you went into a meditative state and were able to see the energy around you, I want you to see beyond, and when that happens, you will experience a strange sensation. Why don't you give it a try?"

Ana took a deep breath and stretched her neck before staring through the cage. The rabbits went back to their business of chewing on green celery stalks. Their fluffy, round bodies radiated heat, and Ana was surprised she could sense it. She stared at their cheeks pulling back with quick movements as they ate their meal. Rapid thumping grew louder in her ears and she realized it was their heartbeats.

While her focus intensified, everything else around her fell away. It was similar to one of the many times she passed out from overexerting herself before Chance healed her heart. At least the moments leading up to passing out, when all she could hear was her own breath and everything around her fuzzed out. It was in those moments, as she stood fixated on the rabbits, it happened for the first time.

Bright blue lines ignited around the hares, their furry bodies faded in her vision and all she could see was their energy. Light poured from the center of the woven sapphire outline and she sucked in a lungful of air at the beauty of it. Soon the mapping faded and she was left staring at the animals. Her energy had depleted and she leaned against the cages to rest.

"How did it work for you, Ana?" Lifen asked beside her.

"I think it worked. I mean, I saw a whole bunch of blue lines all over the animals and glowing light. That was tiring."

"Very good, you just mapped your first animal. It is normally very draining, but if you meditate for a while you should be reenergized. I built my home in this location for a reason. It has a strong magnetic field here, which is naturally revitalizing to shifters and healers."

"Oh, that's the same as Balam. I heard him and Chance talking about it."

"If you'd come with me, I'll show you a special place you can sit to refocus your energy inward." Lifen walked to a door at their side of the building. She said over her shoulder, "I'll be right with you Ryan, since I see it's too hard for you to pay attention to your own work."

When Lifen wasn't looking, Ana saw him sneer at their mentor. She held open the door for Ana. They exited the space and entered a covered patio with large windows. It was cold and drafty, but that was due to the concrete floor and thin walls. Ana shivered and rubbed her arms.

"You can sit on the chaise and go into a meditative state like you did earlier. Draw in the chi around you—don't worry, you're too far from the boys to affect them. This will refill your reservoir and you will be ready to shapeshift."

"Chi?" Ana asked.

"Energy."

Ana moved to the padded outdoor sofa and tucked her robe tightly around her legs before sitting down.

"Come in when you're ready," Lifen said.

The door shut behind her and she knew she was alone. She wanted to get back to work, so she closed her eyes in preparation. After calling to it all day, she was getting much more familiar with connecting to her energy reservoir. It crackled at her attention and her chest radiated warmth. She took a deep breath and looked out the wraparound windows. Bright, white snow covered the earth outside. Exposed tree boughs were caked with what looked like fluffy frosting, only leaving the rough, brown bark of the trunk. Energy motes swirled up from the ground, weaving throughout the landscape, and even around her in the enclosed patio.

Despite her multiple freak-outs earlier, she couldn't help but grin. It was awe-inspiring. If only everyone could see what she saw. It was truly amazing.

With her eyes open, she funneled in the energy around her. The circling light particles pulled toward her as if she were the sun and they were in her gravity field. As they joined with her, the exhaustion she'd experienced when she mapped the rabbit went away and a euphoric sensation replaced it. Although she was a little light-headed, soon she was perky again and ready to take on the next challenge.

This was pretty awesome. If only she'd had this ability when her heart was ill, she would've been able to do whatever she wanted. Had it been this way for Chance? She thought back to his training sessions and doubted he'd been able to regenerate his powers quite like this. It was a benefit of being a shifter healer.

After at least an hour, Ana stood up and went back into the building. Again, her eyes struggled with adjusting to the change of light, but after a minute she made out Lifen and Ryan standing about ten feet away.

"That was fast. Who are you, Superwoman?" A dark expression spread across Ryan's face.

"Do you feel up to continuing, Ana?" Lifen stepped away from him and said over her shoulder, "You need to study it further before you try it again, Ryan."

He braced his hands on either side of the terrarium and grimaced at the glass. Ana recognized his expression—Chance had worn it many times when he was frustrated. She felt bad for him, and wished for his sake she'd taken longer coming inside. She returned to the rabbit's enclosure and kept her back to him, trying to offer some amount of privacy.

Lifen joined her and when she looked at her mentor, a sparkle of excitement could be seen in her eyes. "I am very proud of you. You are a natural."

A clatter of wings above them drew her attention. Two small finches were flapping around a nest in the rafters. Clearly they had adopted the building as their home as well.

"Are you ready to shift?"

"Yeah, I'm ready to give it a try."

Lifen laid her hand on Ana's shoulder endearingly. "Once you are more skilled you do not need the animal before you shift, you need only to refer to its mapping in your memory. But it is best for you to begin with the animal before you. There is less room for error. With your attention on the hare, reference its mapping and call on your energy—the rest should happen naturally."

Ana took a shaky breath, nervous and excited all at once. She hoped it would be as easy to shapeshift as it was to map a new form. She attempted to clear her mind and to call on the blue lines that she'd seen only a short time ago. While she fumbled with the shape, she ignited her core and its warm yellow energy flowed through her body, from the top of her head to her fingertips. She felt like a running engine. Her motor was in gear, ready to go, and she only needed direction.

Chirping echoed through the vaulted ceilings and she tilted her head back. Ana's skin prickled delicately at first, but then her body erupted into a push-and-pull battle with her powers. A strange sensation coursed through her and for a moment she wasn't sure if it would turn painful. Organs rearranged themselves while her structure and skin changed completely. All of this happened so quickly she was surprised she was able to experience all of it while it happened.

Then there was stillness.

Ana looked up at her mentor who loomed over her like a tall giantess. Her mouth was moving and she realized Lifen was talking, it just sounded different in her ears.

"Exceptional. Taking on a different animal group so early on. How do you feel?"

What was Lifen talking about? Ana lifted her shoulders. They pulled differently than she was used to, but they felt fine. Her face was itchy. When she lifted her hand to rub at it, gray feathers brushed across her eyes instead.

Feathers? She stared down at the floor, and amongst the folds of her robe were two brown bean poles for legs. Her beak touched her feathered chest as she gazed at her spider-like feet. *I'm a bird.*

Ana couldn't believe it. She really had tried to become a rabbit and of course, she turned into something else entirely. Well, she would need more practice if she could be trusted to shift into what she intended to. She was just thankful she hadn't hurt herself. Would it be worth changing back to human form just to try it again?

Lifen seemed pleased to see Ana shift into a bird, but she was probably just spinning the fact that Ana had screwed up. Ana didn't particularly want to take the shape of a hare, but she wanted to know that she could do what she set out to do. Sure, birds could fly and feel weightless in the sky . . .

Her tiny heart pumped wildly and she realized she'd taken the form she'd always dreamed of. She would have screamed in happiness if she could have, but instead, a high-pitched chirp came out of her. She lifted one of her legs and stepped forward onto the brown fabric, teetering a little. Continuing to move forward, she walked away from Lifen and down the corridor. It was strange being so low to the ground. Everything towered above her and appeared so different from her new perspective.

Ana's feet scurried ahead, taking her with them. She reached a wide opening to her right and ventured through. Loud clomping and neighing echoed in an open arena. Large shapes moved across the dirty ground.

"Would you like to try to fly?" Lifen's voice came from behind.

She tilted her head sideways and looked at her mentor out of one eye. Lifen lowered herself slowly and let her finger rest just in front of Ana's feet.

This was the moment Ana had been dreaming about since she was a child. The freedom flying brought was only make-believe, or so she'd thought until she'd met Chance. Even then, she never could have imagined it would become a reality for her. She stepped onto Lifen's finger, her claws clutching tightly so she wouldn't fall. Her mentor lifted her gradually, and she couldn't help but extend her wings for counterbalance.

"I recommend when learning how to fly, you grip with your feet and hold on while you flap your wings. When you feel like you have enough vertical thrust, let go. But do not be disappointed if you have to work on this. There is skill involved with maneuvering yourself in the air."

Ana tightened her grip on Lifen's finger and straightened her wings. She lifted up and down awkwardly. It took her a moment to get used to the fact that she wasn't waving her arms around at all but doing something entirely different. She closed her eyes and recalled one of the many dreams she'd had over the years.

A rhythm developed and a pattern of movement. Her feet pulled at Lifen's finger while her wings propelled her upward. Feeling confident and a little adventurous, she let go after a particularly strong downward motion. Up she went into the air, above her mentor's head. Her wings flapped effortlessly and kept her afloat.

"Wonderful, Ana!"

She rose higher above Lifen's head and decided it was time to move. Ana tipped her body forward, cupped her feathers out and let the air carry her across the arena. She couldn't help but giggle, which came out in soft chirps. Her body moved lithely and while she grew more comfortable, she cut sharp corners, climbed vertically and held herself in place. It was even better than her dreams.

After her excitement died down, she realized there were two horses trotting around the large space below her. It had to be Derek and Jordan, but which was which? One was prancing along the length of the arena just in front of Lifen, and the other was standing with its head lifted as though it were trying to watch her. Well, maybe it wasn't too hard to figure out who was who.

Ana circled down to the chestnut colt that was watching her and outstretched her talons to grab onto his back. His muscles twitched where she landed, so she scurried up his spine to his head. Derek's snout lifted and she tipped her head sideways to look down at him. A neigh broke loose and her chirps intermingled with it.

Her enjoyment was cut short when she recalled the last time she was on a horse. It felt wrong being with Derek and guilt consumed her. She shouldn't be enjoying herself while Chance was out in the wilderness, held hostage by the sickness. Ana would never be able to help him if she lost focus. She was far from controlling her powers. There was no room for failure.

CHAPTER 14

It was mid-morning and Chance had been traveling north with Batukhan for days. They'd been making pretty good time, but it would probably take another couple of days before they reached the border of the United States, something he felt somewhat relieved about. There hadn't been many people along the route they took, which had its positives and negatives. It was easier to move without concern of their movement being halted, although it was harder to find food and water and Chance refused to eat in the form of an animal. He had no interest in eating other animals or who knew what else. A line had to be drawn somewhere.

They stopped at a small pond to take a drink and stretch.

Chance returned to human form and questioned Batukhan. "Are you sure we shouldn't cut west? It seems like it'd be quicker that way."

His companion shifted from canine to man swiftly. "I wouldn't drink that in human form. Dogs have better gut and mouth enzymes to filter any unfriendly bacteria. And no, we've kept inland along the eastern side of Mexico, just out of sight of the gulf for a reason. If we cut west now, we'll be sorry. The central region is so dry. It is unpleasant traveling conditions. Once we arrive in Texas we can move west."

How do you know what his intention is? Be on guard.

Suspicion clouded Chance's thoughts. "How do I know you're not just leading me into a trap? You say I should trust you, but I have no way of knowing if I should."

Batukhan settled at the edge of the water and sat in the pose he always resorted to when talking with Chance when he was agitated. Very calmly, he responded, "I am an open book to you, young Chance. Please ask me what you wish to know."

Chance removed his backpack and pulled out something to snack on. "Tell me about Lifen. How do you know her?"

Might as well get to the point. He wanted to know if Ana was in danger and if he should be concerned. Plus, he was sick and tired of people keeping secrets from him. He didn't like being left in the dark—it was time to take control of the situation.

A sorrowful expression flashed across Batukhan's face and he closed his eyes. "I know the pain of being separated from your love."

"And that would be Lifen, I'm guessing?"

"It is best I start at the beginning of this story." Batukhan flipped a tiny pebble into the small basin. He watched the ripples multiply and lap against the soil rim. "Long ago, over eight hundred years back, I was a soldier in Genghis Khan's army. Our numbers were not overwhelming, but we were strong and had a cunning leader to guide us. After he united the Mongolian tribes, he led us in an invasion of the western Xia province, and with some persistence, we overtook the capital. The emperor, having no support from the neighboring Jin dynasty, submitted to the Mongol reign and became a vassal state. To show his loyalty to his new ruler, the emperor gave his daughter, Chaka, to Genghis for marriage. Chaka had her own maid to tend to her needs."

Chance's curiosity was overwhelming, and the intensity of it surprised him. *Remain silent and he will reveal more.*

"I was a messenger in Genghis Khan's army and we remained in the capital city for some time before moving on to the next campaign. I had just come into service as a young man, and everything was new and exciting. I was proud to aid our great empire. As focused as I was on my future with Khan's army, I could not help but be distracted with Lifen's beauty and grace. I do not think she noticed me from any other soldier that roamed the Mongol camp. But while going about my duties one day, something happened that was quite a surprise to me. I discovered my abilities for the first time. It happened quite suddenly and without warning.

"Before I continue, I should give you further knowledge about my culture. You see, Genghis and many of my people believed in Tengerism. We believe everything has a spirit: the water, animals, plants and even these rocks beneath us. Shamans are masters of the spirit world. It is said that they can take on animal form while they are doing spirit work. I had no knowledge of my family being shamans because my relatives made no mention of it. You see, after a young age I was raised by my mother's family, since my parents were killed in one of the nomadic tribe attacks, and they never spoke of my father's ancestors to me."

"Tell me about the first time you shifted," Chance prompted. The cultural information was already oddly familiar to him.

Batukhan paused to study Chance and then continued speaking, his eyes never leaving his face. "My first time was while I was just leaving Khan's tent to take a message to one of his generals stationed outside of the capital city. I was passing by Princess Chaka's tent, which was empty. She had a small dog and while I passed by the threshold, the creature ran out and followed me. I collected it to return it and that was when I shifted for the first time . . . and it was then that Lifen returned to retrieve something for the princess."

For the first time through his storytelling, Batukhan smiled. "It was not humorous, but now in retrospect; I find it so. Lifen knew my secret and she kept it dutifully, though she owed me nothing. I think my heart became hers in that moment. Things were so simple for a while, but as I have learned, nothing stays this way for long. She and the princess were left at the city instead of being taken to the next military campaign, since Khan rarely slowed his movement throughout the east. For years, when I came to the city with messages for the emperor, she would prowl away with me in secret. She loved to watch me shapeshift and learn about my abilities."

"So what happened? Lifen's a shapeshifter too. That doesn't explain how she got her powers and why, if you were so in love, you aren't with her now?"

Chance realized he was only a few feet away from Batukhan now. He'd inadvertently crept steadily forward the entire time his travel partner had been telling his story. From the look he was giving Chance, he was fully aware of his movement around the water basin.

Batukhan's face darkened. "War. We were separated by war and the choices I made and my selfishness. I'm sorry, I find myself growing thirsty from all of my talking. If you can forgive the needs of an old shifter, I will tell you more about my shameful past later. It would be nice to cross the border by nightfall, do you not agree?" Without waiting for an answer, Batukhan shifted into a dog and began to lap at the water.

Without warning, the all-too-familiar sensation of a memory washed over Chance. He grew anxious. One of the last ones he'd experienced was more than painful. Reliving the death of Balam's wife from her killer's perspective was enough to rattle anyone. He'd take another one of his grandfather Niyol's memories of life on his ranch in Montana any day.

A smell overcame him. Something was burning. It was similar to the aroma of a campfire, but it also reminded him of burnt hair, a very offensive and recognizable fragrance. Chance's surroundings came into view, although his periphery was fuzzy, like looking through the bottom of a glass.

He was standing at the edge of a forest. The trees were unfamiliar to him. It didn't look like the jungle in the Yucatán or the timberlands of Idaho. He had never set foot in this place before. The land sloped down into a valley covered with grass and a large fortress, partially obscured by smoke and mountain.

Shouts rang out in a different language, but he knew what they were saying. "It has fallen! Xia will be ours!"

Soldiers ran ahead of him. They wore intricate coats tied with leather belts and cone-shaped helmets covered their heads. Black mustaches and trimmed beards decorated many men's chins. Their round faces closely resembled Batukhan's features.

Chance looked down at his bloodied hands and cuffs. His stomach turned over at the sight of it. What now?

A dog whined and he swayed on his feet. The disorienting sensation lifted and he realized he was staring at his own hands. They were dirty but not saturated with blood. Batukhan barked at him and Chance waved him off, taking his time to shift. He didn't know what he'd just seen, but it had frightened him.

*****

Ana moved her dinner around her plate. She didn't feel much like eating. Her body was starved for protein since she'd burned so much energy earlier, but she'd lost her appetite.

After shapeshifting lessons Ana had been heartily congratulated by Derek, but the others practically ignored her. Jordan had given her a flat "congrats" and proceeded to draw Lifen's attention to his latest accomplishment, although Ryan hadn't even looked at her. She was ecstatic about taking bird form for the first time but was not at all pleased it had been by accident. It also appeared her success had come at a price. From what she gathered, Ryan hadn't been successful at taking on his new reptile form. She seemed to have a ready friend in Derek, but she'd blown it today with the others. It wasn't as if she even liked Ryan that much, but she knew she'd inadvertently hurt him, and that she couldn't live with.

"Pass the dressing, Jordan," Ryan said.

Ana watched Jordan reach out of his way to take it from in front of Ana and pass it to Ryan. Outside of a few comments directed to each other, dinner had remained eerily quiet.

Lifen lifted her cup to her lips and broke the silence with a question. "How was your first day, Ana? I hope you're finding yourself at home here."

How was she supposed to answer? After her long stay in Mexico and the traumatizing events that led to her quick departure, all she really wanted was to go home to her mom and sister. To hide out in her small, dark room that looked out into the evergreens. All today had really shown her was that she had a long way to go in controlling her powers. As long as she was having failures, she couldn't truly celebrate her accomplishments.

"Such a long pause," Lifen said, surprising Ana. "That doesn't bode well."

She hadn't realized she'd taken so long to respond.

"You've been great. I've learned so much already and it's only been a day. It's beautiful here, it's just . . ."

"You are homesick and frustrated. Many of my students have experienced the same thing."

Ana shrugged and nodded, not wanting to speak just yet since her cheek had begun to quiver and talking would just break the dam she'd carefully built up through the day.

Ryan shook his head and muttered. "What a rough life."

All she wanted to do was go to her room and be alone, but before she could move Derek cleared his throat. "So, Ana," he asked, "what do you do in your free time?"

She stared incredulously at him. *Besides crushing other shifters hope,* Ana thought sarcastically to herself. Wasn't it just best to end the dinner before she did something else to upset someone, including herself? Ana took a deep breath and let it out slowly before answering. He was only trying to help.

"Well, I love stargazing. It's kinda my thing. It relaxes me when I'm stressed or sad."

"Maybe you need to pick up the hobby, Ryan." Derek grimaced coldly and braced his hand next to his plate.

Ryan stood up and said with a snarl, "Shut up, man. Stay out of it."

Lifen watched everything in silence and turned to Ryan with a peaceful expression.

"The great lesson of patience can be a hard one, but it is rewarding. It is said that Chinese bamboo is very unique and special. The farmer must plant and tend to it diligently, season after season, irrigating and fertilizing the plant even when it looks no different year after year. To look at it you would think it was dormant and there is no reward for the labor. After persisting for four years, on the fifth year, the bamboo grows over eighty feet high in one season. You may wonder how this is so, when for so long the plant appears unchanged. But to be able to allow for such abundant growth, the bamboo must first send out its roots to be able to support itself. This is the same with shapeshifting. No matter how much you might want to grow, it is more important to lay the groundwork before you start expanding, so you do not fall down.

"Ryan, I think it may be wise for you to calm down and find your center. The feelings you are experiencing are normal, but you must be mindful of your actions. I cannot train someone who is not willing to remain in control of himself. Take your food away and meet me in the meditation room."

Ryan glared at both Ana and Derek and then dropped his chin to his chest when addressing Lifen. "Yes, Lifen."

All eyes were on him as he turned and left the room. Ana noticed her heartbeat had elevated and closed her eyes to calm herself.

"Some need more help than others," Lifen commented with a sigh. "So, Ana, you enjoy stargazing. Are you familiar with astrology too?"

"Um, not as much. I just like the stars themselves. I've learned about different constellations though. I think it's fascinating how different cultures have different stories for the same constellations."

"It is similar to shapeshifting. So many stories . . ."

Lifen set her fork down and stood gracefully. The boys got to their feet and Ana joined them.

"I must go assist Ryan. Ana, if you would like me to show you a special place for your stargazing, I can take you at eight o'clock."

Ana thought about sitting alone in her room and shrugged, deciding stargazing would be a preferable choice right now. Maybe it would make her feel better. "That'd be great. Thank you."

After Lifen left, Jordan picked up her dirty plate as well as his and paused to address Derek. "Your turn to do the dishes."

His eyes were dull and his shoulders slumped, which was more pronounced on his lanky frame. Ana observed him leave and muttered to Derek. "Boy, I really did everything wrong today. I made Ryan feel like a failure and Jordan clearly thinks he's not the favorite anymore. I honestly didn't mean to . . ."

"Hey, don't freak. Ryan's moody all the time and Jordan could use an ego check. But what about me? You didn't mention how hurt I am that you didn't thank me for the pony ride." Derek smirked and started gathering all the food dishes.

Ana chuckled. "Wow, that was inconsiderate of me. Do I owe you a quarter or something? Here, let me help you with that."

They carried the dinner left-overs into the kitchen and Ana opened the dishwasher. Derek put away the food while she rinsed and scrubbed the dirty dishes.

"Seriously though. Don't worry about the guys. They have their own baggage and you can't help that. Anyone can see you're not trying to rub it in their faces. And c'mon—you're different, and *awesome*. You're like Lifen, and you're new, so you're her focus. Can't help that. They'll come around, or not—whatever. You focus on your job—continuing to rock the shifter world."

Ana locked the dishwasher and leaned against the counter. "Thanks, Derek. Ever wished that your life was easy? Like, just once?"

"I know the feeling."

"Well, I'd better get ready for Lifen. As much as I don't want to ruffle feathers, I really don't want to miss out on some stargazing. I could really use a night under the stars. I've been feeling weird, like I've changed in some way and I just need to . . ."

"Don't have to explain. Go get ready and I'll see you in the morning."

"Thanks, Derek." Ana left him in the kitchen and went to get on warmer clothing. Wherever Lifen was taking her, she was ready to assume it wasn't indoors.

While she waited for eight o'clock, she used the candle to practice her energy work in the living room, getting no further than she had that morning. Time slipped by and before she knew it, Lifen's voice filtered through the open space. "Are you ready, Ana?"

"Oh, yes. Sorry, hold on." She blew out the flame and stood up, letting the blood circulate in her legs before joining her mentor near the front entry. "Where are we going? How many layers do I need?"

"You are dressed fine. We are not going outdoors—not into the freezing cold before you are more familiar with regulating your core temperature. I have a special space upstairs that should meet your stargazing needs."

Lifen walked down the hallway to her room and opened it up. Ana hadn't seen the interior of the bedroom yet and peeked in curiously. It was similar to her guest space, although it was larger and there was more art on the walls. A particularly large-framed illustration hung on the wall and caught her eye. Two colorful birds faced each other and an array of tail feathers circled down into an arch.

"People in the West refer to it as the Chinese phoenix, but to my people the male is the feng and the female, huang. Together they are the fenghuang. They represent the union of yin and yang—two opposites coming together. The different colors of its tail feathers represent the five virtues: charity, honesty, knowledge, faithfulness and propriety. Its body represents the six celestial bodies. The head is the sky, its eyes are the sun, its back the moon, its strong wings carry the wind, the feet are the earth and its tail the planets. I look on it every day . . ." Lifen's delicate fingers touched the glass and she wore a melancholy expression.

"It's beautiful. Is it a shapeshifting form?" Ana asked, thinking of the thunderbird.

Lifen laid her hands flat over her stomach and brushed them downward, as if to wipe away dust or dirt, but there was none that Ana could see. Her flowing dress was just as pristine as it was when she woke Ana early that morning.

"It is a form that has been seen in many lands, but I have never been fortunate enough to meet a shifter with the ability. Come this way."

Lifen led Ana to the end of the room and across from what appeared to be her bathroom. She slid open a rice paper door and motioned Ana to follow her. Inside, a circular stairwell rose straight up through the ceiling to another level. Ana followed Lifen, curious to see what she'd find.

A room, if you could call it that, was encapsulated with glass, similar to a lighthouse. It spanned about eight feet in either direction and meditation pillows were stacked on the reed mat flooring.

"Wow. This is yours?" Ana asked and tilted her head back to stare out the glass ceiling and at the stars above.

"Yes, I had the roof built at an angle so snow wouldn't collect on it. I come here to meditate privately. This is where I was when you visited me in your dreams."

"Oh." Ana stepped forward, touched the cool glass, and a blossom of condensation fogged it over from her warm breath. Two-thirds of the sky was visible from Lifen's perch and the lake shone at the foot of the mountain in the moonlight.

"Would you like a pillow to sit on?"

Lifen had set a cushion on the floor and curled her legs into the meditation pose. She held one out to Ana, who accepted it and placed hers beside her mentor's. As soon as she was settled, Ana tried to find star clusters that were familiar.

"I don't see Orion from here. The eastern sky is blocked by the side of the mountain. Polaris is just below the horizon, and I can see most of the Litter Dipper, but the handle is hiding. It might rise enough in a little bit."

"You know a lot about the stars."

"More than some, but my favorites are hiding. You hear so much about Roman and Greek constellations, but what about from where you grew up?" Ana realized that she didn't actually know where Lifen was from. She'd never asked.

"In China the stars are arranged very differently. From the center point, the North Star, the sky is split into four symbols and each of those creatures guards their quadrant of the sky. The azure dragon protects the east, the vermillion bird the south, the white tiger the west and the black turtle secures the north. Each symbol is partitioned into seven mansions and they're used to track the moon's movement."

It sounded fascinating to Ana, but what she really wanted to hear was a story. Outside of their beauty, Ana was drawn to the stars because of the myths and folklore surrounding them.

"Are there any important stars or planets? Any good legends?"

Lifen wrapped her arms across her chest and said with a touch of bitterness in her voice, "One of the most commonly told tales is the story of the weaver girl and the ox herder. It is told to children and celebrated by fools during the Chinese Valentine's Day."

Ana's eyes widened and she couldn't help but stare agape at Lifen. Had she just heard her right? "Um, what do you mean?"

Lifen's dark eyes stared up at the sky and reflected the moonlight. "It is a silly love story with a sad ending. I no longer fill my head with ideas of true love. It is not possible for a man to love a woman unconditionally. Impossible."

Ana was unsure what to do or say. She didn't want to upset her teacher, but she was taken by surprise. How could someone truly feel that way?

Those were only words for the heartbroken.

"I am sorry," Ana whispered.

"For what?"

"That you feel that way."

Lifen turned her almond eyes on Ana and gave a pitying smile. "I can see you are a romantic. Well, I will tell you the story and you can decide for yourself. Happiness and a perfect ending are impossible."

Ana hoped she was wrong.

Lifen continued. "Long ago, it is said a poor orphan boy was left to be raised by his elder brother and sister-in-law. Time was not kind to them and they passed from this Earth, leaving the boy with a meager farm and an old ox. Every morning the boy would wake and till the fields and plant his crops. It was a simple life, but with his ox by his side he was satisfied. Little did the boy know, the ox was no earthly

145

animal. It was an immortal who had been banished from heaven for the wrongs he had committed. Having spent much time by the boy's side, the beast decided the boy was a good and honest being who deserved a wife. So, one day he encouraged him to go down to the stream near their home. The ox said he would find a good woman and the brook would bring him a treasure.

"When the ox herder arrived at the stream he discovered seven exquisite maidens bathing. Just like the oxen, these women were no mortals—they were the daughters of the Emperor of Heaven. As wrong as he knew it was, the boy hid behind some bushes and watched them because he was too nervous and shy to approach. One maiden in particular caught his eye, the youngest of all her sisters. While the day passed, each of the girls left and returned to heaven, all except the youngest. She was stubborn and tired after a long day's work and wished to have more time to herself. She was a talented weaver and her father had bid her to weave rainbows and clouds to make the world beautiful every day.

"Before the weaver girl could leave the stream, the ox herder went to the opposite bank and found her pile of clothing. Ashamed, but sure of his love for her, he stole them and hid them from sight. When the weaver girl came out of the brook he was there waiting. He said, 'If you marry me, I will return your clothes to you. I have fallen in love with you and promise to treat you well.' The girl knew she could not return home without her clothing, and after studying him she decided he had a kind heart. After thinking it over for some time, she shyly agreed to marry him. They lived happily for the next few years and she bore two children with him. While she enjoyed her time on Earth, she no longer wove clouds or rainbows—she was too focused on her family. This did not go unnoticed by her father, who sent the weaver girl's grandmother to bring her back to heaven.

"The husband was devastated to see her taken from him. When his friend, the ox, saw how upset he was, he said, 'You have always been good to me and I hate to see you so sad. If you kill me and take my magic hide, you may fly up to heaven to get your wife back.' The ox herder thanked his old friend and did as he said. He collected his children and they took to the skies, chasing after the weaver girl. The grandmother turned back to see him following them. Worried she would not be able to lose him and tired from running, she took out a hairpin and scratched out a river of stars that he could not pass, which is the Milky Way. Trapped on the opposite side from her husband and children, the girl was forced to continue her work for her father, weaving colorful clouds and rainbows for the world below. You can see her there—the star of Vega, and her love is Altair, on the opposite side of the river." Lifen lifted her finger, pointing out the stars that shone perfectly above.

"That's such a sad love story," Ana said in response.

"Aren't they all?" Lifen turned to look at her with a melancholy expression.

"I don't know . . . it can feel like it sometimes." Ana considered how confidently Lifen told the story. She must have heard it many times. The ending was so abrupt though, it couldn't be complete. "So, they never got to be together again? The weaver girl and the ox herder?"

Lifen sighed and blinked up at the stars. "Oh, it is said that her father took pity on the lovers and on the seventh day of the seventh month, all the magpies make a bridge across the river so they can reunite once a year. On that day my people celebrate the Qixi Festival, our Valentine's Day."

Ana stared up at the two stars separated from each other. She felt a connection to the weaver girl and to Lifen, who had clearly experienced her share of pain. As favorably as she'd treated Ana, her mentor hadn't appeared comfortable enough

147

to talk about her past. Ana was dying to ask, but worried it would cut the evening short.

"It's almost Shakespearean. Like Romeo and Juliet. At least the story doesn't end with their deaths. I can't imagine how hard it would be to see your love and not be able to be with him."

"It is more painful than you can imagine. But nothing compares to the pain of being betrayed."

A tear fell from Lifen's cheek and Ana felt like hugging her but instead, placed her hand over her mentor's. Her energy swelled within her and she whispered, "I'm sorry."

Lifen squeezed.

"Healing is natural to you, Ana. You do not need to send me your energy, but I do appreciate it."

Ana frowned. "What?"

"You do not realize what you just did? You reacted to my emotions and reached out with your energy to soothe my psyche. Women are so different from men. We wish to bring harmony to the world and everything a man does only causes imbalance and destruction."

"I'm not sure I know what you mean." Up until the point she'd met Chance, she'd felt similarly about men. After all, her father hadn't been the most reliable or nurturing, and where was he now? Chance, however, was extremely compassionate and she trusted him with her life. Maybe Lifen had simply had a long line of bad experiences.

"Long ago," Lifen said, "I knew the pulse-racing excitement from being with the one that held my heart. I knew the chill down my spine from his warm breath on my cheek when no one was looking. That was the time when I romanticized about the weaver girl and ox herder and believed in the strength of love. But my long life has proven time and again that men only wish to seek power, riches and the esteem of others."

Ana lifted her knees, wrapped her arms around them, the perfect place to rest her chin. "Well, what about the guys? Derek, Ryan and Jordan. You must've trained other men too. Do you think they're all evil or something?"

"Evil? No. I feel it is most important for me to select promising shapeshifters so that I can mold them and teach them kindness and patience. So that they do not grow up and seek to sway the movement of the world in the wrong direction, or worse, be used by powerful men who only wish to see themselves built up into gods."

Ana could see that. It made sense, especially if there were power-hungry shifters in the world. "I like Derek. He seems to be a nice, genuine guy, although he doesn't appear to get along with the others all the time. It's obvious Jordan just wants to please you, and Ryan—he's got issues, but even though he keeps doing things to upset me, I think he's just in pain. Deep down, I bet he's a softy...*real* deep down." Ana laughed.

"Yes, I selected Derek because of how protective he is of women. He listens to what I say and accepts it, which is probably due to his being raised by a strong woman, but he doesn't get along well with other men and has had issues controlling his temper. Jordan seeks approval, which is his weakness. His parents never paid attention to him or spent time with him and he's hungry for it now. I am trying to work with him on that. He is kind, but is pushed around easily. He may remain with me for some time until he is ready to enter the world. Then there is Ryan. When I found him, he was living on the streets. His parents kicked him out when they discovered what he was, too scared and disgusted to look at him."

"That's so sad. I feel really bad about earlier. I was so excited today to learn as much as I could, I didn't even think about how it would be for the guys. I watched Chance struggle with different forms and get frustrated. I should have known better—I didn't mean to appear like a show-off or rub it in anyone's face. How is he? He doesn't hate me, does he?" The agony on his face when she came back into the training building from recharging her energy had stayed with her.

"He will be okay. I guided him through a meditation to calm his chi and bring him back to center. I have a special technique that assists me in the process. And no, I do not think he hates you. Frustration and impatience are a shifter's enemies, and he has been struggling with moving on to reptile form, something he's been very eager for. You see, I brought Ryan here to try to guide him, to keep him from going down a dark road. He has been here the longest and I imagine he will remain here when the others are ready to leave."

"How do you know when they're ready to leave?"

"When their actions are not guided by greed, selfishness or self-gratification and they are prepared to protect others who need protecting."

It sounded like a hero training camp or something. But Lifen hadn't mentioned her. "What about me?"

Lifen pursed her delicate lips together. "Ana, you are very different from them or any other shapeshifter. You are also a healer, a being whose intuitive abilities help others. You can sense when something is wrong and you want to help. Like me, you were brought to this life not by your own choosing. At first I thought I was cursed when I woke, my clothing torn, wet with blood, but no injuries in sight. I had gone to the other side and was prepared for death. For a very long time I couldn't understand how I'd become what I am. I never truly trusted another shapeshifter, so I taught myself what I could and had to discover my other abilities. This is why I feel it is such a blessing that we found each other—that you reached out to me in your dreams. No one can understand as well as I can Ana. No one."

While Lifen spoke about her death and reintroduction to her life, Ana couldn't help but revisit those moments when she too thought she'd been dead—the peaceful calm that fell around her, soothing like being swaddled by your mother, and then the sensation of flying over the mountains. It was like nothing else she'd ever experienced. No dream could put a candle to it. The chaos and emotional agony that followed had been unreal when she'd woken to find Niyol collapsing over Chance's lifeless body.

Ana knew Lifen spoke the truth. Not even Chance could fully understand what she was and empathize with her like Lifen could.

"I'm glad we found each other too."

CHAPTER 15

A sparse forest surrounded her as she ran low to the ground, ducking under scrub and leaping over rocks. A shadow ran alongside her. It wasn't chasing her but was a companion. She could hear a roadway nearby, and see its snaky gray form cutting through the wilderness. Her ragged breath and thundering heartbeat echoed in her ears.

Soft music overcame her senses and the hum from the highway fell away. Lyrics from a familiar song grasped her consciousness and the gravel under her paws evaporated into fluffy clouds. Ana stretched and her down comforter crinkled from her movement. She opened her eyes and stared at the ceiling.

It was still too early for the sunlight to pour in through her high, narrow windows, but her room was far from inky black. Ana lay in bed listening to her music for a minute before turning it off. She had set her alarm early the last couple of mornings to get up before the guys so she could practice her energy work with the candle. It continued to be challenging, but she wasn't about to give up. It only made her work harder.

After a quick shower, she slipped into a pair of jeans and a loose knit sweater. Her slippers moved silently over the bamboo floors as she walked down to the living room. She spent an hour at the coffee table drawing in the energy around her without affecting the flame of the candle. After working on it for four days, she was beginning to see improvement. She remembered what Balam had told Chance about his abilities being like a muscle that had to be exercised and used. If that was the case, then she intended to work on it daily. Just like true exercise, it was tiring and when she was done she was ready for breakfast.

When she entered the kitchen she started the electric kettle. Morning caffeine was in order, especially if she wanted to perk up for their group meditation and energy work. It was the way Lifen liked starting the day, and Ana could see why. The windows facing out to the mountains and lake were truly picturesque and relaxing.

Ana opened the fridge and stood there for a moment, staring blankly at the contents while she decided what to eat. A few containers of yogurt were stacked on top of each other and she grabbed one since it involved the least amount of steps. Tear off the cap, and eat. *Voila!*

While she opened a drawer for a spoon she studied a statue that was inset into a cubby in the wall. She'd noticed it before, but hadn't taken the time to really look at it. A carved wooden man, sitting on a seat, stared out at her. The figure appeared quite aged. The grain was nearly black, but golden highlights shone along his face, hat and hands, which were holding what she guessed were a bowl and a stick.

Ana touched her finger to his bowl and muttered, "Good morning."

"Morning."

Her eyes widened and she cocked her head. That was impossible ...

Snickers and laughter came from behind. She turned around, feeling very sheepish.

"If you were wondering, no, statues can't talk," Ryan said with a smirk. He was enjoying it just a little too much, but she let him have his fun. In some way she felt like he deserved it.

"Then how do you speak?"

Ryan struck his best Greek god pose and raised his eyebrows. "I know I'm sculpted, but I didn't think you were into me."

Ana hadn't intended it that way, but whatever. She was happy to see he came fully dressed this morning, which wasn't always his mode of operation.

Ana waved to the little wooden man. "I hadn't really paid any attention to it before. He seems so serious. Why is he in the kitchen? Seems like an odd place for art like this."

"He's there to make sure you don't overeat. Please don't—it would be a shame to ruin that body of yours."

It was either mean and rude behavior, or flippant comments from Ryan, never anything serious or heartfelt. She sighed. "Sorry, I would have thought you'd know something about him since you've lived here for so long. I'm going to make some tea—you want any?"

"Sure."

He pulled the tray of eggs out of the fridge and set them on the counter beside the stove, and then he grabbed a pan from the cupboards. Without looking at her he said, "He's the kitchen god. Lifen's told the story so many times I practically dream about him, which is sick. I mean look at that face." He tapped an egg on the side of the counter and dropped its yellow core into the skillet.

She couldn't believe it. Was he actually going to talk to her like a human being? She didn't want to ruin the moment so she busied herself by taking out two mugs for tea.

"So, long ago, there was this dude who had it all—the love of an honest woman and a booming farm. They were happily married until the guy fell for this young hottie, who he became totally infatuated with. He wanted to upgrade for a younger model and abandoned his wife. His mistress got bored with him and left him for another man, and the dude had nothing, but he totally had it coming to him, right? The heavens saw his adultery and punished him by taking away his sight. One day, while the dude was stumbling around begging for money, he smelled some seriously tasty food. He followed his nose to the door of his ex's house, but he didn't know it was her. She recognized her husband and felt sorry for him, so she welcomed him in and gave him some food. While he was chowing on the tasty food, he started telling his story and became real sad for how he'd treated his wife. The heavens gave him his sight and he opened his eyes to see her standing in front of him. He was so ashamed that he threw himself into her kitchen stove. She tried to save him, but could only grab one of his legs."

By the time he was done telling the story, he'd finished cooking his eggs and scraped them onto a plate. Ana finished steeping the tea and poured it into both mugs. She pushed one toward him and lifted hers to take a sip. "So, why's he in the kitchen? To remind people to behave?"

"Basically. Every December just before the Chinese New Year I guess he reports back to the Jade Emperor on the activities of your family. He's offered rice, and honey's smeared on his lips to bribe him to give a good report. I guess it's good luck. Lifen does it every year and tells us his story when she thinks we're being selfish, or full of ourselves."

Ana laughed. "So, you really do hear it often then."

Ryan smirked and grabbed his food and tea.

"What's so funny?" Derek asked while he strode through the doorway.

"I was telling her Lifen's favorite story," Ryan said.

Derek laughed. "Ah, the kitchen god. He's kinda like Santa Claus—he's always watching to see if you're naughty or nice."

"That's bad news for you guys," Ana said into her steaming cup.

Ryan's expression turned bitter. "Says Miss Perfect. *You* wouldn't have anything to worry about, would you?"

Ana didn't know what to say. She'd tried lightening the mood by being playful and it had backfired on her. Maybe she shouldn't bother.

Jordan popped his head in the kitchen and announced, "It's almost time to meet up. You guys ready yet? Lifen doesn't like it when we're late."

Ana stared at the clock on the stove and scooped a spoonful of yogurt into her mouth. Derek rolled his eyes at Jordan's comment and busied himself scouring the cupboards, presumably for a quick breakfast.

"You'd better get a move on then, Jordan," Ryan said, leaning against the oven and taking a bite of his eggs. "Don't worry Ana, she wouldn't get mad if *you* were late."

Ana swallowed another quick bite and dropped the remaining yogurt into the trash. She'd lost her appetite.

***

"Today I think we're going to do something different," Lifen announced with an amused smirk on her face.

They had just done their morning meditation, connecting with their energy cores. Ryan had arrived a couple minutes late, which scored him a reprimanding grimace from Lifen. Ana wondered if he'd done it on purpose. Just to make a point.

The boys looked questioningly at each other, as if they were trying to read each other's minds.

"What do you mean, different?" Jordan asked curiously.

"After talking to Ana last night, it made me think," Lifen said. "Something that might help everyone is a little teamwork."

Everyone, except Derek, glared at Ana. She stared at her hands and wished she were invisible. Being noticed wasn't her thing. But being noticed *and* hated was agonizing.

"I have taken a piece of my clothing and hidden it on our mountain range within a five-mile radius," Lifen said. "No wandering off the property. Don't think about heading to the ski slopes again, Ryan."

Ana could hear Jordan whispering. "This'll be easy."

Lifen stood with her arms crossed and a faint grin played across her lips. "It might not be as easy as you think, because for this challenge you may only choose one animal form and you must remain in that state when you *all* retrieve the item you're tracking and bring it back home to me."

"Cool—this is cake." Ryan uncrossed his legs and jumped to his feet. He put his hand out to help Ana, and when she reached for it, he faked her out and shrugged. "Don't slow us down, and we'll show you how it's done."

What a gentleman. He was really making it hard to like him. Maybe it was his superpower.

Derek got up. "Man, why do you gotta be that way? Here, Ana." He helped lift her to her feet.

"That will not be how to succeed in this challenge, Ryan," Lifen said. "You must work together. I will be watching." Lifen led them out of the meditation room and instructed them to get changed into their robes and meet back at the front door.

While Ana slipped out of her clothing and into her cover-up she worried about the animal form she'd take. It was only her first week in training and so far she'd only become a finch and a rabbit. She knew that wasn't anything to complain about, but she didn't want to be the reason they didn't complete the challenge. It may have had nothing to do with saving Chance, but if she was going to live here for the time being, she would rather get along with Ryan and Jordan. She was being hard enough on herself without all their comments and looks too. It was doing a number on her self-confidence.

Ana tightened the knot of her cloth belt and walked down the hallway in her slippers. The guys were already waiting at the front door along with Lifen, who was clothed in another flowing silken dress. She wasn't wearing a jacket or even a scarf, although a pair of fashionable leather boots tightly wrapped her feet. Ana guessed they were more for display than necessity.

"Are you all ready for your challenge?" Without waiting for an answer, Lifen turned around and went outside.

Since early morning, clouds had begun to fill the sky, blanketing the sun with a gray veil. A chill brushed up Ana's spine when the air touched her skin. She wrapped her arms across her chest and followed behind Jordan and Ryan as they trailed behind their teacher.

Derek walked beside her for a few steps only to mutter in her ear. "Don't worry. You'll do fine."

She hoped he was right. They were probably used to doing these sorts of things, but she wasn't. Despite her worry, a flutter of excitement was building in her stomach. All the times she'd watched Chance run off into the forest as a bear, or scamper away as a monkey, fulfilling some new and interesting test, she'd envied him. Even if he wasn't there, she'd try to make him proud. Ana imagined it was him moving beside her, that it was his shadow overlapping hers on the walkway. How long had it been now since she'd last seen him? Two weeks? Or more? Maybe it hadn't been that long, but it felt like an eternity. Since she'd met him they hadn't been away from each other for more than a day. Her dream, or whatever it was, had left her feeling melancholy. She just wanted to smell his spicy scent, or touch his lips again. Her cheek quivered.

Not again. Pull it together, Ana. If the guys see you they'll give you a hard time.

"Are you paying attention, Ana?" Lifen asked.

They were standing in the driveway and at the top of the walkway. Everyone had formed a semicircle around Lifen and she was staring at Ana now.

"Yeah, I am now, sorry."

"Good," Lifen said. "You must obey the rules of this challenge. Follow my scent away from the house in search of my shawl. It is within this mountain range, and within view of the lake, so if you leave the area in search of some *fun* as you call it, Ryan, then you will not be allowed to join in on shifting lessons for three days."

"Seriously?" Ryan muttered and threw a hard-packed snowball off the mountainside.

"Yes, I am serious. Plus, you must select only one animal form to assume for this exercise. Until you return home, this will be the *only* shape you will take. You must all get to the shawl together. You are not to leave any individual behind. I will be monitoring you, so if you break any of the rules, I will know. Do you have any questions?"

"We can take *any* animal shape?" Ryan asked, looking pleased.

"Yes, any animal shape. You may all take a minute to discuss your plan before you begin."

"I know what form I'm taking," Jordan said.

"Great, but I don't think being a brownnose counts as an animal," Ryan retorted quickly and ran his fingers through his hair. "I know what I'm doing, but I'm not discussing it with you losers. I'll be able to move quick and track without a problem. The question is, what's the newbie gonna be? Think you can shift into an animal that won't get swallowed by the snow?"

Ana bit her lip and wondered the same thing. She'd been practicing the rabbit and finch over the last few days, although she knew she had some other mappings available to her. Chance's experiences were open to her, if she could unlock them, and if she had the capability to manifest them.

Derek held his hand up. "Lay off her, man. How're we going to work as a team if we can't even make a plan? I was thinking about shifting into a bighorn ram—I'll be able to climb the mountains without a problem. Please tell me someone is shifting into something that can track well."

"I've got it covered," Ryan answered.

"And don't worry, Ana. Whatever you can do, we'll make it work. Okay, let's try to stick together and remember why we're out there—to find Lifen's shawl." Derek rubbed his

159

palms together and eyed the cloudy sky. "Let's hope it doesn't start snowing."

Ana stood beside Lifen and watched the boys close their eyes in concentration. White hairs began to grow out from Derek's chocolate skin while he shrank down and collapsed onto his hands and knees. His ears elongated and long horns curled out from his forehead. Within seconds, a ram was standing on Derek's robe in the snow. He lifted his legs tentatively and made a soft bleating sound.

She may have seen it many times, but it was still just as awesome watching a human shift into an animal. Ana scratched the top of the creature's head and rubbed his nose, remembering the tingling that often remained on the snout. A billow of steam came out of Jordan's mouth and he untied his belt just as he began to grow in size. His pale skin turned chestnut and shiny fur covered his large body. A horse's muzzle stretched out and nearly bumped into Ana and she had to step back to avoid getting hit. Jordan clomped his hooves on the ground and neighed.

"Bigger isn't always better, man." Ryan swatted the horse's back. He loosened his robe and looked at Ana. "Try not to get too excited."

"I'll try."

Just like the other guys, fur erupted all over his skin, covering his tattoos and obscuring his body. She wasn't sure if it was a dog at first, but when he faced her with his broad shoulders and regal face, she couldn't help but laugh. Some girls might find a wolf sexy, but she preferred bears.

"It is your turn, Ana," Lifen said.

Ana's amusement evaporated and she looked at Lifen. It was time to make up her mind. She wasn't sure if she'd be able to take the form of a larger animal like the guys had selected. As much as she liked taking flight as a bird, she didn't think it was a good choice right now and a rabbit might get trampled underfoot by accident. What else was an option?

Memories of animal visitations washed through her thoughts. Last spring her worries revolved around her health and a looming heart transplant. Now she was healthier than she'd ever been, but Chance's life was in the balance. Even though it was a painful time, falling in love and hoping for a happily ever after when it wasn't in the cards, she missed those precious moments with Chance. Every day with him had been a blessing and was cherished.

Her mind was made up. She discreetly wiped away the moisture from her eyes and took a deep breath. Ana closed her eyes and the warm glow that radiated from her chest flowed throughout her body. The animal mapping that had been passed from Chance to her became her focus. Its shape, illuminated with blue threads, formed the embodiment of the furry mammal.

Ana thought about Chance sunning himself in animal form in the field below her stargazing rock and his bear heartline necklace that shone against his fleecy white chest. It had been the clue that led to her suspicion of his supernatural secret. While she experienced her memories, a familiar tingly sensation ran through her body. She shrank down onto all fours and stared at her red paws tangled in her robe. As gingerly as she could she stepped out of the fabric pile and stretched, then rubbed her snout on her leg, trying to chase away the itch.

"A red fox. Now if you are all ready, you may get started."

Shadows fell across her body and Ana looked up into the faces of her teammates. The wolf and ram jumped out of the way of the horse, which carefully spun in a circle. Ana lifted her nose and sniffed the air. Although Lifen hadn't instructed her how to track, she tried to recall what Balam had taught Chance. She suspected Lifen didn't care about how well they tracked, but more about the means they took to complete the challenge. That they worked together.

The smells that brushed past her nose were familiar, but so much more vibrant. She recognized Lifen's scent as well as the strong, sharp bite from pine trees. An earthy aroma from the rocks and soil hung heavy on the air and she could even taste the moisture collecting around her.

Jordan moved across the driveway, toward their training building. Ryan and Derek turned to look at her before following after. Ana's first steps in the snow left the pads on her paws cold and wet, but she kept surprisingly warm. While they moved in a line past the edge of the property, she wondered how strange they might look to an outside observer.

It became apparent how awkward a choice the horse form was once they moved along the steep mountain. Although the ground was covered with a foot of snow, just below the surface was gravel and slick rocks. The thick tree line was nearby, but below their altitude and wrapped around most of the western side of the lake. She hoped Jordan would have an easier time once they reached the pines. He quickly fell to the back of the line, just behind Ana.

Ryan took the lead with his snout in the air, which Ana assumed meant he was tracking Lifen's scent, although she had no way of knowing for sure. As long as they could keep up in this way, then they just might have a chance at completing the challenge.

Snow clung to Ana's underbelly while she leapt into the footprints left by Derek and Ryan. Some sections were deeper than others and she wished she'd picked an animal with longer legs so she could have simply walked through the snow instead of being forced to jump through it.

She wasn't sure how much time had passed but they'd made it to the southernmost point of the lake. The edge of the milky blue water was white from the ice that had begun to form over the last week of freezing temperatures. Lodgepole pines surrounded them and although they provided good protection from erosion, sections were so dense Jordan had a challenging time winding his way through.

A breeze blew past and Ana thought she detected Lifen's familiar scent on the opposite side of the lake. Ryan seemed to notice it too, since he picked up the pace, running along the lake's perimeter. The irregular edge of the water split into channels that hid within the forest. Through this shallower section, the ice had hardened through most of the water, but at varied thicknesses, based off its opacity. If it weren't for Jordan's weight and Derek's hooves, she guessed they'd be able to cut across the surface of the lake.

While she glanced over her shoulder at one of the inlets across the bay she noticed a large dark shape moving in the trees. She paused mid-step and focused her eyes. A bear. Her heart squeezed in her chest and she ran closer to the edge of the shore. The beast was standing on its hind legs and staring up the mountain. It looked like there was a lump on its back . . . was it a backpack?

Chance.

Without any further thought, Ana scrambled across the frozen lake, her paws sliding out beneath her as she went. She kept to the white sections of the ice, careful to avoid the translucent, thin parts. Her heartbeat thundered in her ears at the thought of being reunited with her love. He'd changed his mind about Lifen helping him and he must have tracked her all this way.

Claws scratched on the ice behind her and she tilted her head sideways to see a gray wolf racing after her. He probably thought she was going after Lifen's shawl, but there was no way to tell him otherwise. She wasn't about to stop now, not when she was so close to reuniting with Chance.

When she neared the far shore, her paws broke through a patch of thin ice covered with snow and she dipped into the frigid water. She yelped and clawed her way out, dripping wet. Ana stepped onto the embankment and shook her body, sending droplets flying in every direction. She jumped through the snow toward the bear and stopped at its feet. It was then that she noticed it wasn't wearing a backpack.

The beast snorted and a deep rumble reverberated from its chest. Ana took a step back and noticed two silvery faces peering out at her from within a cavernous hole in the ground behind the grizzly. Then realization sank in.

Not only was this not Chance, it was a mother preparing for hibernation and Ana had just stirred the hornets' nest. The mama bear stomped forward and swung out her paw, narrowly missing Ana's snout. She froze, unsure what to do. Ana had been so certain it was Chance, she wasn't prepared in that moment to defend her life.

From behind she heard growling. The sound broke her from her trance. A gray muzzle hovered over her head and she felt fur brush against her back. Ryan's leg lifted and pushed against her chest. She took the hint and scurried backward, out from underneath him. While she backed up, the grizzly lifted to its hind feet, an impressive three hundred pounds on display.

This wasn't good. They needed to get out of there fast. The wolf kept his body low to the ground, his hackles raised. From the sounds coming from his mouth, his lips were parted in a toothy grimace. Ryan took a cautious step back.

The bear lunged forward and ran at him. Ryan parted his teeth and bit at the large shaggy beast. Ana watched in horror. She couldn't let him get hurt. An idea formed and she acted fast. Instead of going back to the lake and safety, she looped around to the cave opening. Curious little faces peered out at her.

All it took was one squawk, and mama bear stopped advancing on Ryan. Her paws pressed into the snow and she spun around to return to her kids. At the sight of the thundering grizzly, Ana tore through the snow, back through the trees, and toward the lake. She hoped Ryan had taken the opportunity to get out of there, because she didn't want to have to face that angry mother again.

Ana raced onto the ice and scanned the surface. The regal form of the gray wolf plodded toward her. She was so happy they'd come out of the experience unscathed she could have done a flip. When he met her, he dropped his head down to stare her in the eyes. She returned the stare, hoping he wasn't furious with her. All he needed was one more reason to dislike her and any possibility for them to become friends was out the window.

A strange hooting bark came from his chest and he put his paw over her neck. She couldn't be certain, but she had the feeling he was laughing at her. If she could have laughed she would have. There was nothing else to do in that situation. By the skin of their teeth they'd avoided getting turned into a rug for some grizzly cubs.

A horse whinnied and they looked through the forest above the lake. A ram and a brown colt stared back at them. Ana didn't want to wait around to see if the bear held a grudge. She plodded up the mountain to meet her friends with Ryan right behind her.

Derek and Jordan stared at them with wide, unblinking eyes as if to say, "What were you thinking?"

Ryan wasn't fazed and jogged ahead of them with his snout in the air, back to tracking Lifen's scent. It wasn't as if she could answer any questions anyway, so Ana plodded after him. The soft footsteps in the snow and steady breathing let her know the others were close behind.

After a few minutes, they caught up to the gray wolf, which had stopped in the middle of a small clearing. This part of the mountain was fairly steep and covered with lodgepole pines, although just above them only snow-covered rocks paved the way to the top of the mountain. Ana wondered why he'd stopped and switched her attention to her sense of smell. She closed her eyes and tried to block everything else out. The pungent aroma of the pines was strong, but she could definitely identify Lifen's scent. She lifted her nose, followed it a few steps forward and bumped into a scratchy tree trunk.

When she opened her eyes, Ryan shook his head side to side. He lifted onto his hind legs and placed his paws on the tree while staring into the boughs above them. Ana backed up to focus on what held his attention. Jordan didn't have enough room to move so he just held still, looking to the others in silence. Derek trotted to the far end of the clearing with Ana and made a funny bleating noise.

She wished she could talk, that any of them could talk. What was Ryan doing, and what did he see? While she studied the frosted pine tree she noticed something moving in the breeze. A dark piece of fabric brushed against a snowy branch, high above them at the top of the tree. Lifen's shawl.

Ana glanced at Derek's long, white face, and saw that he too had located their target. They moved to the base of the pine, joining Ryan, who was attempting, futilely, to claw his way up the trunk. There was no possible way for Ana to get to the top of the tree. Not unless she grew wings and flew, and that would be breaking Lifen's "one animal" rule. Derek seemed to be thinking the same thing as he stared at his hooves, buried in the snow.

Jordan snorted and Ana thought of an idea. She looped around the horse and tried leaping onto his back but instead collided into his rounded belly. Having fallen onto a fluffy white cushion of snow, Ana shook off her soreness and righted herself. Ryan's steamy breath rolled over her fur and she stared at him. He was staring at Jordan's back and then at the tree. After one last look, he ran back the way they'd come.

Jordan's big brown eyes blinked and he turned to follow the wolf from the clearing. Frustrated that the others gave up so soon, Ana paced around the trunk. There had to be a way to get the shawl. Unless it was impossible in the forms they'd taken. Maybe it had required more planning ahead of time.

Maybe they should have discussed four animals that had different abilities and traits.

She wasn't the type to give up, but without the guys, there wasn't any point. Derek stood staring at her, and she realized just how creepy ram eyes were. His body was positioned to follow the others, but he was waiting for her. Ana sighed and gave a little yip, which was the closest thing to a groan she could muster, and followed him away from the clearing.

They wandered slowly back the way they'd come, avoiding their detour across the lake to the bear den, and all the way back to Lifen's driveway where she stood, with her arms crossed and a frighteningly serene expression on her face.

"Welcome back," Lifen said. "I see you returned without my shawl. This wasn't exactly a practice in teambuilding, was it? Never mind, it's time to shift back. Ana, here you go." Lifen opened up Ana's robe for her.

Ana stepped around to the opposite side of the cloth, where she was hidden from view from the boys, and focused on her human form. It was easy shifting back. It was always easy returning to normal, like releasing a breath after holding it for an extended period of time. The cold wintery air brushed against her exposed, pink skin and she slipped her arms through her robe and wrapped it around her quickly to avoid more goose bumps.

Lifen held out a robe for each of the guys, who shifted quickly and covered up without anyone seeing more than a bare arm or leg. "I watched the entire time. You boys gave up far too easily and thought you knew the best forms to take without even discussing it as a team. I often wonder why I bother training men. You are so set in your ways—selfish and egotistical. I am never surprised when you fail."

Snowflakes began to fall from the sky, which created a feathery crown on all of their heads. A piece touched Ana's eye and she blinked in pain. She felt Lifen was being unfair to the boys. Maybe they weren't perfect, but they didn't deserve such condescension.

"Ryan saved me," Ana said. "I thought I saw Chance, but I was wrong. It was really a mama bear getting ready for hibernation. If he hadn't stuck with me, I'm not sure what would have happened."

Lifen turned her stony gaze to Ana and she held her breath. Sharp, stabbing pains permeated her feet from standing in the snow, but she was afraid to move, unsure if she'd angered her mentor.

"I am disappointed to learn you were chasing after the ghost of your boyfriend, Ana. I thought you were trying to lead the others straight to the shawl. Why you would risk your life for an undeserving man, I do not understand."

Ana's heart thundered in her chest and her throat tightened. How could Lifen be so cruel? Afraid of saying something that she'd regret, Ana pinched her lips together and breathed heavily from her nose.

"You all must be tired. You may go inside and make yourselves lunch. I will not join you, but I will expect you for an afternoon meditation at two o'clock. Clearly you all need more focus."

The guys turned in silence and started down the stairs. Ana gathered up her boots from where she'd left them sitting in the snow earlier, and followed the guys down. She didn't turn to look at Lifen again. She was too upset. By the time they got to the front door, her feet were bright pink and nearly numb.

Derek rested his hand on her shoulder and offered her a sympathetic grin. "Why don't you grab a shower? No offense, but you look like you could use it. Just a quick one and we'll eat some lunch."

Noiselessly, she nodded and dropped her boots at the entryway with all the other shoes. She shuffled down the hallway and Ryan walked with her until he got to the stairs heading down to the lower level and the boy's rooms.

"Thanks Ana," he whispered.

She couldn't believe her ears and turned around, but he was already gone. Ana went into her bedroom and closed the door. As soon as it latched, off came the wet robe into a pile on the bamboo floor. The cool air hurried her, and she pulled out some fresh clothes from her dresser and rushed into her bathroom.

Ana didn't waste any time getting into the warm water. She just stood under the shower's steady stream, letting its heat chase away the chills. Her hair plastered to her face and she placed her hands on the tiled wall. The pain she'd locked away erupted into tears and she felt her face pinch up into a silent cry.

Would she ever see Chance again? And if she ever did, would she be prepared to help him? It felt like Lifen was trying to keep her from learning what she needed to. Like she was trying to keep her from Chance. Was she such a miserable person that she needed to make everyone else around her unhappy?

Ana began to doubt her choice to follow and trust in her new mentor instead of chasing after Chance. She hadn't learned anything about healing yet. She knew it'd been less than a week, but still.

Lifen's words burned through her mind. *Why would you risk your life for an undeserving man?* Chance was the most deserving man she knew. He'd saved her life twice and she loved him. How bitter would you have to be to hate men so much?

Ana shook her head and reached for her shampoo. Maybe she was just being emotional. It had been a shock running into a bear preparing for hibernation when she'd thought, or maybe hoped, it'd been Chance. It had also been disappointing not completing their challenge. Who knows, maybe Lifen was just as disappointed as Ana was in their performance and she was taking it out on them. Either way, Ana didn't feel like waiting any longer to learn about healing. This was why she was here. Shapeshifting was awesome, but it wasn't going to help her save Chance. If Lifen wasn't going to help her, then there wasn't any point in her staying.

By the time she finished her shower, Ana had calmed herself down and was resolved to ask Lifen about healing lessons. She missed her mom and sister and wouldn't mind heading back home, although it scared her when she seriously considered it. If she went home, it would mean she'd failed.

The only way to get through this was if the guys were on her side. It was time to draw a line in the sand. She'd had enough of Ryan's comments and Jordan's resentment. They weren't on opposing sides and it was time to stand up for herself.

Ana ran a brush through her hair quickly after her stomach made a threatening growl. She threw on some clothing and her slippers and felt almost human. Voices echoed down the hallway as she approached the kitchen. All three of the guys were there, busy with food prep. Derek and Ryan were on either side of the island sharing supplies, making the largest sandwiches she'd ever seen. Jordan was curled over a skillet, frying up some eggs and what she could only guess was Canadian bacon. The smells hit her nose and her belly groaned its demands.

First things first. Ana cleared her throat. "I have something to say." The guys looked over their shoulders and she plunged ahead, not letting her nerves get the better of her. "I know my coming here hasn't been a good thing for you and I'm sorry I've caused issues for you guys, but I don't have a choice. I came here because I had nowhere else to go for help. Chance is out there with the sickness and time isn't on his side. Lifen's the only one I know who can teach me what I need to know. Ever since I got here, I've been made to feel like

I don't belong. The truth is, I have no idea what I'm doing. All of this is scary and I'd rather have friends with me who know what it's like being different—who can support me and each other when we're having a bad day instead of being made to feel bad about who I am. For the record, I'm *far* from perfect. I make mistakes all the time, and hopefully this isn't one of them. So . . ."

She waited for their reactions and looked at Derek tentatively. He gave her a subtle nod and didn't answer, clearly knowing her speech hadn't been directed at him.

"Okay," Ryan said.

"Yeah?" Ana ventured a look at him.

"But I won't change who I am and I can't promise my mouth won't get me in trouble." Ryan winked at her and Jordan gave her a reserved nod.

Ana sighed. "I'd never ask you to change who you are, just stop with the Miss Perfect comments."

"Great! Now that it's settled, let's eat!" Derek said.

"Good, because I'm so freaking hungry!" she announced and cradled her abdomen.

"Well, I hope you don't mind," Ryan said, "but Derek and I've been building you a mega-sandwich. If you don't like any of the ingredients, well, just close your eyes while you eat it." He pressed down on the top half of half a French bread loaf. Meat and veggies bulged out the sides. He cut it in half and handed her the plate.

Ana looked at Derek who gave a nod and grin in encouragement. She couldn't believe it. Ryan wasn't even slipping in any inappropriate comments. Yet.

"Wow—that looks awesome! I wouldn't complain even if you put sardines in it." She accepted the plate and stared wide-eyed at her lunch.

"Thanks for the idea. Next time, girlie."

"Hey, Jordan, how close are you over there?" Derek asked over his shoulder, "Let's all sit together."

171

"Yeah, it's done," Jordan said. "Just gotta plate it."

"What about drinks?" Ana asked and went to the fridge. She pulled out a container of orange juice, tucked it under her arm and then grabbed four cups.

They all wandered into the dining room and set all of their food on the long wooden table. Ryan flung out a bag of chips before he took his seat. Jordan pulled up next to Derek, so Ana sat next to Ryan. The room went quiet except for the sound of chewing. Everyone was too hungry to make small talk.

It wasn't until she'd eaten half of her sandwich that Ana paused to say something. "Sorry guys. I totally shouldn't have run off like that. I bet you thought I was trying to cheat or something. Anyway, I just wanna to say thanks, Ryan, if you hadn't followed me and backed me up, I might have had to test out my healing abilities. And your sandwich is awesome by the way."

A piece of lettuce hung between Ryan's lips while he chewed a large bite. With his mouth full he said, "That's cool. It was fun. I thought you were out to showboat us, but then it got exciting. Glad to get some action finally." He set his sandwich down and wiped his mouth with the back of his hand. "And thanks for trying to stand up for me . . ."

"No problem." Ana stared out of the floor-to-ceiling windows at the snow falling outside and rubbed her temple. "So, I've talked to Lifen a little and it's pretty obvious that she's not a big fan of men, but that was nuts earlier. Seemed really unfair. Does she say things like that to you guys regularly?"

It was Derek's turn to pause and answer. "Yeah, she's got her bad days. We sort of try to avoid her triggers on those days and try not to rock the boat."

"What are her triggers?"

The guys shared a look and Ryan said with a grin, "Selfishness, dishonesty, weakness of character. So, basically us."

"And here I thought she was super nice."

"It freaked you out that she tore you down, didn't it?" Ryan said. "Not used to that, I can see. Must have a mommy and daddy who love you." He popped a chip into his mouth and reached into the bag for a handful. "It's nothing new to me. I mean that's what I grew up with. I probably would have been kicked out of the house even if I wasn't a shifter. That just gave them a good excuse to toss me out."

Ana studied his face. Ryan wasn't joking around or being cocky for once. She could see the pain in his eyes and her heart went out to him. "They kicked you out because you're a shifter? That's . . . I'm so sorry."

"Yeah, when I was sixteen. They didn't like all my tats or my skateboarding. I don't think they really liked me, period. Had to take care of myself, but that worked out well. I didn't have to deal with them anymore. Lifen found me living on the beach near Santa Cruz when I was eighteen. Even though she may be hard on me, I know it's because she just wants me to become a better person, so I guess it makes it bearable. Mostly. I make her work for it though."

"Just so you know," Ana said, "you're wrong about me having a mom and dad waiting at home for me. My mom may be annoying, but she's the best person I know, and my dad left when I was younger because he wasn't getting along with her and he couldn't take the stress of my heart condition." Ana curled her finger over the neck of her shirt and pulled it down so they could see the top of the scar that ran the length of her sternum. She was thoroughly impressed when Ryan didn't make a smart comment about her undressing. "I was born with a heart condition. If you can believe it, I almost died from it. Actually, I did. Chance gave his life to save me."

173

"Wait, I thought shifters couldn't heal? That's what Lifen told us . . ." Jordan said with a frown.

"Oh, but they can. It's just not something easily controlled. If you start a healing connection, I guess it's hard to disconnect. It's not natural to shifters and it's dangerous to try. His grandfather warned him about it."

As painful as it was revisiting those sad times, it wasn't nearly as bad as she thought it would be. Maybe it had to do with the fact that she felt comfortable talking with the guys. Or maybe it was because she wanted to offer something in return for Ryan's honesty.

"Um, I'm confused. I thought your boyfriend was alive?" Derek asked and scratched his tight brown curls.

"He is. After he sacrificed himself for me, his grandfather did the same for him. Niyol willingly gave his energy to Chance so he could live."

Ryan shook his head. "Dude, that straight-up sucks. Sorry about that. And now he's got the sickness?"

"Yeah, but not from his grandfather. His cousin apparently had the sickness and had been hunting us down. He found us in Mexico and just as he was about to try to kill me for a second time, Chance killed him to protect me. That's the Reader's Digest version."

Jordan's eyes were wide and she could only imagine what frightening thoughts were racing in his head. Maybe Lifen didn't talk about these sorts of things. Ana and Chance had had no idea there were shifters in the world set on killing others for power.

"Somewhere in that story does it explain how you're a shifter?" It was only a matter of time before Ryan would go back to being himself, but that was okay. She wanted to tell them. It was time.

They all stared at her and appeared to be holding their breath, eager for an answer. "So, I guess when Chance healed me, it took all of his energy and his sacrifice planted the seed of his powers in me, and because I'm a woman I naturally have the healing abilities of a woman as well, or at least that's how it was explained to me. After my heart stopped, I woke up after the most incredible and real flying dream I'd ever had. We discovered he hadn't only brought me back to life, he'd healed my heart. We thought that was all until I shifted into a horse. I was desperate to get to Chance when I thought his cousin was going to kill him. It was a crazy day—one I can't forget."

For once, Ryan wasn't ready with a smart retort, and Derek couldn't seem to think of anything to ask. Jordan appeared to be having a frightening realization that there was a lot more to the world than Lifen's small shapeshifter preserve.

And he was right.

CHAPTER 16

Chance was tired of running. For days they'd been traveling north, and now they were in Texas. Despite their grueling pace, Batukhan made sure they stopped regularly so Chance could rest, which he said was important so the sickness didn't progress, but Chance kept losing sight of why he was sticking with Batukhan. Part of him, a very large part, wanted to strike out on his own and go as fast as he could in whatever direction that led him to Ana, but the voices in his head were constantly at odds. The softest one, and the most familiar of all of them, urged him to continue on his journey—to meet the person Batukhan was taking him to. It was Niyol's distant whisper in the moments of waking that held him to his companion.

Chance's paws were dusty and his pads stung. He was looking for the caves that a sign had announced a short ways down the road. It was quiet here. Not much traffic now that the sun had dropped to the horizon. There was a certain amount of risk of getting picked up by animal control running alongside the highways and streets, or even getting hit by a car, but it was the easiest way to make good time and to find food. Not that gas station sandwiches could really be defined as food.

The road veered off and a small metal sign with the symbol of a cave marked the intersection. Chance turned down the gravel lane and Batukhan followed. He picked up the pace and couldn't hold his tongue in his mouth any longer. It rolled out into the wind, flapping free. He was beginning to get used to moving in canine form.

After a few minutes a small, empty parking lot came into view that was surrounded with trees. Chance continued across to a pathway that led to a rocky hill and stopped. His energy flared and his skin tingled. The fur that covered his body disappeared and he rose to his feet. Chance stretched his arms above his head and dropped his backpack to the ground. Soon he had on a pair of jeans and a T-shirt.

While Batukhan finished pulling on a long-sleeve, he said, "A good place to camp for the night. In many cultures, caves are considered portals to other worlds and magical creatures live in them."

"Well, I guess tonight that's true. So, tell me why we aren't staying at a hotel again?" Chance combed his fingers through his shaggy, black hair, pulling free dirt and burs.

"I have told you, Chance. It is not safe for you to be around people in your current state. You do not want to hurt anyone, do you?"

"No." It was like he was trapped in a moving prison. He guessed Batukhan was right, but he resented being treated like a criminal and sleeping on the ground really sucked. The sooner all of this could end, the better.

He slipped the strap of his backpack over his shoulder and started walking to the mouth of the cave. His vision blurred and he stumbled to a stop. Another memory began to form in his thoughts and he grew anxious. He never knew what to expect and he didn't like being forced to watch against his will.

His skin burned in the sunlight. Long black hair hung around his shoulders while he leaned down behind a large rock. The scent he'd been tracking was strong here, but so was the aroma of blood.

Please be alive, Mai.

Nastas's heartbeat was elevated and he was having a hard time steadying his breathing. He was staring at a cave in the rocky hillside ahead of him and attempting to adapt his vision to see farther and more clearly. There was no movement, but based off the thoughts tumbling around in Nastas's head, he was certain Mai was there.

Father would know what to do, but he's not here. What if it's another shapeshifter? Or what if it's a skinwalker?

The stories Chance had read on the Internet rushed back to him. He knew that term. He'd thought it was the Navajo name for a shapeshifter. Except all of the stories about skinwalkers were negative and frightening. What if it referred to shifters with the sickness . . . like him? A chill went down his spine.

There's no time to get Father. Mai could be hurt or dying. I have to help her.

Nastas quickly formed a plan. He set the bird he'd killed onto the rock he was hiding behind and removed a small, sharp knife from his belt. Nastas raised his arm and cut along his forearm. Bright red blood bloomed from the wound and he pressed his arm to the rock, letting it saturate the stone. He wiped the blood from his blade and held it between his teeth. With his eyes closed, he mustered all of his energy and a blue mapping illuminated in his mind. The familiar tingling sensation rippled through his body and his skin felt like it was being poked with needles. The discomfort of his self-inflicted wound eased, and he knew his cut had healed.

Nastas extended his eagle wings and rose to the air, careful not to drop the knife that was held in his beak. He climbed higher and higher until the cave was far below him and he rode the currents down toward the rocky hills behind the opening in the rocks. His claws gripped at some scrub growing on the dusty hillside and began a slow and steady descent, careful to be as silent as the wind.

Movement came from the opening of the cave. Nastas scurried to hide behind a small boulder and then peeked around the side. A large hairy shape walked out on two legs. Its nose lifted to the air and it began to move toward the rock he'd marked with blood. While the beast had its back turned to him, Nastas continued down the rocky face until he reached the top of the opening of the cave. From there he could hear soft whimpering and an eerie gurgling noise from within.

Mai.

The large hairy beast reached the bloody rock and held up Nastas's bow in his large humanoid hands. Nastas had never seen anything quite like the animal before, but they'd heard stories recently about the howler from neighboring tribes. Chance knew exactly what it was, however, and couldn't believe it.

The sasquatch turned around and started back to the cave, but moved very slowly. He was scanning the wilderness and appeared very busy trying to pick up Nastas's scent. Nastas pressed his body down against the stony lip of the cave and listened for the beast's approach.

A man's voice called out, "I know you are out there, young shapeshifter. Do not think I don't know your game. I have been watching you for days and think you would be a fine host, if you can kill me. But that is always the test. Either way, you're mine."

Nastas risked it and lifted his head enough to look over the edge. No longer was the large hairy beast standing there, but a brown-haired man. His skin was much paler than Nastas's and he appeared to be older, possibly in his twenties.

"Your woman is dying. You might want to hurry."

The man got closer to the opening of the cave and just as he passed below, Nastas pinched the blade tight in his beak and coasted on his wings down a few feet. Before he reached the ground, he shifted back to human form, grabbed the knife from his teeth and drove the blade into the base of the man's neck. Nastas's adversary fell forward with a yell and Chance watched in horror as his head bashed into a rock.

A burst of blue light radiated out from the man's body along with a shockwave of air. It pelted into Nastas, reminding Chance of the moments after Markus's death. A rush of power flooded his soul, making Nastas lightheaded for a minute. He sputtered and coughed.

The world was a little brighter and more colorful. Smells and sounds overwhelmed his senses and a laugh broke free, echoing off the walls of the cave.

When the rush subsided, Nastas's gaze fell on a lump a few feet away. Long strands of hair had fallen free from the bun on the top of her head. Dark blood ran from her mouth and onto the rock she was wrapped around. Her eyes were wide and unseeing.

"Mai?"

There was no answer.

You don't need her. She was weak.

The voice echoed in Nastas's mind and Chance recognized it immediately. It was the same, nameless guiding force within him.

"Chance!"

The scene inside of the cave dematerialized and Chance realized he was being shaken. The twilight sky and dark shapes of the trees surrounding him welcomed him back from the memory sequence. Batukhan was standing before him and was gripping his shoulders, staring worriedly into his eyes.

"What? Leave me alone!" Chance wrestled free of his grasp.

"That was a long one. What did you see?"

"What do you mean? I was just spacing out—I'm hungry."

Batukhan led him into the cave and motioned for Chance to sit down. "You may be trying to fool yourself, but not me. I know what it is like experiencing memories of other shifters. That is why I am taking you to my friend. That is why we must hurry."

Chance settled against the rocky wall and opened up his backpack. He pulled out his water bottle and a crushed bag of chips. The only person he'd really talked to about the memories was Ana, but she wasn't here and he couldn't talk to her. He wasn't sure if he should trust Batukhan. The voices in his head argued if he was trustworthy.

One thing he was sure of was the fact that he couldn't take much more of these memories. Why couldn't he channel happy thoughts and not murders? The only time he was free of them was while he was in animal form. It was quieter then.

"I can see you don't want to talk about it. If you do not, then you should at least try to center yourself after it happens. Feed yourself. Do you have enough protein? After you eat, let's meditate. Calming your energy and reconnecting with it is a priority when there is so much noise in your mind."

Batukhan held out a protein bar to Chance, who accepted it and tore it open. He was starved, and swallowed it down in three bites. After he ate an apple, a bean and cheese burrito left over from their stop at lunch, and a beef stick, he felt much more human.

The entire time Batukhan kept a close eye on him, something Chance was well aware of. He didn't much like a sturdy Mongolian staring at him, but there wasn't anything he could do about it but try to ignore him.

"Close your eyes. It is time to meditate."

Chance did as he was told and took deep breaths, allowing himself to relax.

He is trying to hypnotize you into complacency. You must stop this. Are you his cattle? What about Ana? What if she's in danger? It is your job to protect her.

Ana's face traced his thoughts and his heart actually hurt thinking about her. How many days had it been? Weeks? Too many. Traveling by dog was slow going and he just wasn't confident Batukhan was looking out for his well-being. What if he just wanted his friend to help kill Chance? This was crazy. The advice he'd had from his grandfather and great-grandfather was to be wary of other shapeshifters. Always be cautious.

The only thing Batukhan had done to display trust was giving him food and not killing him. Yet.

After a quiet period, they both lay down to go to sleep. Chance was tired from running all day and as soon as he tucked his backpack beneath his head, his eyes shut and all of the voices fell away into silence.

***

Life stirred around the mouth of the cave. Birds chittered and the distant sound of cars on pavement brought Chance from his deep sleep. The comforting, deep whisper from Niyol welcomed him back to consciousness.

Remain at peace, be true to yourself. Listen to your instincts and be patient.

When he opened his eyes, shadows clung to the ceiling and sunlight crept across the dusty ground. Batukhan sat cross-legged, facing out. His formidable form kept Chance's face in shadow.

"Good morning, Chance. How did you sleep?"

He groaned and lifted himself to his feet. "As good as you can on the ground."

Chance brushed the dirt from his clothes and thought longingly of his bed at home. He could almost smell the bacon and eggs his mom used to cook for breakfast on the days she didn't work. He begrudgingly took a granola bar from his backpack and tried to imagine a heartier start to his day. Who knew how long he'd be traveling this way. If Batukhan had his way they'd remain sleeping in the dirt and eating out of their bags. He definitely didn't need a pillow top mattress, but living like this left a lot to be desired.

"I think we can start heading northwest toward New Mexico. Do you have enough food to last you until lunch time?" Batukhan turned his head but didn't look at him.

Chance looked in his pack again, pulled out an energy drink and took a swig before answering. "Yeah, but I'll need something more than a bruised apple and protein bar for lunch. We'll definitely need to stop."

"Let us prepare ourselves for our journey." Batukhan rose from the ground and stretched.

"So, I know you don't want me to be around people 'n all, but why can't we at least rent a car or something? I've got the money. Wouldn't we make better time?"

"That is a good question. Shifters who have the sickness fare better when they remain in animal form. Have you noticed the voices aren't as loud when you're a dog?"

Chance didn't need to think about it. "Yes, it's much quieter."

"This is why we are traveling in this manner. Unless you have any other questions, let's prepare ourselves to leave."

They quickly got ready and were soon on the road again, running along the dusty shoulder in canine form. It was a long morning and when they stopped at midday, Chance was ready for a rest.

Behind a gas station and a pair of dumpsters they shifted into human form and pulled on their clothing. Short of having a little extra grime on his skin, he looked like any average teen. He pulled out his tennis shoes from his bag and noticed his cell phone. Since leaving Balam's home in the Yucatán, he hadn't checked his messages. He didn't have any battery life left in it and he hadn't exactly had the opportunity to stop and charge it. His parents had probably checked in and would be wondering where and how he was. Besides that, he was afraid to hear Ana's voice and the pain that would be impossible to miss. Even if he got better, would she ever forgive him for abandoning her?

"What is that?"

"Just my phone." Chance slipped it back into his bag and zipped it up.

"Mmmm."

"What, do you have a problem with phones too?" Chance asked in agitation.

Batukhan eyed him. "You will be tempted to see your family and friends, but I recommend you wait to speak to them until you are in control of yourself. I can hold it for you so you are not tempted."

"No, you're not taking my phone." Chance slipped his backpack over his shoulder and sauntered around the brick building. He was hungry, tired and seriously annoyed with his travel companion. Who did he think he was, his mom?

The gas station had a Mexican fast food restaurant attached and Chance was eager to have something other than prepackaged meals that tasted like plastic. He ordered ten burritos and ate five while Batukhan watched him warily, like he was some kind of ticking time bomb.

Chance put the remaining food in his pack. "I've got to go to the bathroom. Be right back. Could you get me some waters?"

"Yes." Batukhan watched him move away to the far end of the convenience store.

The men's room was empty when he walked in, which was a good thing, because as soon as he stepped inside his vision grew fuzzy and he stumbled against the wall. Another memory absorbed his thoughts and his breathing quickened.

Instead of standing in the bathroom, he was biking down a rural neighborhood street. Chain-link fences lined the small, one-story homes and loud music poured from the window of a parked car.

He turned to look behind him and spotted a large black crow on a telephone pole. Wind combed through his hair and a lock fell across his eyes when he turned to face the sidewalk. Clouds streaked across the sky and a chill was in the air.

It's him. I know it is. Mom thought we'd be safe here, but he always finds me.

Chance recognized Markus's voice in his head. This memory took place in a different town from last time, he was almost sure of it. It was more rural than the last one.

Markus's blood pressure was rising. The veins in his neck were throbbing painfully, and it was transferring to Chance. He gasped for breath against the bathroom wall and stared blankly at the stalls as the memory continued.

Markus pedaled ahead, turned down a dusty gravel street and kept his eyes ahead of him. Down the road he could see a gleam of metal shining in the sun. An Exxon sign came into view and the small service station was empty of cars. He pumped his legs and then coasted up to the building.

I don't want to move again. I can't put Mom through this again. It isn't fair to her. If grandfather kills me like he did with dad and Ricky she'd lose it. She'll have nothing left. I can't let that happen.

Fear transformed into resolve and Markus climbed off his bike and went to the door. A bell chimed when he went inside and he put his hand into his pocket to pull out a five-dollar bill. He grabbed a soda from the case and a candy bar from the small display rack and threw them on the counter.

After he paid the attendant he asked, "You got the key to the bathroom?"

The old man behind the counter handed him a key hanging off a metallic tire rim. "Bring it back, you hear?"

"Yes, sir."

Markus took it, lumbered back outside and sniffed the air. Rain was coming, he could smell it. He rounded the corner of the building and approached the bathroom door. A black crow flew down to the gravel and cawed at him. Markus paused and turned his back to the cinderblock wall. He kept his eyes on the bird while it stared at him.

Chance realized just how rural the town was in that moment. He hadn't seen a passing car on the dusty road since Markus's memory began. There were only bushes and trees

185

nearby, no other businesses or homes. A few rooftops were visible, but he knew they were alone. So did Markus.

"Come to visit me again, grandfather? Take me to the zoo and get an ice cream cone?"

A black feather floated to the ground as the bird stretched out its wings and shifted into a man's body. His head was not that of Nastas, but of a grotesque beast. A wolflike face with a wrinkled maw pulled back to reveal sharp teeth. Fierce eyes flashed at Markus and fear grabbed at his chest like a vice.

"You can't scare me," Markus whispered.

The frightening beast's face shifted until Nastas's almond flesh was revealed. His eyes gleamed as he stared at his grandson. "I don't believe you. I know my face gives you nightmares. I hear you crying into your sheets when the moon is high. You can't escape your fate. You will be mine, just like your father and brother before you."

Markus remained quiet, but his mind was racing. *I can't let him kill me. I can't let him hurt Mom again. It's either me or him.*

"You've got a foolish look in your eye. I'd rather let you live a little longer so you may grow more powerful before I kill you. It is better for me that way. But if you'd prefer dying today . . . I can arrange that."

"Ever since I learned I was like you, I decided I wouldn't give you what you wanted. I don't shapeshift or use my powers, I'm nothing to you. Why don't you just leave me alone?"

Nastas smirked. "I can't do that."

Markus edged toward the bathroom door and tried grasping the key between his fingers but the tire rim got in the way.

"Nothing like a good chase, but you've got nowhere to go." Nastas's sneer elongated while he shrank into a cougar. The tan cat padded forward, and let its mouth drop open.

Markus ran to the door and fumbled with the key, slipped it in and turned the knob just as Nastas reached him. Pain ripped his back and Markus yelled in surprise. While he pulled open the door, he turned around to see the cougar's claws implanted into his back. More than the physical agony, his energy was being sapped. Panting with fear, Markus lunged into the bathroom and tried shutting the door behind him. His grandfather lost his hold on him, but was already halfway into the dark, dirty room.

Markus stumbled back, away from the predator and watched it creep in toward him. The cougar reached out and clawed at his leg, tearing his jeans. He exhaled sharply and thought to himself, *This is your last chance. Don't let yourself be a lamb for the slaughter! Move!*

He dashed around the animal and dove for the door. He could hear the animal behind him, but he remained focused on what he needed to do. Markus flung himself against the outside of the door and pushed with all of his weight, trying to shut his grandfather into the bathroom. A screech called out beside him and he saw the cougar's head lodged between the door and the wall.

Markus's blood thundered noisily in his ears as he planted his foot against the base of the door and the ground. He turned to place his palms against the metal door and wracked his mind on what to do next. While he stared at the large metallic disc dangling from the key that was still in the knob, he realized his life was in his hands. With his foot and shoulder planted securely, he slipped the tire rim from the keyhole. Gripping it tight, he raised it up and with all of his strength, brought it down into the wild cat's neck. Metal cut through flesh and stopped at bone.

The cougar's head was thrust to the ground and blood washed the dirt. Its mouth fell open and eyes stared unblinking. Markus's heartbeat rattled uncontrollably and he took a shaky breath. Without warning, a burst of blue light and wind radiated out from his grandfather's body. Markus dropped the tire rim and fell back against the door, the burst of power and energy surging through his core. Dizzy and lightheaded, he shut his eyes.

I told you, you'd be mine. One way or another.

The memory faded and as Chance leaned against the restroom wall, he tried to get oriented. He wasn't reliving Markus's life anymore—he was in a gas station with Batukhan. What he'd viewed in his head wasn't really happening now. But even though it hadn't been real, he felt the stomach-turning rush from Nastas's death and the voices in his head.

What was he doing?

Markus's thoughts echoed in his head and he pushed away from the wall. Just like him, Chance had no intention of being led like a lamb to the slaughter. He gripped his shoulder straps and swallowed hard.

It was time he struck out on his own. He didn't know who Batukhan was or what he really wanted with him, but he wasn't going to just hand himself over to be killed like a fool.

The door opened and a police officer walked into the bathroom. Chance nodded to him as he brushed by and formed a plan. If he was going to make a clean getaway, he'd need some help.

"Excuse me, sir? There's a man outside the bathroom who's got a gun in his bag and he threatened to kill me."

CHAPTER 17

The flame licked up toward the ceiling. The candle had melted halfway down and wax was pooling at its base. Ana sat cross-legged before it, still and focused. It was early morning and no one else was up. She had been practicing in all of her spare moments, eager to control her abilities. If this was the key to learning about healing, then she'd put every ounce of effort into it. Failure was not an option.

In her meditative state, she was aware of the energy motes swirling around her. Careful not to disturb the candle's flame, she drew in the power surrounding her. For the first time, the bloom of light wasn't affected. It continued to lick at the air, undisturbed from Ana's actions. Her concentration broke and she let out a laugh.

Finally! Was it too early to go knock on Lifen's door? She still felt the sting from her teacher's condescending remarks the other day and wasn't eager to agitate her again, no matter how off base she thought it was.

While she smiled at the flame it doubled in size and her eyes widened in surprise. Had she done that? She quieted her mind and paid attention to her energy, which she realized was now radiating outside of her body. The flame continued to grow and react to her. Ana focused and reversed the flow instead, pulling in the glowing light around her and the candle's teardrop of fire reduced back to what it was.

"You are very determined, Ana. I am impressed."

Ana looked over her shoulder. Lifen was standing at the entrance of the living room wearing a colorfully embroidered robe. Her pale skin shone in the darkened room.

"Good morning, Lifen. I've been practicing and I think I've got it! I can control the energy around me."

"It also looks like you've discovered the beginning stages of healing too. How to push your own energy outside of your body."

Ana lifted herself off the floor and stood up. "Does this mean I get to learn about healing now?"

Lifen stared at her.

"You promised," Ana whispered, fearing her mentor's silence.

Lifen's acerbic voice frightened her. "I never made a promise. I told you that you would be ready to learn about healing once you were able to control the energy around you. I see much impatience within you."

She continued to study Ana, whose feelings were erupting into panic and fear. "However, I do see your intentions behind your actions, which confirms my initial impression of you, Ana. You will be a great healer because you are a kind person."

Ana was afraid to say anything, not wanting to agitate Lifen again. She would do anything to be able to learn how to save Chance. Being berated by her mentor stung, but she'd take it if it meant getting taught about healing.

Lifen turned to leave and said over her shoulder, "Are you coming?"

She didn't need to be asked twice. Ana blew out the candle and scurried after her mentor. They went to the meditation room and Lifen slid open the rice paper doors. The first rays of sunlight had begun to peer over the mountains and were visible from the windows.

"The boys will be waking soon, so we need to get started. Please close the doors and take a seat."

Ana did as her teacher asked and settled on a cushion on the floor. Lifen went to the small cabinet, took something out of a drawer, and then sat across from Ana.

"There are many forms to healing. I will teach you one of the more basic elements today. You are able to see energy around you and have now learned to control how to draw it into your body. This technique alone takes healers months to learn. You are special."

Lifen held between her fingers a small knife. An intricate design was etched along the blade and the milky, translucent handle had a floral pattern. It seemed to be very old, but it wasn't rusty or dull. Ana watched her mentor in surprise while she lifted the blade to her forearm and slid it along her flesh. Blood surfaced along the incision on Lifen's skin and she looked up at Ana.

"It stings a little, but you can heal me."

No matter how many times she saw blood, she couldn't adjust to it. She was sickened at the sight, but strangely drawn to it all at once. It upset her to see the wound, although she couldn't have walked away if she wanted to.

"When healing, it is important not to draw from only your own energy, weakening yourself, but to pull in the energy around you. Beginners find it useful to have contact with the injury when they start, but as you evolve you will only need to be near to direct the energy into the recipient. Healing is similar to shapeshifting in that both require the ability to map an animal. Once you have pulled in enough energy, and you are in touch with the mapping of the injured person or animal, you can begin the healing connection. It should be gentle, and if it isn't, then you need to disengage immediately so you do not cause damage to yourself."

"But I didn't think it was possible to map a human. . ." she said with her eyes glued to the bloody cut.

"You are correct that shapeshifters and healers cannot map humans, but that is because we are human and it is ingrained within us. You already know the proper form of man. Now if you are ready, please begin."

While Lifen had been talking, Ana had already begun to draw in the energy around her. She couldn't take her eyes away from the cut on her mentor's arm. All Ana wanted was to fix what was broken. Her energy surged and she could actually see it reach out to her teacher's arm and connect, like a long glowing feeler. At the same rate she was absorbing the power around her, it was funneling off to Lifen in a beautiful electrical arc. Before her eyes, her mentor's pale skin created a puckered seam that extended the full length of the cut.

"Very impressive. I have not seen anyone as suited for healing as you are." Lifen wiped the blood from her arm. "A scar remains, but you will learn how to remove those with time. I can fix it, do not worry. You may let go of the connection."

A dew of perspiration beaded at Ana's forehead and she realized she'd been holding her breath. She inhaled and disengaged the flow of energy with a little effort. The glowing light that had been arcing between them dissipated and Ana was left feeling numb.

"After a healing, it is important to meditate and reconnect with your energy core. Do not neglect yourself, or you will grow imbalanced. An imbalanced healer does not remain a healer for long."

Ana nodded and closed her eyes. She did feel a bit tired and a nap sounded better than anything, but she did as her mentor instructed.

"With time you can even remove your own scars if you wish it."

Ana automatically lifted her fingers to her sternum, and felt the ripple of flesh beneath her shirt.

"Only if you wish it."

Not only had she never expected to be cured from her heart condition, she never thought she could be free from her physical scars. Ana was thankful to Chance for saving her life, and was happy to be alive. She would have thought that after a lifetime of embarrassment, the marks that remained on her chest from her surgeries would be easy to say goodbye to. But now that it was being offered to her, it wasn't such an easy answer.

After a few minutes, she realized her thoughts were keeping her from relaxing and meditating, so she let go of her angst and focused instead on the energy around her and the yellow power within. Rejuvenated and no longer in need of a rest, she discovered she was extremely hungry. Her stomach growled and she cracked open one eye.

Lifen smiled at her. "Healing will also make you hungry. I think I hear the boys moving around. Why don't you go eat breakfast and we'll do more again soon."

Ana got up off her cushion and thanked Lifen before leaving the meditation room. She found all of the guys in the kitchen preparing breakfast.

"Hard at work already?" Ryan asked, but she didn't get the feeling he was giving her a hard time.

"Learning a little healing," Ana said. "I'm finally able to control myself when pulling in energy. Now I won't hurt you guys during meditation."

Ryan raised his hand and gave her a high five. "Sweet! That's always a plus—not hurting your friends."

The fact that he'd called himself a friend didn't go unnoticed by Ana.

"Good job, Ana. Congrats!" Derek said and Jordan chimed in with his congratulations.

"Thanks!" Ana said. "Anyone started the tea yet? I can brew a pot." Ana wove through the kitchen, feeling truly at home.

***

Ana woke slowly, her eyes combing the ceiling. Daylight poured into her bedroom from the small windows at the top of her wall. She sat up suddenly and grabbed for her phone on the side table. She'd slept in and only had enough time to throw on some clothes before meeting the others for meditation. Breakfast would have to wait.

Another week had gone by and she hadn't had another dream of Chance. She was growing anxious about his safety. Was he hurt? Or worse, had he hurt someone? Not knowing was eating her up. She constantly vacillated between happiness and guilt. One moment her excitement for accomplishing something new would take her to a new height, but in the next, her sadness over Chance being lost from her brought her to an extreme low. The guys tried to roll with it, understanding that when she grew quiet, she needed space.

Ana pulled on a shirt and sweats and ran a brush through her hair so it wasn't as tangled. A pair of socks warmed her feet before she nestled her toes into her slippers. Just as she reached for the doorknob, a quick tapping sounded from the other side of the door.

"Ana, you awake?"

She opened up to find Jordan's concerned face.

"I slept in by accident. Coming now."

"Lifen really doesn't like it when we're late."

Ana pulled her hair into a ponytail and squeezed Jordan's arm. "We don't want her in a bad mood. Thanks for coming to get me."

The others were just getting to the meditation room when they walked in. Lifen was waiting, sitting cross-legged with her back to the windows. She was wearing a serious expression and Ana shared a worried glance with the others, who seemed to have picked up on their mentor's frame of mind.

"Good morning," Ana said brightly, hoping to start the day off right.

"Let's get started."

Wordlessly, they all sat on cushions before her and closed their eyes. Ana was comfortable absorbing energy around her friends now that she had control of it. She hadn't had another healing session with Lifen, and she was anxious to learn more. Chance didn't have a cut finger he needed healed—she knew it was far more complicated than that. She was eager to practice again, but she didn't feel comfortable hurting herself or asking one of the guys to, either. So, she continued to focus on shapeshifting lessons, no matter how unimportant they seemed. It appeared asking Lifen about another healing lesson was out of the question today since she wasn't in the mood, but she really didn't want to wait any longer. If the opportune moment presented itself, she'd be ready.

They meditated for half an hour before Lifen told them they'd be working in the shapeshifting arena yet again. Ana sighed and lifted herself off the floor. While the guys went to get changed into their robes, she ran down to the kitchen and grabbed a granola bar from the pantry. With it hanging from her mouth, she stripped in her bathroom and pulled on her robe, no longer shy of her own skin.

At the front entry she slipped on her boots and followed the guys up to the large metallic building. She went down the corridor of stalls and cages, feeling a bit depressed. Ana never would have thought learning about shapeshifting would have been so unpleasant. Maybe it was the fact that she hadn't sensed Chance in a while, but she didn't want to shapeshift just then.

She stopped in front of the osprey enclosure and stared at the bird of prey. Its golden eyes returned her stare while it held still on its branch. After a moment of studying her, it blinked and gazed at the wall.

Ana whispered, "I wish I weren't here too."

If she had to be around anyone, she'd prefer hanging out with the birds. Although staring in at a caged bird made her sad. She'd always loved them for the freedom they represented. She felt just as free as the birds in Lifen's collection. Something to look at and admire without a proper job or value.

A scuffle down the corridor drew her attention. Within the folds of a robe, a lizardlike creature flicked its tongue out. Patches of pink skin intermixed with the dark green scales in a strange pattern.

"No, Ryan," Lifen said, with her hands resting on her hips. "Shift back before you hurt yourself. Reptiles are not natural to you. I do not understand why you persist having such issues."

The animal curled under the fabric and began to grow in size, lifting up the robe as it enlarged. Ryan's shaggy blond hair lifted above the collar and his hands came out the sleeves. He tied his robe and braced himself against the wall of tiny glass terrariums.

"I'm trying my best. I want to learn reptiles. There's something about them—I just want to get it right. I don't know why I can't do it!"

Ana realized she was staring and turned her head to face the wall.

"You need to do what I've instructed you to do. Maybe we should go back to mammals for now. You don't seem to be ready for this yet, Ryan."

"What if I try a different type of reptile? I'm not giving up."

"No, the iguana is the perfect starting point. It isn't too complicated."

Ryan groaned and Ana looked back. He punched the wall beside the cages and swore as loud as he could.

Lifen held up her palm. "You must be patient then. Calm yourself."

He closed his eyes and rested his head on the glass of the terrarium. Ana focused in and everything began to glow. The energy currents around them, floating from the floor to the ceiling, swirled in heart-stirring harmony. Each of the animals flickered with soft blue light and beside them, Lifen glowed like the full moon. When Ana turned her attention to Ryan, she noticed his luminescence was weaker than their mentor's by far, and a wisp of light curled away from him into the air.

Ana was curious. That couldn't be normal. Maybe that was why he wasn't able to shift into a reptile.

Ryan was staring through the glass of the terrarium again, ready to give it another try. His brow wrinkled with concentration and his hands were pressed against the wall on either side of the iguana's cage. The energy leak didn't seem right to her, so she reached out with her power and connected to his. It was similar to when she'd healed Lifen's cut, but different still. She felt a wound, a hole in the skin of his energy and pushed her healing light into him, trying to seal the leak.

Ryan shrank down to the floor. A pile of fabric curled around a green snout that peered out from the folds of the robe. He climbed out, triumphant, his long, forked, pink tongue tasting the air around him.

The connection was lost and in a daze, Ana smiled. "Awesome! Great job, Ryan!"

"Ana!"

Her heart skipped a beat in surprise and she put her attention on Lifen's voice, the source of the interruption.

"Come with me. *Now.*"

Her mentor swept toward her and as she passed by, grabbed hold of her arm, and led her to the door. They burst out into the cold, dry air and Lifen didn't stop there. She continued all the way to the opposite side of the driveway, where the stairs led down to the house.

If it were possible for flames to ignite in her irises, she was pretty close to it now. Ana thought she'd seen Lifen agitated before, but she was wrong.

"What do you think you are doing?" Lifen said through pursed lips.

"I . . . don't know," Ana stammered. "What do you mean?"

197

"You were just trying to adjust Ryan's energy. You have no place doing that. *I* am the teacher and *you* are the student. I am the one that knows what's best for all of you. You haven't lived for more than twenty years and you think you know everything already. My lifetimes could lap yours around the sun many times over."

"Wait, you mean he had an energy leak on purpose?" Ana shrank away, just a little bit freaked out at Lifen's intensity. She wasn't one for a fight. She'd rather walk away than deal with confrontation.

"You breathe a word of this to anyone and you will be on your own. Not only will you ruin your own education, but theirs. Male shapeshifters have far more energy than the average person. You know this. That increase of power in their youth is a challenge for most to control. Mixed with their feelings and ego, it can create a monster. I have found through my years of aiding youngling shifters, that if their energy doesn't peak too quickly it helps them through their most important stage of learning. So, I create a small puncture in their energy field so it never grows too big before they are ready. None of them are ready."

Ana didn't know what to say. What could she say? She guessed the logic was sound, but still, it just seemed backwards. Although she'd known Chance to be a bit impatient and he had his moments of frustration, he'd always behaved himself. He never did anything inappropriate with his gifts. That she knew of.

She had a realization. "Wait, is that why I feel like a shock whenever I touch the guys?"

"Yes, it is. I hadn't realized you could sense it." Lifen closed her eyes. When she opened them, the anger that had been so alarming was gone. She put her hand on Ana's shoulder and the edges of lips curled up.

"I hope you understand, Ana. I have lived for hundreds of years and I've met my share of shifters. I may sound bitter, but it is for good reason. More times than not, their inability to keep their powers in balance has caused death and destruction. Shapeshifters are an endangered species, and healers, well, are even harder to find. This is why I was so excited you found me—that we found each other. You are unique and you have the power to change the world for the better. I know this is confusing, but I need you to promise you will keep this a secret. It is for everyone's good."

Ana didn't know which end was up. If Chance were here they'd talk it over and figure it all out. He'd know what to do. She had no idea if she'd made the right choice coming here with Lifen, but all she knew was this was the only place for her to learn about healing. At present, that was the only thing that mattered to her. Or, it used to be. She'd made friends. Friends who mattered to her and she didn't want to see them hurt.

With reluctance, Ana nodded.

CHAPTER 18

Ana woke to a text from her mom.

If we aren't seeing you for Thanksgiving will we see you for Christmas?

It was only ten minutes before her alarm was set, but her eyes were heavy with sleep. She'd stayed up late looking at the stars from the living room windows, trying to calm her mind, but it didn't work. She hadn't wanted to ask to use Lifen's private gazing tower, because she didn't want to be around her. The only thing she was prepared to ask for was healing lessons and she was waiting for her opening.

Her eyes blurred when she stared at the glowing text. As much as she wanted to see her mom and sister, there was no way she was about to leave. She wasn't entirely confident Lifen would let her leave if it came down to it, but it didn't much matter to her. She was staying until she found out what she needed to know, and if Lifen refused her that knowledge, only then would she leave.

Work's been going well. Christmas is busy here—but I will come home soon. Promise.

After she sent her response, she tucked her hands, phone and all, under her pillow. She considered having a sick day to sit in her room alone, but knew it wouldn't fly. Not with a healer in the house. She might as well get up and put her feelings into something else besides brooding in private.

Ana got up and took a shower, which helped a little bit. She got dressed, put on her slippers and went down to the kitchen. Cooking wasn't her passion—she'd prefer leaving that to someone else—but today, she felt like doing something for the guys.

She opened the fridge and saw there wasn't much to pick from. She'd had her mind set on scrambled eggs but it wasn't going to happen today. There wasn't enough fruit to make a salad, so she went to the cupboards to scavenge. The only thing she could think of to make was oatmeal and she found some blueberries in the freezer. Something to add a little color and flavor when it was done.

"Wow, you're cooking breakfast?" Jordan asked as he joined her.

"Yeah, I hope you like oatmeal. There's not much left in the fridge. I wanted to do something nice for you guys."

Jordan sauntered over to the pot and switched off the burner. "Thanks, Ana. I let Lifen know we were running low on supplies. Looks like it's time for her to make another grocery order."

Derek and Ryan emerged in the doorway.

"Did I hear Ana cooked breakfast?" Ryan asked with a grin. "Is it safe to eat?"

"I saved it from being burnt," Jordan said.

Ana joined him at the stove. "What? Oh, no! Glad you got here in time."

"So, what do you think Lifen has worked out for us today?" Ryan asked while he braced his hands against the counter. "Who wants to bet she's in a bad mood?"

Ana spooned out a large helping for everyone and sprinkled the blueberries on top, saving one to pop into her mouth. As soon as it touched her tongue, it began to melt and the sweet juices awakened her taste buds. "I don't know, but I've been waiting for a good day to ask about more healing lessons. I can't take another crabby day. I didn't come here to just shapeshift."

Ryan and Derek exchanged a smirk and Jordan accepted his bowl of oatmeal before muttering, "Tell us how you really feel."

Derek flashed his dimples and laughed silently.

"I'm serious," Ana said. "I haven't had a dream of Chance in over a week. I don't know what that means, but how do I know he hasn't gone all crazy-Markus-like? I have to help him and Lifen doesn't seem to care about any man, least of all Chance."

Derek put his arm around her. "Sorry, Ana. That really sucks. Don't know what you can do but try to grease her up. We'll see if we can't help out too by being on our best behavior. Right, Ryan?"

With a sweep of his hand, Ryan tucked some of his stray blond locks behind his ear. His blue eyes met Ana's and his constant smirking face grew serious. "I'll do my best. What sort of dreams are you talking about?"

Ana realized she'd never said anything to the guys about her special dreams or whatever they were. It was just something else that made her different from them. She hadn't said anything previously because she didn't want one more reason for Ryan and Jordan to resent her, but now that she'd landed on Lifen's naughty list many times and the guys seemed to have warmed up to her, she figured it couldn't hurt to share.

With their bowls in hand, they walked into the dining room and Ana took a bite before saying anything. "No, I'm not talking about regular old dreams. After Chance saved my life and put all of his energy into me, awakening my powers, I started dreaming of this place." Ana waved to the windows and the icy lake outside. "I saw the lake and heard Lifen's voice in my head. I asked her about it on the way here and she said that healers can sense emotion, and sometimes thoughts floating around someone's head—but close up, like in the same room. She said that when I was dreaming, I found her and visited her, like telepathically. Something like that. And since Chance left I've had these dreams of him. Not all of them have been good, but at least it's a way to know if he's alive or not."

"Whoa, that's a trip," Ryan said, holding his spoon in the air.

Ana ventured a look at the guys and they were all staring at her in awe. "Have you ever heard of shifters or healers having unique abilities? Or am I just a freak?"

"If you're a freak, then I don't know what we are," Derek said.

Jordan leaned forward and his eyes were alight with excitement. "The research I've done about it would suggest that it's happened before. I'd have to look into it more though. What did Lifen say about it?"

"I don't know. When I asked her about the dreams, she told me it wasn't something she could do. That she'd sensed me visiting her, but past that, she wasn't really in the mood to tell me more."

"Don't you want to know though?" Jordan responded.

"Well, yeah. I guess so, but that hasn't been my focus. It's not going to help me save Chance. What I need is the knowledge she has about healing. I don't want to get her cranky if she doesn't have to."

"I hear you. Okay, so today we'll all do what we can to get her into a good mood so you can ask her about healing. Right, guys?" Derek's eyes narrowed as he stared at Jordan and Ryan.

Ryan finished his oatmeal and answered, "I'll do my best."

"No different from any other day," Jordan said.

"Thanks guys." Ana hoped luck was on her side.

Derek and Jordan spooned their last bite into their mouths and got up to leave. Ryan leaned in and whispered to her, "Hey, I've been meaning to ask you. Did you have anything to do with me taking iguana form? Lifen seemed bent out of shape, so I wondered . . ."

Ana took a moment to answer, not sure what to say. Her conversation with Lifen was still fresh in her mind and she still didn't know how to feel about the energy leak situation.

At the time, she'd only wanted to assist her friend and she didn't regret helping him, even if it got her in trouble.

"S'okay. Your silence speaks volumes. Just wanted to say thanks—I don't know what you did, but it worked."

***

Lifen met them at the front door after they cleaned up from breakfast. Ana noted her calm disposition and gave her a bright smile.

"Today I thought I would give you the opportunity to prove yourselves again. Last time you failed to work together, but I hope that today you find the value of working as a team."

The four of them exchanged weary glances and then returned their gaze to Lifen. Butterflies churned in Ana's belly and she felt her breakfast testing the boundaries of her stomach.

"I have hidden an item of my clothing within this mountain range. You must work together to retrieve it and bring it back to me. You are to stay together to accomplish this task and you all must choose from the animal forms you took last time."

Ryan crossed his arms and scowled. "But last time you put your scarf in the tree and we couldn't get to it. That totally wasn't fair."

Derek shot him a warning glare, which he conveniently avoided.

"You did not work together before you began, and you did not plan how you were to accomplish the challenge. It was not my fault you did not work as a team and you gave up too quickly."

Ryan grumbled to himself, but refrained from saying anything more. Ana watched Derek's complexion turn from cocoa to brick red while he grimaced at Ryan. His fists tightened and she worried he wouldn't be able to keep his cool, but somehow he contained his anger and closed his eyes. Her next concern was Lifen. Had Ryan just ruined the possibility of cornering her with her request for more healing knowledge?

She didn't want to wait to find out. "I was just talking with the guys at breakfast and we know we can do it together. You won't be disappointed in us today, Lifen. We will work hard for you."

A slow smile spread across Lifen's face. "Thank you. I accept your offer. I don't want you working hard for me, but for yourself. Most of all, I want to see you work as a team. Go get your robes on and we will meet outside at the top of the stairs in five minutes. You are allowed to talk and plan as long as you need to before you begin. Once you shift, you are to remain in that form until the challenge is over."

Ana nodded to the guys and they all chorused their thanks to Lifen and started down the hallway. Before going downstairs to his room, Ryan stopped. Derek bumped into him as he brushed by. Ryan waited until Derek's door shut before he said to Ana, "I'll really do my best. I didn't mean to. . ."

She locked eyes with him and found a seriousness there that she didn't often see. "I believe you. And hey, Ryan, friends help each other. That's how that works. I'd do the same for you."

He gave a small grin and followed the guys to the lower level.

As fast as she could, she stripped down out of her clothes and wrapped herself in her robe. She hurried back to the front door and slipped on her boots. The guys were only seconds behind her and they ventured up the zigzag walkway to the stairs that led up to the drive.

Lifen stood in the snow barefoot. Her sage-colored silken dress rustled in the breeze and her pale skin glowed white in the reflected light of the snow. Ana imagined that her mentor must have known love in her lifetime. Her ageless beauty would have brought her many opportunities. The gentle expression on her face was the same misleading peacefulness that had lulled Ana to trust her when they'd first met. Not that Ana considered her mentor a wolf in sheep's clothing exactly, but her placid appearance certainly covered a tormented heart.

Ana smiled brightly at Lifen and prepared herself for what would likely be another hard challenge. There was no way she could give up or let the others do so.

"If you are all ready, you may discuss your plan. The rules are the same as last time, but now you must select the same animals you used before. You cannot leave our valley, you are to stay in that form until the end of the challenge and you have to work together to succeed. Do you understand the rules?"

"Yes, Lifen," Jordan said first.

The four of them stood in a circle and Ana held the lower half of her robe tight, trying to prevent the chilly draft from touching her legs. It was freezing, but soon enough, she'd be covered in fur and warmer than she was now.

"What's the plan, Ana?" Derek asked.

The others stared at her, waiting for her response. "Uh, okay." She paused and thought it out. "So, clearly we don't have to come up with new animals—that's all settled. Jordan, you've got horsepower and strength behind you. You're the largest out of all of us so you won't be able to squeeze through thick forest and it's dangerous for you to go across extremely rocky areas. Derek, you're a natural rock climber and you've got great ramming abilities, but because of your hooves we should stay clear of ice. My form is small and I'm probably the most nimble out of all of us. Ryan, the wolf has a strong jaw, and you would be our best tracker, so you should take the lead. We can't cut across the lake just yet. It wouldn't be safe for Jordan or Derek because they could break through. I don't trust the thickness of the ice—it's still too early in the season. Remember, we have to stay together, so if we have to go another way because someone can't make it, then we turn around and try another path. There's no giving up. Between all of us, there has to be a way to accomplish this. I believe in us. We're not just your average group of misfits. We're misfits with skills."

"Mad skills," Ryan chimed in.

"Any questions?" Ana asked.

"Nope, I think the godfather has spoken." Ryan winked at her.

Jordan tilted his head. "The godfather?"

"She's our alpha. Alpha Ana. AA."

Derek laughed. "I like it. Let's do this for Alpha!"

One at a time they shifted into their animal forms, and before the minute was out, a horse, ram, wolf and fox stood in a single-file line on the driveway. Ryan led them off the snow-covered concrete and down the mountainside. Ana took one last look over her shoulder at Lifen, who watched them drop out of view in silence.

They moved diagonally south along the range. The snow was quite deep from the last couple of weeks of winter weather and Ana found it challenging to spring into Ryan's footprints, so Jordan trotted ahead of her and shuffled his hooves through the white powder. He left behind him a narrow trench that was far easier for her to navigate through. Derek's wiry, cotton-ball puff of fur was almost camouflaged, except for his gray horns that twisted out from his face and the cloud of steam that surrounded his nose and warmed Ana's heels.

Clouds moved in and covered the sun, forcing the temperature to drop severely. Except for Jordan, who had shorter fur, they were all equipped to handle the cold. While she moved behind him, she noticed his abdomen twitch in shivers and she hoped they'd be able to finish quick before he turned into a horscicle.

The path they took appeared to be exactly the same as last time. Once or twice, Ryan paused with his nose in the air, and then continued on. They rounded the southernmost point of the lake and had to weave around a particularly rocky section, an area that Ana and Ryan had avoided before when they'd run across the frozen water to the bear den. Although it was Ryan's job to track Lifen's scent, Ana could smell it too. So far, everything had gone extremely smoothly and she was waiting for the other shoe to drop. There was no way that Lifen would just give them her shawl. She wouldn't make it that easy, no matter how much she wanted them to succeed.

Almost in answer to her fears, a few minutes after they headed north on the eastern side of the lake a very familiar scent met her nose. Bear.

Both the bear's and Lifen's aroma intermingled and grew stronger with every step. Ryan's ears perked up and his hackles rose down the length of his spine to the root of his tail. Jordan reared and Ana could see the terror reflected in his eyes. She stopped short so as not to get trampled by his large hooves and Derek bumped into her.

Ryan turned to look at them and instead of going straight toward Lifen's scent, he moved up the mountainside while he continued north. Each of them walked single file behind him, ears erect and eyes scanning the terrain. They stopped just past a cluster of tall pines and Ryan stared down toward the lake's edge.

Ana craned her neck in the same direction, searching for what he was looking at and then she found it—a piece of maroon fabric hanging from a branch midway up a tree that towered just above the bear's den. Perfect.

How exactly did Lifen expect them to get to her shawl? And how were they going to do it without getting killed? Hopefully the mama bear had already tucked her cubs in for their long winter sleep and wouldn't hear or smell them coming.

She glanced at her friends and they appeared to be having the same thoughts she was. Their disbelieving stares were evidence enough.

It was possible though. It had to be. Why would Lifen put it in a place with no possible way to get it down? Did she want them to fail? Ana chewed on that thought for a moment and shared a look with Ryan.

There was no way she'd let them fail. She didn't care if Lifen believed in them or not, because Ana did. Not only that, she had to do this for Chance. If she had to force Lifen into a good mood just to request more healing lessons, she'd do it. This was going to happen.

Ana leapt through the snow and moved down the mountainside slow and steady. Ryan's gray nose appeared beside hers. He kept sweeping his gaze from side to side, clearly in search of an angry mama bear. When they reached the bottom of the slope they stopped, although they didn't have to wait long for Derek who was right on their heels. Jordan, however, had to switch back and forth since the grade was too steep for his large body. All together, they moved cautiously toward the tree that held their treasure.

They stood with their muzzles pointed into the air, staring at the maroon flag that hung high above them. If Ana were a bird it would be easy, but changing forms would break the rules. None of them had hands or claws to climb the tree.

What if Jordan stood under the tree and Ryan jumped onto his back? Could they reach it then? Ana visualized it and besides it looking comical and absurd, she didn't think they'd have the height they'd need. Just out of reach. She scanned the area. Was there anything that could help them?

Then she saw it. The pale, gray trunk of a dead tree nearly ten feet away on the slope of the mountain. It could serve as a bridge if they could knock it down. She bounded through the snow to reach its base and stared up its length.

The others followed her over and waited for some sort of sign. How could she communicate her plan? She reached her paws up to Jordan's front knee, making sure she had his attention and positioned her rear quarters to the trunk and kicked at it. His big brown eyes blinked at her and for a moment. She wasn't sure if he'd understood what she was trying to tell him, but he pointed his body up the hill and measured his distance to the tree by reaching out his back leg. Ana realized she was in the wrong place and plunged through the snow to stand with Derek and Ryan, who were out of the way.

Jordan snorted and steam clouded the air in a swelling burst. His front quarters flexed and in a surge of power, his back legs fired out and impacted the trunk of the tree. A loud shot rang out and echoed across the lake. Ryan's and Derek's ears pinned down to their heads in reaction. It took Ana a minute to recover from the noise and then she remembered the tree. A serrated crack ran through the impact point and it tilted awkwardly toward the lake. It wouldn't take much more to push it the rest of the way. Jordan surveyed the damage over his shoulder and kicked out again with both hooves, but not as hard this time. The narrow stalk of the dead pine snapped off and fell into the branches of the trees down the slope.

Although it landed close to the intended branch of the tree that held the shawl, it needed to be moved another four or five feet. As Ana considered the options, a noise broke the silence. A deep, rumbling groan.

A dark shape emerged from a mound in the snow between them and the foot of the lake. The grizzly's long snout pointed at them and they remained stock still. Ana considered the situation. They weren't actually in human form, although she wasn't entirely sure they didn't smell like humans as well as animals. She knew better than anyone that bears had superior olfactory senses. Last time they'd met mama bear, Ana had run straight at her with Ryan on her tail. The grizzly must have felt threatened, but if they stayed out of her way, then maybe she'd go back into her den. Or maybe she'd recognize their scents and she'd want the last word.

As quickly as Ana rolled her thoughts around, the bear appeared to do the same. Go back into her den with her cubs, or get rid of the freak show at her front door. She might have chosen the first option if she didn't remember them, but apparently she did.

Mama bear rounded the embankment that was her home and rose up on her hind legs. Even twenty feet away and downhill, she was impressive. Ana glanced at her and then the maroon fabric in the tree. They were so close now. She didn't want to leave.

Ryan edged down the hill, just in front of them. His hackles were up and his head down in an aggressive stance. He shot her a look over his shoulder as if to say, "What are you waiting for?" and she sprang to action. She evaluated the fallen trunk and knew it had to get moved, but worried Jordan was too powerful for the task so she turned to Derek, who was still staring at the bear. She rose up on her hind legs and touched her paw to his horns. His yellow eyes focused on her and she scampered to the gray tree shaft and placed her nose on the wood.

Derek dropped his head and Ana moved aside just as he came thundering into the trunk. His thick, curled horns rammed into the pine. Its end brushed along snow-covered branches and came to rest at the root of the limb that held the shawl.

The noise and movement seemed to agitate the grizzly. She made more deep noises that stirred in her chest and poured from her toothy maw. Ryan held his ground, like a valiant guard.

Ana studied the length of the fallen trunk and climbed onto the base. She knew she was small enough to do it, but she wasn't entirely confident in her tight-rope skills. Her paws found footing, sure and steady, but it was icy and she didn't want to fall. Halfway across, a wiry limb curled into the air, blocking her path. She reached her front right paw out and tried to wind around it, but lost her balance. Ana dropped off the beam and landed with a puff in the snow below. Frustrated and angry, she lifted her head up and shook off the white powder.

Movement from the bear drew her attention. It was getting closer to Ryan and all the while, making deep growling threats. They didn't have the time for her mistake. Maybe they just needed to go and come back. She didn't want Ryan to get injured or killed. It wasn't worth it. She yelped.

In response, the wolf growled at her and advanced on the bear. She wished he wasn't so pigheaded. Ana scrambled up the hill to the base of the fallen pine and tried blocking everything out. All she saw was the straight path to the shawl. It was waiting for her and all she had to do was go and get it. Step by step she eased along the trunk and when she got to the point where she'd fallen before, she kept on moving, not giving it another thought. Finally, she reached the end and looked at the maroon fabric that was dangling from the branch above her. She lifted onto her hind feet, felt the cloth brush against her muzzle and jumped up, snapping it between her teeth. When she didn't fall like she'd expected, she realized the shawl was snagged on the branch.

Now what? What am I going to do? Panic set in. But her panic quickly turned to anger. There was no way she'd let go now. Flailing her lower body, she started twisting and swinging, determined to get them out of there. Her abdomen flexed, she arched up and suddenly she was falling. Again her body landed in the soft snow and she was ecstatically happy. Her excitement turned to horror when she heard the howling.

Bright red painted the snow and Ryan's front leg hung limp. The grizzly was preparing for another attack when a loud slap echoed across the valley and a pile of snow fell nearby. Ana didn't stop to find out what it was. She ran to Ryan's side, nudging him up the hill while the mama bear turned to find the origin of the noise. Another bang, but not as piercing, came from the opposite direction.

Ana lifted under Ryan's injured leg and helped him up the hillside away from the grizzly. His weight pressed against her back and she braced her legs just in time, nearly getting pinned down. He struggled going up the steep slope. Once they dragged themselves to level ground, Ana expected to see the guys, but they weren't there. She looked over her shoulder to see if they were being pursued by the bear, and was thankful to observe the bear had returned to her den. But that didn't explain why Derek and Jordan weren't there.

Ryan sat back on his haunches and sniffed his bloody leg. Ana returned her attention to him and tried to get a closer look at the damage that had been done. Her stomach turned at the sight of his wound. More than anything, she wanted to shift back to her human form to heal him. Her soft whimpers were dampened by the cloth hanging from her jaws.

She knew it wasn't necessary. He'd be as good as new once he changed form, but it really bothered her to be so near an injury but unable to do anything about it. As if to put her concerns to rest, Ryan stood back onto all fours and took a few steps.

A neigh came from nearby and they both turned their heads to find Jordan coming from between the trees below them. Ana was only partially relieved. Where was Derek?

She did a one-eighty, searching the wilderness for his white fur and coiled horns. Movement caught her attention and she sighed in relief, which appeared as a plume of steam pouring from her snout. Derek leapt over a snow-covered rock and hurried to their side. His head tilted as his eyes focused on the wolf's bloody leg.

All three of them stared at Ryan in silence. A question hung in the air. Would they be able to make it back now that they had the scarf?

He ignored the attention that was cast his way and limped forward. Ana knew every step he took had to kill, but he did it anyway. If there were a way to get him onto Jordan, then maybe they could get him home that way. No, she knew he'd never let Jordan carry him on his back. He had too much pride.

On the way there, he'd led the party with his muzzle in the air, tracking Lifen's shawl, and now he took the lead again, but this time it was more like a funeral march: every step slow and tentative, painting the snow with a faint line of blood. He made it north along the lake, nearly to the latitude of the house, but once it was time to go uphill, his leg wouldn't cooperate. Ana and Derek took turns giving him support, lifting up under the front of his body.

Finally, they reached the top of the bluff and the edge of the driveway. Lifen was waiting for them with a smile on her face. Ana might have immediately thought of herself if it weren't for Ryan, but in that moment, she didn't care how happy or proud their teacher was. She wanted to see her friend recovered.

Ryan stopped midway across the plowed drive and sat down. Lifen plucked his robe from the ground and brought it over to him, holding it open. He turned his head away and ignored her presence. Instead, he looked at Ana and lifted his leg.

She couldn't believe it. He was seconds away from shifting back to human form and being healed and he wanted to give her the practice. Ana wasn't the only one who was surprised by his actions.

"You want Ana to heal you, Ryan?" Lifen asked with her eyes wide.

Ana didn't want him to wait any longer. She dropped the maroon shawl on the ground and raced across the driveway to her crumpled robe. She touched her snout to the fabric and considered shifting before anyone noticed, but Lifen hurried over and shook it out and held it up. Like going home again, Ana shifted back to her pink, fleshy form. The cold air nipped at her skin so she wrapped herself in the cloth and tied it tight.

Derek and Jordan took turns shifting back and slipping into their robes, but by that time Ana was already by Ryan's side. She stood beside him and cleared her mind of the guys talking and just how cold she felt wrapped in wet fabric. Her yellow core glowed from within. She became aware of the energy within her as well as the power around her. The gray wolf pulsed with blue light and she stared at his wound.

With her hand out, she pushed her energy in a stream to him. When it connected, she felt a gentle tug and she visualized the corrected mapping. Before their eyes, the exposed flesh on his leg stitched back together and the fur grew back. The only sign of an injury was the blood that stained his pale fur.

Ryan stood up on all fours and licked Ana's hand.

Ana laughed. "Ooh, gross. Seriously? There are better ways to say thank you!"

Lifen helped him with his robe and within seconds his blond hair poked up above the cloth. He tied it and stretched the arm that had been hurt. "I was just thinking the same thing."

Ana walked up to him and gave him a hug. "Thank you, Ryan. You really didn't have to go through all of that, but I appreciate it. Really."

"What, we don't get hugs?" Derek asked jokingly.

"Of course you do." Ana gave both Jordan and Derek a hug too. "Thanks, guys—great job."

"I am pleased with all of you," Lifen said. "You worked as a team and you followed the rules even though one of you was injured." She looked directly at Ryan. "I see much growth and I am happy."

The guys all briefly glanced at Ana and gave her a nod. By helping her get Lifen into a good mood, they'd put their differences aside and helped each other. She was thankful for their friendship and hoped it would be enough to get what she needed from Lifen.

CHAPTER 19

Chance got off the bus and flung his backpack over his shoulder. He took a deep breath of the fresh pine scent and looked down the quiet street. It was nice being back in Clark Bend. He'd missed it.

It had taken a little work to backtrack to San Antonio to catch a bus to Idaho. He hadn't seen any sign of Batukhan, not since he left him in police custody at the roadside truck stop. Hopefully that was a loud enough message that Chance didn't want his help.

In a few minutes, he'd hopefully be reunited with Ana. He assumed she'd come home. After all, where else would she go? Chance wandered down the street and ducked into the bank. He searched the teller's faces but couldn't find who he was looking for.

"Excuse me, can I help you sir?" The receptionist asked a bit too brightly.

"I'm here for Melissa Hughes."

The woman pressed her lips together and lifted her phone. "There's a young man to see you." She cupped her hand over the receiver. "What's your name?"

"Chance."

"Your last name?"

"Morgan."

"A Mr. Chance Morgan is here to see you. Yes, okay." The woman hung up the phone and pointed to an office door. "She said come on in."

Without saying thanks, he breezed past her desk. Before he got to the door, Melissa emerged with a curious expression on her face.

"Hi, Chance. It's been a while since I've seen you. How've you been?"

"Okay. I got separated from Ana, but I'm back. Is she at the house?"

Melissa frowned and crossed her arms while she leaned against the door frame. "You haven't talked to her then?"

Chance grew agitated. "Where is she?"

She took a moment responding, and when she did, it was clear and calm. "She took a job in Canada. Maybe you should try calling her first to see if she wants to see you. She seemed pretty upset when she visited—didn't want to talk about you."

Her last comment stung and he clenched his fists instead of answering her. He forced a smile, which probably appeared like a grimace and muttered thanks before turning around and leaving the bank.

While the glass door closed behind him, he fished out his phone from his pocket and dialed Ana's number. He didn't really want to talk to her over the phone. He'd wanted to just see her and her loving glow. Now, he had no choice.

The call went straight to voicemail.

He cleared his throat and stammered, "Hey, Ana. I'm here in Clark Bend—thought I'd surprise you, but you're not here." He paused and closed his eyes. "I miss you, more than you know. Can you call me back? I want to see you."

Chance slowly pulled the phone from his ear and hung up. Maybe she was screening her calls. What if she didn't want to talk to him? After all, he had left her alone in Mexico without any explanation.

But she loved him. She had to understand why he abandoned her.

It didn't matter. He'd find her and make her understand. Chance looked over his shoulder at some passing cars and thrust out his thumb.

After a minute, a sedan pulled aside and he jumped in. First he'd go home to repack and grab his truck.

***

218

Memories from the past rushed back to him as he walked down the gravel driveway. Melting snow lay in piles amongst the trees and it felt ten degrees colder in the shade on the mountain. For a reason he couldn't explain, he grew anxious the closer he got to the house. It had been months since he'd been home and he couldn't count how many weeks it'd been since he talked to his mom and dad.

There were ten unanswered messages in his voicemail from Aiyana alone and another five from Ben. He could guess what they said, and he didn't feel like hearing it. At no point had he felt like getting back in touch with reality. It seemed so far away from his world now. What was he supposed to say anyway?

When he neared home, he could see his shiny black truck beside the shed, but his parent's cars were gone. Perfect. He'd expected his dad wouldn't be there but wasn't sure if his mom would be at the hospital or not. This way he wouldn't have to answer any questions. Maybe he'd leave a note for them.

Chance pulled the spare key out and let himself in. The familiar aroma welcomed him as he stepped through the threshold. Nothing had changed since he'd left.

He leapt upstairs to his room. His mom clearly hadn't contained herself in his absence: the bed was made and there wasn't a piece of dirty clothing in sight. Unlike how he'd left it. He emptied his bag on the bed and picked out the necessary items, like his wallet, passport and the remaining gold coins he hadn't cashed out that Niyol had left him. He hid all but one in his sock drawer and put it back in his bag.

If he was going north, then he'd need warm clothing. He pulled out jeans, long sleeve shirts and a sweatshirt, as well as fresh socks and underwear. It had been nearly three years since he'd discovered he was a shapeshifter. Since then, in an evolution, he'd become less and less susceptible to the cold. He didn't need the clothing so much to stay warm as he needed them to fit in to his environment. Not many oddballs walking around in shorts in fifteen degree temperatures.

When he was done packing he went to his desk, pulled out a piece of paper and jotted down a quick note to his parents letting them know he was fine, but heading out to track down Ana. They'd been separated and he needed to make things right between them. He placed the letter on top of his dirty clothing just as he heard tires on the gravel driveway outside. Chance peered out his window and saw his mom's sedan driving up to the house.

He pulled on his backpack and waited for the sound of her coming up the front steps. Chance looked downstairs from the crack in his door and watched her come inside. Aiyana's hair was braided down her back as usual, and she was humming to herself. Taking him completely by surprise, he felt her energy, crackling just below the surface. Nothing strong like a true shifter, but significantly more than the average person.

He supposed it made sense. She was, after all, his mom and Niyol's daughter. Before he killed Markus he hadn't been able to sense other's powers, but now ...

A hunger awakened in him that he hadn't felt since Batukhan had stopped him back in Mexico. *She can give you the power you need to become truly great. It's not much, but it will help. She would want this for you.*

Aiyana moved through the entry and disappeared in the direction of the kitchen. Chance opened his door and stood on the landing, listening to the radio that was turned on downstairs. Just as his foot touched the first step, a soft rattling noise came from inside his grandfather's room.

His curiosity got the better of him. Aiyana wasn't going anywhere. He could take a minute to check and see what it was. Chance soundlessly turned the knob and walked in, shutting the door behind him. His eyes combed the space.

Everything was just as it was after he'd passed away. The bed was made and everything was in its place.

Movement at the window drew his attention. A bird was flapping awkwardly at the glass and pecking at the wood. He may not have thought more about it except that the animal had a huge amount of energy radiating from its body. A shapeshifter.

Chance approached the window and stared at the creature. From Niyol's desk, he picked up a letter opener and then lifted the latch, letting in the blue bird. He held the dull knife in front of him and watched it land on his grandfather's bed. It tucked its wings to its body and a few stray feathers struck out on one side.

The feathers disappeared quickly as the bird augmented and grew into a fleshy human. Batukhan adjusted himself and used a blanket as a cover.

"Why are you here?" Chance whispered. "I thought I made it clear that I didn't want to stick with you any longer."

"I don't think it is best for you to come home and be around your loved ones yet. Not until the voices are removed."

Chance lifted the letter opener. "I don't trust you. I won't be herded like cattle for the slaughter."

Batukhan blinked. "I don't trust you either right now. I never finished telling you my story. I think now is the best time. Have a seat and I'll tell you my sad tale."

Without moving his eyes from him, Chance quietly pulled out the chair from Niyol's desk and sat down.

"I told you that I was a soldier in Genghis Khan's army and that I started out as a messenger. Lifen knew of my shapeshifting abilities and she was the only one who knew my secret. Well, my abilities gave me the opportunity to excel through the ranks of the army. No one was faster than I at delivering messages. When I gave important information to Khan about opposing armies' attack plans, something I came by when flying overhead, I quickly became a valued secret soldier. I could sneak anywhere undetected and execute enemies, something I was used for on a regular basis. I often took the form of the blue wolf when taking lives or the eagle when traveling. My new position kept me from visiting Lifen, and years would go by between visits." Batukhan's arms flexed as he spoke and his expression turned bitter. The hardened edge Chance had detected upon their first meeting was made more prominent now.

"On one unfortunate mission I met another shapeshifter and I barely escaped with my life, although he wasn't so lucky. When I killed him, I took his power and from then on I heard the echo of his voice wherever I went. I was a changed person. I enjoyed things I never used to. I grew self-important and pleasured in the company of beautiful women in the cities I visited." Batukhan stared Chance in the eye and paused. "When I returned to the capitol of Western Xia, I stopped to see Lifen only out of habit. It was clear she was saddened by the changes she saw in me, but I did not care because I was drunk with power. She begged me to run away with her, to live a simple life in the hills, away from warfare and temptation. But I didn't have the strength of character to listen to her. I was selfish and greedy. My love for her was outshone by what I thought was more important—political power, my value to Khan and the wealth of women, money and drink. To remember it now, it gives me pain."

Batukhan stopped to rub the top of his head and the muscles in his neck pulled tight. The lines of his face seemed to deepen and his eyes were lined with guilt. The sound of the radio downstairs thumped through the floor and he continued to speak softly. "Pain is necessary for growth. If you can learn from my mistakes, then you must listen to me now."

Chance thought he might actually jump up and grab him, but he settled in his spot on the bed and wrung his hands together. "It had been over ten years since I'd met and fallen in love with Lifen. Many things changed in that time. Western Xia broke their alliance with Mongolia, questioning their military might. They infuriated Genghis Khan, who swore the annihilation of their people. It took him years, but he destroyed garrisons and cities until he reached the capital and watched his enemy's army destroyed. Satisfied with Xia's defeat, Khan left the summer heat to oversee a campaign against the neighboring kingdom. At the time, I had been sent ahead to check on the enemy's forces. When I returned, I discovered his plans for murdering Xia's emperor and family. Khan had already stopped just short of genocide, and he wouldn't be pleased until he saw them wiped out. I was ordered to join the other forces who'd been sent to ransack the palace, but when I hesitated, I was threatened with hot silver poured in my eyes before dying a slow death.

"The whole way to the city, I was tormented about what to do. I knew that deep down I still loved Lifen, but I didn't want to disappoint Genghis. I flew as fast as I could to the capital to hide her from Khan's soldiers, or maybe it was to carry out my orders and to save myself from my master's fury. I only remember glimpses from when I arrived at the palace. I can recall Lifen's bloody, clawed up body and her still heart. After reaching my energy out to save her, I was a razor's edge from death, but that is all I know. Whatever happened left a hole in my memory and my powers. I've never been able to fully transform into an animal since then—you may have noticed my limp." Batukhan grabbed his leg. It appeared the weight of the world was held in his heart and displayed on the lines of his face.

Chance recalled Batukhan's animal forms never seeming quite right. "Yeah, I noticed. But you obviously healed Lifen. You made her into a shifter healer, or did that come later?"

"I made her what she is. But I'm not proud of it. For a long time, I thought she'd died that day. My compatriots found my body and brought me back to the closest

223

Mongolian encampment where I took months to heal. My misery kept me from healing. I returned to Genghis's war party, feeling lost and confused. It was there that I saw her again, and in those moments, time slowed and I thought she was a ghost. When she saw me, I realized she was real and I was so happy, but she made it very clear she never wanted to see me again. She claimed I'd killed the Princess Chaka, herself and countless others in blue wolf form, one of my favorite shapes for taking lives. Even though I'd brought her back to life, it was inconsequential. The damage was done. She disappeared and I realized what I'd become. I went in search of a healer who could free me from the personality that was trapped in my head. I vowed to earn atonement for the people I'd hurt and the pain I'd caused in my youth. I may never gain penance, but I won't stop trying. I tell you this, Chance, because you are at a crossroad. I know your situation, because I've lived it. I know you love your Ana, like I love Lifen. Do not make the same choices I did. You must protect her and your family from yourself until you are healed. You do not want Ana's blood on your hands." Batukhan held his hands out and Chance could almost imagine them covered with red.

Listen, Chance.

Niyol's soft whisper swept through Chance's thoughts and his heartbeat quickened. He stared at Batukhan's face and saw only honesty reflected back at him. Chance pinched his eyes shut.

Don't listen to him. He only wants to toy with you before he kills you. Never trust another shifter.

The same voice Chance had grown so accustomed to argued back. Only problem was, he didn't want Ana's blood on his hands, or his mother's. He recalled what he'd been tempted to do just before Batukhan had distracted him and his stomach turned in disgust. Too many personalities were at war in his head and he just wanted it to end. He wanted peace and quiet. Chance turned the letter opener in his hands and stared at its gleaming point. There was one thing he could do to end it definitely. He could silence all of the voices now.

I won't let you.

"Okay," he whispered. "Help me, but help me fast. I can't take any more of this. I'd rather be dead than risk hurting anyone. Do you understand?"

Chance opened his eyes and Batukhan was staring at him.

Batukhan gave a nod. "I do. Then we must get moving. We should not be too far from our destination. Drop your bag out the window and we'll fly down. My pack is just below."

When they were safe outside and preparing to leave, Batukhan held his hand out to Chance. "Your phone. It is best I hold onto it for now. So you're not tempted."

Without thinking, Chance reached into his backpack, pulled it out and dropped it into Batukhan's palm. Maybe he was more himself than he'd been in a long time, but when he thought about Ana and her striking green eyes, he had a sinking feeling, like he'd never see her again.

And if he remained this way, he hoped he wouldn't.

CHAPTER 20

Ana held the phone to her ear and had to sit on the bed when her knees weakened. The voice she'd only recently heard in her dreams was on the other side of the line. It had been over a month since she'd last been with him. When he'd looked at her with a frightening hunger and flew away over the green canopy of the Yucatán.

Her heart squeezed tight in her chest and skipped a beat. He wanted to see her. She could have jumped for joy, but instead a tear traced down her cheek. Ana put her phone on the bed and held her towel to her chest. Drops of water fell from her hair and tapped on the blanket.

The shower had warmed her after the cold adventure outside with the others. She'd been so happy about completing the team challenge for Lifen. Jordan and Derek had volunteered to make lunch if Ryan and Ana would clean up. She hadn't even expected Chance to call her. Not now. Not after so much time had passed. What had changed?

As tempted as she was to return his call immediately, she thought twice. Maybe she should run it by the guys first. She trusted their opinions, although she wasn't so sure about mentioning it to Lifen. So, she dried her hair as fast as she could and pulled on her clothes. She half ran, half glided down the hallway in her slippers with her phone in her hand.

Ana found the guys in the dining room eating. A plate of food sat untouched next to Jordan's seat. She flopped down in her spot and said in an excited whisper, "Guys, I just got a message from Chance!"

All three of them exchanged a wide-eyed glance before looking at her. Derek was the first to respond. "What did he say?"

"He said that he's back home and that he misses me and wants to see me."

Then it was Ryan's turn. "You didn't call him back, did you?"

"No, not yet. I thought I'd run it by you first." Ana fidgeted her hands.

"He didn't mention his . . . condition, did he?" Jordan asked in his logical, analytical manner.

They all studied her in silence, waiting for her response. Ana's heart fell into her stomach. Maybe if she'd roomed with a house full of teen girls they would have given her the response she was looking for instead of the gloom and doom treatment.

"No," she said.

Derek reached out and touched her arm. "Hey, I think it's great he's not dead 'n all. That's good news."

Ryan sighed and put his food down. His wet blond hair hung into his eyes and she could see that he didn't want to say anything. "I'd love to joke around right now, and tell you that it's pathetic to make up a boyfriend, but c'mon. You came here for a reason, right? You were just talking about needing to learn how to help the guy. I don't know a lot about the sickness, but everything I've heard isn't good. Maybe your luck's better than mine—sunshine and daisies, but you've gotta be real. He could hurt you."

"Good thing we accomplished the team challenge today," Derek said. "Lifen's happy, so you should go ask her about what you need to know. If you wanna see your boyfriend, you'd better know what you're doing."

Ana let their words sink in. As much as she wanted to argue with them, to tell them they didn't know Chance, she had to concede that maybe she didn't either. Not anymore. He'd sounded very much like the man she'd fallen in love with, but how could she gauge anything off of a short message? Maybe they were right. But if they were, then she needed Lifen's help.

She stood up and pushed away from the table. "You're right. I'm going to talk with her now."

Derek waved her back. "Sit down."

"Don't you think you should eat first, Ana?" Jordan wiped his mouth with a napkin.

Ana's stomach gurgled and she realized just how hungry she was after a long morning of activity and excitement. She sat down and picked up her sandwich.

"Okay," Jordan said, "when you go to talk with Lifen you want to be humble and appreciative. You want to show respect and be patient. If you're anxious she's going to send you to the meditation room."

Ryan snorted. "Quick, Derek, make some crib notes. He's sharing his wisdom."

"Shut up, man," Jordan said. "I'm trying to help her."

Ryan's and Derek's eyes widened in surprise. Ana started laughing and the guys joined in.

"Since when did you grow a pair?" Ryan snickered.

Jordan's cheeks reddened and Ana patted his shoulder. "I like this side of you, Jordan, and thanks for the advice. I appreciate it."

Ana ate quickly. When she got up to take the dishes into the kitchen, Derek chased her off.

"Don't worry about it," he said. "We'll take care of it. You go do your thing—good luck."

"Thanks!" She felt like giving all of them hugs but thought they'd get weirded out by it, so she turned down the hallway and tried calming herself down. She could feel her heart beating in her throat and her palms were sweaty.

You can do this, Ana. Just don't get impatient. Be honest.

Lifen would be in one of two places at this time of day. She didn't usually eat breakfast or lunch with them because she often meditated quietly by herself. Ana peered into the meditation room and, finding it empty, went to the end of the hallway to Lifen's bedroom door. She breathed out slowly and knocked.

"Lifen? May I come in?"

A minute passed, and Ana knocked again. She heard movement behind the door before it opened.

"Hello, Ana. I was just up in my lookout room meditating."

"It's a nice day for it. The sun's out—bet the skiers are on the slopes in Banff."

"Yes, I imagine they are. Is there something I can do for you?"

Ana looked Lifen in the eye and answered, "Can I talk to you?"

Her mentor opened the door all the way and welcomed her inside. "Why don't we go up to the lookout?"

Ana followed her through her room to the stairwell that led up to the glass room. She pulled a cushion to the center of the space and sat down cross-legged besides Lifen. It was almost too bright from the sun illuminating the snow outside, but she didn't mind. It fooled the senses enough to make her forget it was winter.

"Your arrival here has been good for the boys. I have seen positive change in them. Even though at the beginning you were concerned Jordan and Ryan didn't like you."

"I didn't really say anything before . . ."

"You didn't have to, Ana. I could sense your feelings. Remember, I'm a healer too."

Ana shook her head. "Right, of course. Well, I like the guys. They're my friends. They're good people."

Lifen turned her face to watch an eagle glide across the air currents outside. "This isn't what you came to discuss, is it?"

"Not really. First, I want to thank you for bringing me into your home and for teaching me. I know you have other students who aren't like me and it's not just a one-on-one education like Chance had, but I'm anxious to learn more about healing. This is why I came here—to be able to save a shifter from the sickness."

Her mentor didn't appear surprised or agitated. She simply stared out at the rugged landscape. Ana wasn't sure if she'd even heard her because of her lack of reaction, until she spoke. "I knew you would come to me, and I've known what your purpose is. You always wished to save him and I've always wished more for you. It must be clear to you that I don't think very highly of shapeshifters. They're simply men with more power, which I have learned in my lifetime isn't a benefit to anyone but themselves."

"What happened?" Ana asked. "Who hurt you so bad?" She hoped her mentor wouldn't shut down about her past, like previous inquiries.

"I once loved a man as much as you love your Chance. It was a very long time ago. So long ago, it almost feels like a dream. I was a handmaiden to the princess of my kingdom. I was proud of my duties and did my job with pride. It was a tumultuous time, wars were common between the kingdoms and the Mongolians were a rising force under Genghis Khan's control."

Lifen's face soured at the mention of the famous ruler and Ana noticed her hands clench. History wasn't her strong suit, but she knew if Lifen was alive that long ago, she had to be at least the eight hundred years the guys had guessed.

"The emperor submitted to Khan's reign and our territory became his vassal state. The princess was offered to Genghis, although she was not pleased with his manner, but she knew her duty to her father and her people. During this time, I met Batukhan. He was a young courier in the Mongolian army and very handsome, although I would not have paid him any notice if I had not discovered his secret. It took him quite by surprise, the fact that he was a shapeshifter.

He seemed so innocent and kind, and my heart was pierced with love." Lifen's face softened and her eyes welled with moisture. The happy expression changed Lifen's face so much, Ana recognized an inner light that she hadn't seen before.

"Batukhan would visit me when he brought messages to the city and our appreciation for each other grew. I would sneak away with him and he'd show me new animal forms he'd learned. His favorite was the blue wolf because of its importance to the Mongols as a symbol of good luck. As his powers grew, so did his rank in the army. I would see him less and less and then he simply changed. I recall him describing a strange burst of light after he killed an enemy soldier and the voice that echoed in his head. No longer sweet and patient, he was self-important and had no time for an innocent handmaiden. On his last visit I begged him to run away with me. We could have had a simple life together away from the destruction. We could have been happy." A tear curled down Lifen's cheek and the light that reflected in her eyes moments earlier flickered out. Lifen's voice turned cold as she continued, "The emperor had offended Khan and war was coming. I thought if we could live a common life in the mountains away from everything he could become the man I had fallen in love with again, but I was wrong."

Lifen's pain was palpable. Maybe it was Ana's healing abilities that made her sensitive to her mentor's agony, but Ana had to hold back her tears. She knew that feeling. So many times Ana had yearned to get away, to simply be with Chance instead of worrying about what trouble would come around the next corner.

A vein in Lifen's forehead grew pronounced and a fire burned in her narrowed eyes. "Genghis Khan was so maddened by the emperor that he went from city to city. My people were killed without remorse. Hundreds of thousands of Tangut voices were silenced. I have known no other so evil, and pray I never meet his equal." Lifen covered her face for a moment, regaining composure, and said through her pale, long fingers, "We hoped it was over. Khan had destroyed our army and had conquered the capital. The emperor was in peace talks with the Mongols, but they had other plans. My fear at the sound of Mongol soldiers killing people in the palace turned to relief when I ran into the Princess's chambers and saw the blue wolf. I thought Batukhan had come to save me, but then I saw Chaka's limp body and the blood that stained his jaw. I begged him not to kill me, but he didn't listen. He turned on me like I had never meant anything to him and tore my chest apart with his claws. After the pain stopped, I was at peace. My spirit was free and winding through the forest in the morning light, but without warning, I was forced back into my body. I awoke to find death all around. Batukhan lay beside me, still as anything, and the poor princess was barely recognizable. I thought he had killed himself and didn't stop to notice my wounds were gone. The only thing I could think of was to save myself. So I escaped the palace and city." The emotion that had bubbled up now submerged to glassy stillness, and Lifen stared at her cupped hands.

Her story was tragic. Ana couldn't imagine the agony of knowing the love of your life had killed you. Although that didn't explain how she'd come back to life. "Wait, but he killed you and healed you? That's how you were turned into a shapeshifter and healer? But how is that possible if he didn't die?"

"It took some time for me to piece it together. Too late, he must have realized what he had done and tried to save me. Somehow, he didn't kill himself doing it, but he must have come as close as you can to death. That is the only way he could have planted enough of his power within me to make me what I am. After everything I went through, I lost sight of my peaceful upbringing, and all I could think about was stopping such a violent creature as Genghis Khan. Knowledge of his weakness for a beautiful face and the curve of a waist was well known, and I used it to my advantage. I hid a dagger on my thigh and went to his camp, offering myself to him. He didn't expect my kiss to produce a wound in his gut, and I didn't expect to live beyond the attack, but with the rush of adrenaline, I shifted for the first time. His screams drew his bodyguards into the tent, swords drawn, but they didn't find an attacker, only a blue wolf. I rushed through the camp, frightened and unsure of what was happening. At the outskirts I spotted him, Batukhan. When I ran into him I shifted into human form. He must have thought he was looking at a ghost. I never expected to see him again. I thought he, too, was as good as dead. He claimed not to recall what happened at the palace, but I reminded him of his deceit and shame. Even though he brought me back to life, his actions were unforgivable and I made it clear I never wanted to see him again."

No wonder Lifen felt the way she did about shapeshifters. Ana had been unprepared for what she'd just heard. It was hard to imagine Chance ever hurting her, although she guessed Lifen never would have imagined it either. Despite everything, it only showed how important it was to help Chance. She had to help him, because who else would?

Ana touched Lifen's hand. "I'm so sorry, Lifen. I can't imagine the pain you've been through. I'm curious though—how did you learn to cure the shapeshifter sickness?"

"I learned about the sickness from another healer I met later in my travels. She taught me how to remove the foreign imprint of another's personality from its host. Since it requires cooperation from the shifter, I haven't had the opportunity to do it many times. Men don't like accepting help from a woman."

Ana hesitated before asking the question. "What about Batukhan? Sounds like he got the sickness. Did you ever track him down to help him out?"

"He did as I asked of him and has stayed away, at least out of eyesight. I've smelled his scent a few times and can only guess he checks in. I cannot forgive his actions."

How could she get Lifen to understand when her experiences had made such deep scars? Could she understand Ana's feelings, or was she too jaded from her own experiences?

Ana took a deep breath before venturing to say what she was thinking and put in as much emotion as she could. "He hurt you and I can understand your anger, but Chance hasn't hurt me. He's only ever tried to protect me from harm. I know he has the sickness and when I see him again he may be a different person, but if I don't do everything I can for him like he's done for me, then I don't deserve to have the powers he gave me."

Lifen blinked at Ana, studying her for some time before responding. "You are surprisingly wise for a youngling. I know my experiences do not mirror your own, so I can understand your need to help. Because of this, I will do what I can to help you, but you must understand how dangerous it is to attempt this form of healing. Like I have said, the shifter cannot fight you, or you risk losing part of yourself in the process. I know you haven't worked with internal injuries and sicknesses yet, so I suppose we can focus on that next. You must be able to see them as clearly as you can see a cut on the arm. This is important for untangling the psyche—you have to see the energy that doesn't belong."

Ana couldn't contain her gratitude and awkwardly reached out to hug Lifen. "Thank you, Lifen! Thank you so much! Can we start now?"

Lifen broke into a smile and actually laughed. "Okay, it happens that I got a call about a sickly fox found wandering beside the highway. I was going to go pick it up this afternoon. You can help me look it over when I get back."

Ana jumped up and offered her hand to Lifen. She lifted her off the floor and gave her a proper embrace. "Thank you so much."

The wait had been worth it.

***

Ana hadn't been allowed into the therapy room, although there had never been the need. This was the first call Lifen had received about an animal that required rehabilitation since she'd arrived there. It was a small, unpainted space and unlike any veterinary practice. There was no need for medical devices or drugs when a healer treated the animals. The only thing that seemed to fit the setting was the metallic table at the center of the room.

Lifen stood beside a medium-sized dog carrier on the table's metal surface. Ana could see a tuft of fur in the shadows between the bars of the door. Her mentor unlatched it and waved Ana over.

"She's really not feeling well so it's safe to leave this open, but I closed the door to the room. I expect she'll have a rapid recovery after you're through with her. We don't want her running out to where the boys are practicing."

Ana was tempted to touch the frightened animal, to feel the fox's soft fur, but she refrained. She didn't want to scare the creature any more than it already was. It couldn't even stand on its feet. It just lay panting on the towel laid underneath it.

"Alright, Ana. It is time to go into a meditative state. Let yourself become sensitive to the energy around you and connect with the mapping of the fox."

Ana used her meditation training and took a deep breath to clear her thoughts. Her butter-yellow core lit up at

235

attention and it flowed throughout her body like her circulatory system. The now familiar energy motes began to glow around her, and then she focused on the sick animal. Blue lines slowly ignited, crisscrossing over its form.

"Seeing beyond the skin of an animal will become second nature to you," Lifen said, "but first you must learn how to do it. Seeing its mapping is the first step. The second step is looking beyond its shape to see its energy. I know you've already begun to see energy in others, but there's more to it than just light. If you allow yourself to focus long enough you should begin to see a pattern and shady spots within the glow. The dark spots signify unhealthy energy and this is what I want you to look for now."

She tried not to let Lifen's instructions distract her from concentrating on the fox. Ana stared at the creature until her vision blurred. The glow from its energy overpowered the blue lines and soon that was all she could see. Minutes passed by, and she tried avoiding looking at Lifen, not wanting the added pressure. The longer she studied the mammal's radiance, the more uncertain she became about the pattern. Was it really there, or was she seeing things?

Ana blinked and refocused her eyes. Similar to pictures she'd seen of salt magnified, tiny crystal blocks pieced together to make an energy pattern. It was something she hadn't been able to see on the surface, but that presented itself upon closer inspection, like seeing your own fingerprint close up. The small crystals created their own pattern within the light, an organic puzzle found in nature. Beautiful and unique.

"I see the pattern," she whispered, afraid to move her attention from the fox, not wanting to lose it.

"Very good. Inconsistencies in the pattern represent issues within. If you scan the entire body of the fox for a break in the rhythm, you should see a shadow or a change in the light."

Ana did as her mentor said and traced her eyes across the animal's body, like a human X-ray machine. When she got to the animal's chest cavity, the crystalline pattern became irregular and jagged. Ana focused closer and saw that the glow of energy did indeed obscure. She reached out her hand and placed it over the fox's rib cage. Its fur was just as soft as she had imagined. The animal lifted its muzzle off the blanket to glance at her. After locking eyes with Ana, it lay back down and gave a shuddering gasp.

"I can see you found the location of the animal's sickness," Lifen said. "The cells are irregular from a cancerous growth. I have hundreds of years' experience treating many sicknesses and injuries. It will take you time to learn. It is always important to know what is wrong before you act because of energy requirements. The cut you healed on my arm was a beginner's ability and did not require you to see within my energy makeup because we knew it was a topical wound. You sent energy into my body and aided it to stich up the cells. Injuries and sicknesses that require more energy for healing, beyond a simple regeneration, make more demands on you. It is also necessary to know the proper mapping of the creature you're healing—knowing human form is second nature to you, but with other animals you need to know the mapping to restore them to health. Then, you must connect yourself with the power around you so it doesn't pull everything directly from your own reserve. And finally, you have to know how to cut off the siphon. If you feel yourself growing weak, you must shut down the transfer. Just like shapeshifting, being able to heal takes practice. Your abilities will improve the stronger you grow with age and strength. Connect with the power around you before reaching out to the fox. Visualize the proper mapping of the animal. You know fox form, so you know what it should look like. Allow the flow to begin. If you get tired, disconnect. Otherwise, you will know when the creature is healed because the pull will slow significantly."

For whatever reason, Ana withdrew her hand from the animal's body, sensing she'd be able to work better from a distance. Instead of studying the fox, she allowed herself to become aware of the swirling energy around her and pulled it inward. When she felt confident, she pushed a fingerling of power out, its yellow light sparkling and shimmering. After a little effort, it connected with the fox.

Calling upon the mapping she'd used to shapeshift into the same animal, she overlaid it onto the sick creature and her power filtered out to do its job. The pace of the flow was much quicker than when she'd healed Lifen. It surprised her and left her breathless, disoriented.

"Focus, Ana. Don't give too much of your own energy, but pull from around you . . ."

Ana fought to regain control. She reached out to the energy that swirled up from the floor to the ceiling, like a lifeline. It helped slow the stream and she pulled as hard as she could to compensate for her own loss of power. She was growing weak and tired as though she were being bled out, but she didn't want to give up. It had taken a lot to get Lifen to agree to teach her more healing skills. She was determined to do this, although she could tell she was losing far more than she was taking in. One step forward, two steps back.

Her lips were numb and her fingers cold. She teetered on her feet, and she fell forward against the table.

"Disengage! Disengage—can you hear me?"

Lifen's voice echoed in her ears. All she wanted to do was close her eyes and go to sleep, but something stopped her. Instead, she went inward, focusing on her core, which was dim and slow to respond. As though she were pulling in a life raft, she withdrew her connection from the fox, and when their energies broke free from each other, she was able to take in a lungful of oxygen.

"Did I do it?" She panted with her face against the cold metal table.

"You are reckless. I was tempted to stop you, but it is best you understand your own limits."

"You didn't answer me . . ."

"You nearly did."

Ana's heartbeat echoed in her ears. Her body was physically exhausted, as if she'd just run up and down the mountainside and then got leveled by a bus. Now hearing she'd put that much effort out and still hadn't healed the poor sickly fox, she was crushed.

"Can I try it again?" Ana drew herself up onto her elbows and looked at Lifen.

Lifen gave her a quizzical expression and lifted her hand over the animal. Ana sensed a flow of energy between her mentor and the fox and choked back her tears. She should have been able to do it. If she'd tried harder, then Lifen wouldn't have had to finish the job.

"You are too weak right now. You need to recover before you try another healing like this again."

Ana couldn't look Lifen in the eye; she was so ashamed of herself. Her mentor might not be disappointed with her, but she was. After her insistence to have more training, she fell short of completing the task.

She didn't really know what to expect when it came to healing—what she'd done so far was nothing compared to what she had just tried. This had been so much harder. She thought of Chance and how he'd saved her life. She could see just how easily a shapeshifter might die attempting it, and that scared her.

"So, is it anything like that when you heal a shifter from the sickness?" Ana asked with her stomach in her throat. She watched Lifen put the fox back into its carrying case and nervously awaited her answer.

The latch of the metal door clanged shut and the fox stared out at her from between the bars. Lifen lifted the gray crate off the table and onto the floor. She was much stronger than she appeared. Her thin, lanky frame would have led most to assume she was weak, but she moved with effortless grace. She turned to face Ana and she could see her mentor's expression was as still as carved stone. This wasn't good.

"Healing a shifter with the sickness is very different from anything we've done. It isn't a cancerous growth, a broken bone or even a stomachache. The sickness affects the psyche. When a shifter dies, their power is released from their body. If another shapeshifter or healer is nearby, it is absorbed by them. This power has an imprint of their memories and abilities. If you absorb the thoughts and memories of an unhealthy shifter, your true self can crumble and reform into a new and evil self."

While the minutes slipped by and Ana slowly began to recoup some of her lost energy, her lightheadedness disappeared, but not her physical exhaustion. She straightened up, still requiring the table's support. "What about me? I've had a couple of Chance's memories, but not many. I can count on one hand the amount of times I've seen one."

"That's because he was healing you when he died, which is very different. It's a positive transference of energy and it's not fragmented or broken. I have experienced a few of Batukhan's memories, but like you, it hasn't happened very often, and it has occurred less and less as time passed."

"So how do you help someone like Chance then, if it's not physical?" Ana experienced a sinking feeling in her gut that left her cold.

"It is connected to the energy pattern that you began to sense today. Every organic animal form has its own unique pattern, and you need to locate the variance of that pattern . . . and remove it," Lifen said abruptly.

What does that mean?

"Remove it?"

"It goes against the instinct of a healer to take away energy, but it is the only way to help a poisoned shifter. Trying to pinpoint the foreign energy is hard, but it is even more challenging to pull it free without damaging the subject's psyche—this is why they must be willing, or else you are likely to do serious harm. It is the opposite action of what you did today, and it is very dangerous to you and the infected."

Ana swallowed. "Why me?"

"Because if you pull the energy into yourself, then you will be infected."

Lifen's words sank in and Ana tried to comprehend it. "So how do you pull it out without absorbing it?"

"You must let go of it once it's free of the shapeshifter. There is no way for you to practice this, which is why I don't want you considering it before you're ready. You are too precious to this world. I do not wish to see you hurt yourself, but I am beginning to understand your tenacity and giving nature."

Lifen moved around the table and wrapped her arm around Ana's waist to help her to the door. Just outside, the echo of animal noises met her ears. Besides her jelly legs, her insides were twisting nervously. The gravity of the situation was sinking in. In no way did it sway her determination to help Chance, but she knew she wasn't prepared to help him. Not only could she hurt herself, she could cause him harm.

If she couldn't even heal a fox, how could she expect to save Chance from the poisoned energy within him? She knew she needed practice, but convincing Lifen to allow her more opportunities would be challenging. Tears threatened to spill out again and her breath grew ragged.

"Why don't you go sit down outside and try to reenergize?" Lifen guided her out the back door to the enclosed patio and helped her sit on the sofa. "Take as long as you need before you come in."

Ana nodded wordlessly and watched Lifen return inside. She turned to stare numbly out the paneled windows and at the snow outside. Tiny white flakes floated down to the ground, adding to the fluffy blanket that already covered the earth. She looked out at the peaceful scene and fear gripped her heart. How could she help Chance if there was no way to practice what she needed to do? And how could she live with herself if she hurt him?

CHAPTER 21

After the turn of events with Chance, Batukhan suggested they move as quickly as possible. While Aiyana was in the shower, Chance grabbed the keys to his truck and they were soon gliding over the river of pavement, moving north to Canada. He felt at ease behind the wheel again. The only thing that would have made it feel like old times was if Ana were sitting beside him instead of a Mongolian shapeshifter.

"So, you have no way of reaching this guy?" Chance asked, casting a glance at Batukhan.

He shook his head in response. "No, he prefers to stay away from society. He remains in animal form most of the time. I think he feels at home in the forest. At peace."

"But how're we going to find the guy?" He didn't feel like playing a game of Marco Polo in the Canadian wilderness and hoped there was an easier way.

"I know the area he likes to go to in the winter. It's just a matter of tracking him down. Have you developed tracking skills yet?"

Chance recalled the days spent in the Yucatán with his great-grandfather and his last day with him. Balam had left with Ana to give him a test, to see if Chance could find them in the jungle. Instead, he'd found Markus on their heels.

"Yeah. I can track. But not when I don't know what I'm tracking."

"Good. We'll get to that when we're ready. First, we need to get across the border."

Batukhan went silent and Chance cranked up his music. It helped drown out the voices in his head and pass the time. They eventually crossed the border and continued north. Batukhan had to pull out a map to remember the way. They drove through the night, taking turns at the wheel. Sometime in the early morning, Batukhan directed him to a turnoff that guided them off the highway and into the trees.

"There shouldn't be much traffic through this area this time of year. We should be able to leave your truck here for a while without it drawing attention. Just go down a little farther and look for a place to park on the side of the road that isn't deep with snow."

The tires lost traction in a pothole, and Chance white-knuckled the wheel while backing up a few feet and speeding forward through the bad section. He hoped it wouldn't be much farther because he wouldn't want to try leaving after another snowfall. An opening next to the road presented itself and Chance pulled off with a sigh of relief.

"Alright, grab your pack. We're in the mountains so you need a good travel form to get you through the snow and one that tracks well."

"That won't be a problem." Chance opened his door and jumped out. He reached behind his seat and grabbed his bag. Like he'd done before, he pulled free the nylon straps from their attachments at the base of the pack and tied the ends together, leaving a large open loop.

"What we're tracking you've never seen before. It has a very strong smell, similar to the dung of a cow and ape. Quite unpleasant. I know he tends to keep to the range we're in now, running north-south. Why don't we move north from here and see if we can't pick up the scent? When it gets stronger let me take the lead, so I can make our presence known. We don't want to get on his bad side."

Batukhan stepped out of the cab and began his own preparations for travel while Chance began to strip off his clothing. Although it was freezing, his body's core temperature remained warm as he undressed. He stuffed his shoes into his bag along with his keys and locked up the driver's side.

"I'm ready to go—make sure you lock up your door," Chance instructed Batukhan while he looped the large strap around his neck and prepared to transform.

He took a deep breath and exhaled, watching steam puff out in a mushroom cloud. The energy within him ignited at his demand and the familiar mapping traced itself through his thoughts. Fur grew in waves over his almond skin, and he towered on his back legs above the top of his truck. The strap of the bag tugged at his throat but remained secure.

Chance dropped to all fours and grunted. Movement from the other side of the truck drew his attention and he looked around the front grill to see an enormous wolf sauntering around to meet him. Its gun-metal blue fur rustled in the breeze and its head came to the height of the hood. Even though Chance knew he'd never seen a wolf that size before, there was something familiar about it.

This must have been the form Batukhan had used when he was a soldier in Genghis Khan's army. It certainly would have done the job in the fear department. The white daggers showing from below his muzzle were a clear threat. Chance saw he had his pack strapped to his back and didn't want to dwell on Batukhan's teeth any longer, so he lifted his nose to the air and took in a deep breath, letting in the layers of smells. As many times as he'd taken grizzly form, he was still getting used to his nose's capabilities. It was like receiving all of the cable channels all at once. Being able to tune the others out and home in on one was the trick. The cutting bite from the pines he discarded, as well as the aroma of the plant life around them and the grease on the hot engine. Batukhan started trotting forward and he followed, keeping his nose up.

Chance knew the smell of cattle almost all too well. Niyol had had a cattle ranch in Montana and he'd often visited him there throughout his childhood. He'd also gone to the zoo a few times. The most recent visit was with Ana when they'd traveled through Denver just a couple of months back, but he wasn't sure if he'd be able to revive the specific smell from the great ape building.

Batukhan ran in the only way he could, half limping, half catapulting himself on his three good legs through the wilderness in a northerly line, keeping away from roads, houses and towns. This was something any shapeshifter got used to when traveling in a predatory animal form, and Chance knew exactly why. The last thing you wanted was to be blown to bits by a shotgun.

A few hours passed and he hoped they weren't just getting themselves lost in the great north, when he caught hold of a new smell. It definitely had similarities to cattle but was riper, like a meat-eater. Maybe this was Batukhan's friend.

Chance pushed ahead of Batukhan and took the lead. They moved like this for at least an hour, the smell continuing to grow stronger the farther they went. Then, Batukhan ran ahead of Chance and turned around to face him. He slowed to a stop and stared at the wolf who trotted ahead and climbed onto a snowy boulder. There, his gray fur disappeared to reveal Batukhan's bronzed skin. He cupped his hands around his mouth and let out a reverberating shout. The sound echoed through the valley and he waited. After a minute, a similar call that was more animal than human answered back. Batukhan gave another screech and looked at Chance. "He'll be here in a minute. Stay still and don't react."

What did that mean?

Batukhan yelled out, "My friend! It is me. I have brought a soul who is sick and can use your help. If you wish to assist him, we would be grateful!"

Chance scanned the trees surrounding them and waited for something to happen, anything. He wasn't sure what to expect, but Batukhan's warning made him leery. Was a minotaur about to walk out of the forest?

Before he realized it, a figure had emerged from the snowcapped trees and was already halfway across the open area where Batukhan had perched on the rock. Chance's jaw dropped open and he would have laughed if he could, but instead a low moan came from his chest. Batukhan shot him a warning glare and he checked himself.

Chance found himself staring straight at bigfoot. Sasquatch. Whatever the proper name was, it was standing fifty feet from him. Suddenly, Nastas's memory traced his thoughts. This creature was just like the one that had kidnapped Mai, Nastas's girlfriend. Chance's amusement quickly dissolved into dread. He had to tell himself it wasn't the same one. Nastas had killed the one who had threatened him.

"Hello, Mac, thank you for showing yourself. I would like to introduce you to Chance, a youngling who would like to free himself from the extra voices in his head. Are you able to help him?"

Batukhan held his hand out to Chance and he wasn't sure what to do. Batukhan had told him to stay still. Was he supposed to shift into human form, or give him his paw in greeting?

The gigantic ape-man turned his eyes on Chance and a chill went down his spine. Humanoid eyes studied him from beneath a veil of long, shaggy brown hair. The bigfoot towered over Batukhan, who was still standing on the small boulder. Its muscular hands hung down to its knees and Chance didn't doubt he could tear tree trunks from the earth. If this was a shifter, he could understand why he came to greet them in this form. It was far more threatening than a *Beware of Dog* sign.

After he stared Chance down for a minute, he turned around and started sauntering off perpendicular from the way he came. Batukhan readjusted his pack around his neck and called over to Chance, "Follow me."

He shifted back into the large wolf form, tucked his gimpy front leg up and propelled himself after the bigfoot named Mac. Chance didn't waste any time and followed after them not wanting to get left behind with his jaw gaping at the snow. They ran for about five minutes and the pace slowed.

Chance smelled the strong aroma of a fire and the curl of gray smoke rose above the trees. Batukhan crested the top of a hill and he disappeared below the horizon. Chance rushed to catch up, his breath ragged in his ears. The wolf tracks led down into a gully that was surrounded with pines, and there at the bottom was a crackling fire held snugly by a fire pit. He spotted a dark opening in the opposite bank. A cave.

His big bear paws sank into the snow and he slowed down the slope so he wouldn't fall on his face, something he'd done before. Carrying around that kind of weight could be hard when going downhill, he'd discovered. Finally he joined Batukhan, who had already shifted back to human form at the foot of the fire. His travel companion pulled out clothing from his pack and began to dress himself.

"You are safe, Chance," Batukhan said with a look of amusement. "You prefer to be a bear or human?"

As a matter of fact . . .

"Either way, I don't think Mac speaks bear. Why don't you make yourself comfortable?"

Before Chance joined Batukhan in human form, he scanned what he guessed he would call a home for the mysterious shaman he'd come to visit. Footprints led into the dark cave and he could only guess that was where he'd gone.

You should not trust them. A shifter cannot trust anyone.

The same strong voice that had persisted at the corners of his mind over the last month or more was pulling on the loose threads, fraying his conscience. He hadn't heard it since those regretful moments at his home in Clark Bend. Things had quieted down a bit after Batukhan had told his story, and Chance decided he couldn't allow himself to learn the hard lessons his travel companion had been forced to live with. If he lost Ana forever, then there wasn't anything left for him. She was his North Star and his guiding light. Without her, there would only be darkness.

Chance closed his eyes, smelled the char of the fire, and grasped to stay in control of his own thoughts, if he could even tell them apart anymore. Just as he tried to silence the hum, a voice he trusted more than anyone's whispered in such a low murmur he barely caught the words. *Patience, Chance. Breathe deeply and clear your mind.*

Right. He did as Niyol often instructed and tried to clear his thoughts by taking long, slow breaths. A low, soft groan rumbled in his chest and without opening his eyes, he let his fleshy human form call him home. The protective pads on his paws metamorphosed, and the ice began to melt under the warmth of his feet. His pack pulled against his neck. He looked up to see Batukhan fully dressed and sitting beside the campfire on a fallen log that had been stripped of its branches and turned into a make-shift bench.

Chance hurriedly pulled a set of clothes out of his backpack and slipped them on. Not that he was terribly cold, but he wasn't one for hanging out in the nude no matter what the setting. After he perched beside Batukhan on the log, Chance turned back to look at the cave again.

Instead of the huge, hairy bigfoot, a tall man appeared from the shadows. His skin was a darker complexion than Chance's, but he shared the same black hair and hazel eyes. Chance thought of the memories he'd seen from both Nastas's and Niyol's childhood and the man standing before him now would have fit in perfectly. That is, except for the fact that he was wearing a gray pea coat with jeans and a Canucks hockey jersey.

Batukhan turned his head and stood up. "Chance, I would like to properly introduce you to Mac. I always pronounce his full name wrong, so I shortened it so I wouldn't offend him."

Mac walked barefoot through the snow and reached his hand out to Chance. His creased eyes held Chance's gaze and he seemed to be trying to determine something.

"Nice to meet you, Mac." Chance tried to ignore the man's stare.

Seriously, it was getting a little excessive. Did he have food in his teeth or what?

"How are you sleeping?" Mac grabbed hold of Chance's chin, yanked it to the side and then peered into his ear.

"Uh . . . well, I haven't been sleeping on a pillow top mattress exactly. The ground doesn't help with good sleep." Chance wrenched himself free of Mac's grip and felt himself getting annoyed. "Why are you looking in my ears? I don't have an ear infection."

Mac folded his hands together. "No ear infection. I am just having a little fun with you. You shouldn't listen to anyone who looks in your ears to cure a stomachache. Don't forget it."

Chance grew agitated and the voices in his head clamored for attention. He was ready to be done with it already. "Listen, it looks like you don't get many visitors up here, and I didn't come to roast marshmallows with you. Batukhan told me you'd be able to help me for real. Is that true?"

Batukhan and Mac exchanged a glance. "You are a very impatient youngling. It is customary to at least sit and share food or drink before asking things like this. So, I will offer you a seat by my fire and I will pour you a drink."

Annoyed, Chance sat on the log beside Batukhan and stared at the golden flames in the pit before them. Instead of letting his frustration get the better of him, he meditated while staring at the organic wisps licking at the sky, each one reaching high and disappearing before its replacement tried to meet an even greater height.

While he was spacing out at the fire, he failed to notice Mac pouring something from a glass bottle into a small shot glass until it was being held out to him. He accepted it and gave it a sniff. It was odorless, but he had a feeling it wasn't water. If Ana were here right now, she'd eye it suspiciously and warn him from taking a sip. But she wasn't here right now, and that was reason enough to slam it back with reckless abandon. If it helped numb him or distance him from the nonstop echo of the other personalities reverberating in his brain, then it was welcome. It no longer concerned him if he could trust Mac or not. If Mac could put him out of his misery, in some way or other, Chance was ready.

"Thank you." He tipped the glass back and the cool liquid burned all the way down. It reminded him of what Balam had given him to aid him to see his *nagual* in the flames of the fire before he got his tattoo. It would do perfectly.

Batukhan accepted a glass from Mac and lifted it to him in thanks. "I see you have continued to live in the same way. Still no interest to live near people?"

"I prefer living in the wilderness," Mac said. "It's peaceful and it allows me to be in animal form most of the time, which is what makes me happy. Although I do like catching a hockey game and a burger every once and a while. And then there's the fun I have with hikers, giving them a taste of the mystical to keep the legend alive."

Batukhan grew serious. "Just be sure not to go too far. There's a difference between a legend and you winding up on a scientist's table. We would never want that to happen."

Mac grinned. "Has anyone caught the howler yet? I have not arrived at my age without knowing how to hide. If I don't want to be found, I won't be. Anyway, tell me about your friend here."

"He's trying to return to his mate," Batukhan said. "I believe that is why he's so anxious, although I never knew him before he got the sickness. I stopped him from feeding on an innocent's power, and I have tried to teach him to calm the voices. I knew you would know how to help him."

Mac's brown eyes studied Chance and he grew serious. He reached out with the bottle and poured Chance another glass of whatever the mysterious drink was. "Will you honor me with your story? How you got the sickness?"

Chance was already beginning to feel the effects of the clear liquid. When he tried to think back to the events that had transpired in the jungle over a month ago, the memory was fuzzy. Not because he couldn't remember it, but because it felt like a bunch of stuffing was filling the space in his head, making it hard for him to think quickly or clearly. It took him a minute to recollect what had happened. The pain and sadness triggered from the incident echoed in his heart, but it held only a dull ache.

He blew a lungful of air between his lips, which made them feel tingly and numb. "I was in Mexico with my girlfriend, Ana, being mentored by my great-grandfather. He was teaching me all sorts of stuff and he even gave me a tattoo of my *nagual.* Everything was going great when my cousin showed up. I thought he was a psychopath before, trying to hunt me down to kill me for my power, but now I'm thinking he really wasn't so bad. He just had the voices in his head like I do now, you know?"

While he narrated the story, he realized just how relaxed he felt. After being on edge for so long, tortured by the voices in his head, this was a nice getaway. It was like he was on an island, offshore from reality and his sucky life.

"And then what happened?" Mac asked, snapping him from his reverie.

"Right, so then Markus caught up with us and killed Balam."

Mac nodded. "Balam was your great-grandfather?"

Chance couldn't remember if he'd told them his great-grandfather's name or not. "Yeah, so Markus killed him and there was this bright light. Then Ana came along and Markus started chasing her and I had to stop him. She couldn't protect herself from him, so I had to do something. And I did. He won't be coming after us anymore . . ."

The words didn't make sense to him. That wasn't right. Markus was still there. Inside of Chance. And now *he* was the one Ana wasn't safe from. To his surprise, he discovered that his cheeks were wet. When was the last time he'd cried? He wasn't sure.

His throat was dry, so he swallowed, which didn't help. "I'm thirsty," he said. "Do you have water?"

Mac poured him one more glass of the clear liquid. "Drink this last cup and I will get you some water. I promise."

Chance did as the bigfoot shapeshifter told him and obediently swallowed it in one shot. This time it didn't even burn as it rushed down his throat. His cheeks were warm, if not flushed, and he was content giving control to the friendly man in the hockey jersey.

"Very good, Chance," Mac said. "I will give you some water now." He picked up a pot from the side of the fire and emptied its contents into a brown mug. Then he grabbed a handful of snow from a few feet away and dropped it in. "It'll be a little warm so take it slow."

Mac handed it to Chance. While Chance swallowed it down, Mac directed another question to him. A very simple question that Chance was able to answer.

"So, Chance. Can you tell me if you hear Markus in your head?"

"Yeah. He's there. His memories aren't very happy." Chance shrugged and took another sip of water.

"Is there anyone else in your head?"

"Yeah."

"Like who?"

"Oh, there's Nastas, Markus's grandfather. Markus killed Nastas because he was stalking him and he knew the only way he'd leave him alone was to kill or be killed."

"Yes, I understand. Those memories must be hard to live with."

Chance whispered, "You have no idea."

"Are there any others?"

"Balam of course, and Niyol too."

"Who is Niyol?"

"My grandfather. His voice is soft and I have to listen hard to hear him. He saved my life—that is why he's with me."

Batukhan and Mac stared at Chance and all he could hear was the crackling of the fire. He didn't mind that they were so focused on him because he didn't really care about much at the moment. He was comfortably numb. Batukhan stood up and wandered over to a wood pile and carefully set two more logs on the fire. Embers sparked and hissed at the disruption and the umber glow brightened, which mesmerized Chance.

"Are there any other voices in your head?" Mac's low voice broke his concentration.

He nodded mindlessly. "So many memories of death. I don't know who else is in here"—he tapped the side of his temple—"but they've gotten around."

Batukhan looked to Mac. "Five voices at least—so many. Will you be able to help him?"

"I can try," Mac said, "but what he really needs is a healer. We can work on pushing the voices back so it will be more peaceful. That will be the best I can do for him." Mac's mumbling was barely noticed by Chance, who continued to watch the firelight dance and flicker before him. Mac raised the volume of his voice and directed it at him. "What I'd like you to do is continue to stare at the fire. I will have you concentrate on Markus first. Picture his face in your thoughts and let his voice come forward. It is time to call him out."

Chance slouched down on the log seat and his eyes blurred. Bright and dark strokes of flame painted into disjointed shapes at first, but then they began to form a face. Scruffy hair hung down and empty eyes stared out at him.

I will not be led like a lamb to the slaughter. It's kill or be killed.

Markus's voice filled his head like a church bell echoing through a valley. Chance shrugged, unsure what to tell the guy.

"Do you see him?"

"Yeah, he's staring right at me—it's creepy." Chance squished up his face until his nose tickled.

"Yes, okay," Mac said. "I want you to use your energy to push him away until you cannot see or hear him any longer. Do you know how to push your energy out? Not many know how."

Chance was vaguely aware of Mac's face beside the fire pit, and his question confused him. Had he pushed his energy out before? He had definitely pulled energy in, but that wasn't what Mac was asking.

"I healed Ana before," Chance said. "I had to push my energy out to her then . . . does that count?" Chance slurred his words and laughed at himself.

"It counts. It isn't exactly the same thing, but while you're thinking about Markus, I want you to push your energy out to him in the fire until he disappears and you cannot hear him anymore. Okay?"

"Right-o."

Chance furrowed his brows and focused on Markus's face in the fire. He tried to think back, but it proved challenging. What had he'd done when he'd saved Ana? The ball of energy at his core was awake and alert, unlike his consciousness. With every exhalation, he pushed his power toward the fire. He imagined himself blowing a pile of powdered sugar off a stack of pancakes. A drop of sweat curled down his nose and he brushed it away. It began to get a little easier the more he worked at it and soon, Markus's face faded away and all that was left was a piece of a log that resembled a nose.

255

"Hello? Are you there?" Chance asked aloud, waiting for an answer. "Nope, Markus is on vacation."

"Great, now I want you to do the same with Nastas, was it? Picture him in the fire and call out his voice."

Chance recalled one of Markus's memories and imagined his angry face. Maybe he could have used one of Mac's drinks to make him a little more chill, he thought to himself. Then maybe he wouldn't have been so bent on killing everyone.

Similar to before, Nastas's features were represented in the flames of the fire and his voice echoed in his thoughts. *You should not do this. Protect yourself.*

Without waiting for Mac's repeated instruction, he went ahead and tried blowing out Nastas's birthday candles. The idea made him chuckle to himself as he pushed his energy out in an attempt to snuff out his face from the fire.

"You seem to know what to do. Is he gone now?"

Chance tilted his head to the side as though he were listening for a bird chirping in the trees. When only silence met his ears he nodded contentedly.

"Who's up next?" He laughed. When was the last time he'd laughed? It sounded strange in his ears, foreign.

"Hmm, who did you say?" Batukhan asked from beside him on the log. "Was it Balam?"

Balam. He really had no reservation about saying goodbye to Markus and Nastas, two people who held only negative memories for him. But he'd never been able to give Balam a proper goodbye. Chance never believed he'd die. He'd lived through the Spanish invasion and a shapeshifter war.

As if sensing his hesitation, Mac said from across the fire pit, "I know he is family and every mentor is important. They make you who you are. But they belong in your heart and not your mind. You need to let go for your sanity."

Chance nodded.

He didn't have to recall anyone else's memories to picture him. It may have been just over a month since he'd last seen him, but the memory of him was fresh. His proud and regal face stared back at him in the fire, although it was nothing like the man in the flesh.

Stay focused, Chance. Don't lose control.

The lightheartedness that was there just moments ago dropped away. With sadness in his heart, he pushed his energy out in slow waves until his great-grandfather's voice was silenced. Chance stared at the fire and the place that had occupied Balam's face. Now, only undulating wisps of flame remained.

A warm hand pressed onto his shoulder and he looked up into Batukhan's eyes. All expression left his face and he returned his stare to the campfire.

Mac filled Chance's shot glass again. "Are you ready for the next one? Niyol?"

"No," he answered with a shake of the head.

Chance slung back the cold liquid and welcomed the severing of threads of his consciousness. It was as though he let go of a heavy balloon he'd been holding on to for far too long. Relief set in.

While he stared at the fire and the shapes within it, a shadow crept into his mind, fast and silent. It lulled him into silence and took hold with a sense of finality.

Chance straightened out of his slouch and surveyed the scene before him. Batukhan was staring out at the forest and Mac had turned his back to set down the bottle. Without hesitation, Chance reached out and pulled one of the fresh logs from the fire, its full underbelly blackened with charcoal, alight with flame. He swung it up and brought it down with as much strength as he had over Mac's head. A loud hollow crack sounded and the bigfoot shapeshifter dipped face first into the snow, not to move again.

The smell of burnt skin met his nose, but he didn't care. Chance tightened his grip on the log despite his sizzling skin and turned to take a swing at Batukhan, but the man was too quick and sprung from his seat, his eyes wide.

"Chance?"

"Maybe, somewhere in here. Your friend did me a big favor. Without the other voices fighting against me it gave me a clear path, so thanks."

Batukhan's surprise was amusing to him. *You know that moment when everyone knows you're the most powerful in the room? Success.*

A memory fogged up his vision and he clung to the log while he planted his feet firmly on the ground. Bright red walls surrounded him. They were decorated with Chinese symbols that were painted in gold. Gauzy fabric was draped over a regal bed. He appeared to be in a Chinese palace. Screams rang out nearby and in the distance.

He dropped the body of a thin woman from his mouth, the taste of copper on his tongue. Her black hair tumbled free from its decorative bun and her maroon blood flowed from multiple wounds on her neck and legs.

He stretched his long, furry legs out in front of him and howled. The sound reverberated off the walls in the room. A woman ran in and called out, "Princess Chaka!"

A look of horror spread across her face when she saw the bloody scene before her and she began to cry. "Batukhan, how could you do this?"

Chance slunk toward the devastated woman, and he would have laughed if he could. There wasn't time to waste. He had orders. No prisoners. No survivors.

He pounced the woman, knocking her over and sank his canines into her neck. Her words came out gurgled. "No, please, I love you . . ."

The memory dissolved as quickly as it had set in, and Chance licked his lips as he stared at Batukhan.

Batukhan began to back away slowly, but it didn't escape Chance's notice. "I do not understand. Why are you doing this?"

"You know, when you were crying your sob story about your woman, and how she'd blamed you for her murder, it all fell into place for me. I thought she looked familiar before when I saw her and now I know why."

Batukhan squinted and shook his head in disbelief. "What? Chance, is that you talking?"

"I thought it was strange that the young maid pleaded with me, saying another man's name. She was so surprised that I killed her, even telling me she loved me with her last breaths. I knew that Khan had other secret officers who were especially gifted with surveillance and murder, but I was never lucky enough to meet you. The others were not so fortunate, sadly."

The expression of confusion turned to horror on Batukhan's face. He slipped his shirt off into the snow and he flexed his arms, in a ready position.

Chance laughed in a strange sort of way. "I am not here for you. I don't need another voice to battle with when I'm so near my prize. But if you wish to have a taste of me, so be it. When you die, you know the truth about your love—but she never will. What a sad love story."

Batukhan growled and hair sprouted in a carpet across his arms while he sank into all fours on the ground. The enormous blue wolf sneered at him, his white dagger-like teeth gleamed white.

"Here puppy," Chance muttered before calling on the same mapping as the beast before him. The burning log fell to the ground with a sizzle, his hand seared with the shape of a C.

His skin prickled with sensation and his power rushed like a fire hose on full. The rush of energy made him euphoric and he wanted more. Saliva flowed from between his canines and he snapped his teeth with pleasure. His gray paws pressed into the snow and a cool breeze brushed through his fur. It may not have been his form of choice, but he didn't mind using it to humiliate his opponent.

Batukhan launched across the distance between them and onto Chance. The force of the impact sent them spilling over the log they'd sat on and into the snow. Batukhan's teeth sank into his neck. He was flung toward the lip of the fire, his fur catching light. Chance yelped with surprise and sniffed at his smoldering shoulder. Then he stared at the lumbering shape of the blue wolf coming to finish the job.

CHAPTER 22

"Chance!"

Ana woke with a start, sweat beading at her temple. She hadn't caught much, but what she did see frightened her. He was being thrown around by another shifter.

He's in trouble.

Her mind raced. She'd seen him surrounded by snow and pine trees. He definitely wasn't in Mexico any longer. He could be home in Montana, or anywhere at altitude. Could he be close by?

She reached for her phone and held it in her hands. *The guys said it wasn't a good idea to let him know where I am until I knew how to help him. Maybe this isn't a good idea.*

The sight of him being tossed into a fire by another shapeshifter was enough to make her fear she'd never see him ever again. Lifen had taught her more about healing and helping a shifter with the sickness. Since it was something she'd never be able to practice without doing it for real, she decided there wasn't any time to waste. Chance needed her and she couldn't just lay around in Lifen's multimillion dollar property while his life was in danger. Not going to happen. Did he ever think about the consequences before leaping to save her?

She looked up her geo location on her phone and dialed his number. It rang and then went to voicemail. The sound of his voice on the message made her heart squeeze in her chest. It had been too long since she'd heard him in person.

"Chance . . . it's me. I just dreamt you were in trouble. I don't know if I'm too late or not—oh God, I hope I'm not. I'm leaving to find you, wherever you are. I'm outside Banff in Canada. I know you're in the snow, so I hope you're not far. Call me when you get this, or you can find me somewhere near the coordinates . . ." Ana mumbled the array of numbers that her phone had dictated. "I love you. Stay alive."

She hung up and set her phone back down on the side table. Without thinking about her recklessness, she slipped out from under her covers and stood at her dresser. How would she travel, and did she even know what direction she was going? She knew the fastest way to travel, but it would be hard to bring her phone or a wrap, unless . . .

Ana searched through her belongings and found a small bag with a thin strap. She placed her phone securely inside and, after another thought, opened a drawer. Although she hadn't been wearing the obsidian necklace that Balam had given her for protection, she'd kept it close. The memory of it left her sad. She lifted up Chance's bear heartline on a leather band and the jade jaguar that he'd left behind at Balam's.

Ana would see him again, and she would return them to him. She hoped the hemlock-laced talisman wasn't needed, but not bringing it wouldn't be wise. Before leaving her room, she took a colorful sarong she'd brought from Mexico and looped it around her neck. As silently as possible, she unlatched her door and looked toward Lifen's room. On tiptoe, Ana crept down the hallway, trying not to think about her mentor or friends and what they'd think when they found her room empty in the morning. Leaving a note would be the kind thing to do, but she didn't want to take the time. Every second might count when it came to saving Chance from his attacker.

She slipped from the house and wound her way up the path to the driveway. Stars painted the cloudless sky. On any other night she would have allowed herself to get distracted by the beautiful palette above her. The frigid air was hardly noticeable and she realized her bare feet didn't register the icy ground at all.

Ana set the small purse and sarong on the ground and faced out toward the lake that glimmered in the moonlight.

Rather than allowing her fear and worry to take control, she focused on what she needed. And that was direction.

She didn't know what she was doing, but she hoped the connection she'd had with Chance when she was sleeping would guide her now. So, she closed her eyes and meditated quietly, calling on the bright light within. Energy flowed throughout her body and the hairs on her arms stood on end. Chance's face skimmed her thoughts. When she reopened her eyes, she realized she'd repositioned herself, facing west.

During her stay at Lifen's, she'd mastered the finch despite her eagerness to learn more aviary forms. Her mentor had insisted on a slower approach to shapeshifting lessons, but in that moment it didn't matter. She had another mapping, thanks to Chance's memories.

The bird's form traced itself in her thoughts. Blue lines etched its shape. Power wasn't lacking as Ana absorbed the energy around her. Her arms transformed into wings and feathers layered over her body like shingles on a roof. When she was done shifting, she stepped on top of her bag and cloth wrap, securing her talons around them.

Exhilarated to take on a larger bird form and eager to take to the skies, Ana stretched her wings out and scooped at the air. She lifted off the ground, which took a little effort with the added baggage, but once she rose above the trees and caught a current, she was off.

So many nights she'd listened to the soothing song of the horned owl in the pines around her house, felt its eyes on her as she gazed at the stars in sadness. Now, it was Ana who would use Chance's nighttime form to guard him from harm.

***

Batukhan leaned back onto his rear haunches, preparing to attack Chance again. He impacted Chance's prostrate body and growled in his ear.

Let him think he's in control a little longer and then end it.

Chance did little to protect himself or attack back. Just as Batukhan was beginning to realize this, a sound that seemed out of place in the setting distracted them both. They looked over at Batukhan's pack.

Ring, ring, ring.

It was Chance's phone. Sure, it could be his mother calling, but then again, it might be Ana. Calling to tell him where she was.

Time to get moving. I don't need to waste my time with this guy any more. He's nowhere near as valuable as Ana.

Without hesitation, Chance pushed Batukhan off of him and he shifted into a cobra. His hood extended out from his head while his forked tongue licked the air. Chance coiled and struck at the blue wolf's abdomen. His teeth sank into flesh and he held on, the worst yet to come.

A flicker of blue lines traced throughout Chance's furry adversary, and he pulled at its energy, like yanking at the loose thread of a sweater. Batukhan's power leached out of him, leaving a green glow in its wake. The blue wolf snapped his teeth at Chance's long, muscular body that hung from his waist, but Chance let go before the wolf could reach him. He swept between Batukhan's legs.

Chance slithered through the snow and thought of a new animal form. One that could help settle the fight now that he'd poisoned his opponent. His narrow body warped and grew into a hunched, yet sturdy, silverback gorilla. Hairy, black knuckles pressed into the ice and he barreled at Batukhan, who had limped around to face his attacker.

Wrapping his long arms around Batukhan, he squeezed as tight as he could. The wolf's teeth sank into his neck, but the pain only excited him more. Ragged breathing rattled in his ear and he knew the wolf was close to passing out, but the creature shrank away until Chance was only grasping at air.

He looked all around and couldn't see anything except a large area of disturbed snowfall where they'd fought. Chance returned to human form and squinted all around. He could feel powerful energy nearby, although that could have been Mac, who was still lying unconscious beside the fire. Wherever Batukhan was, he was hiding and likely wouldn't come out until he'd recovered.

It didn't matter to Chance anyway. Not right now. He had more important things to do. He riffled through Batukhan's bag until he found his cell phone and listened to his message. Ana's concerned voice met his ear and his lips spread wide.

I wouldn't normally switch hosts so quickly, but I've been looking for a woman like Ana for a long time. I hope she's easier to tame.

Chance left his pile of clothes on the ground, slipped his pack around his neck and shifted into the blue wolf. He stalked into the night and stared up at the stars. Somewhere out there Ana was under the same sky, and he needed her.

Like a dagger needs flesh to cut.

CHAPTER 23

Ana hoped she wasn't just following her instincts in the wrong direction. She'd been flying for some time, keeping Chance in her thoughts. Her talons were tired of gripping her purse and sarong, but she didn't want to slow down. She passed over roads and a few buildings, but for the most part, it was just snowy wilderness.

Her left wing dipped down and she moved south in a large arc. When the urge to continue in a circle pulled at her, she let herself drift down to a lower altitude. Forced to sweep her head back and forth to see the landscape with her nighttime eyes, she settled on a shape moving across the snow.

Could it be Chance? She was ready to find out.

Ana glided down at least fifty feet from the animal and found a place to land that wasn't covered in snow—a bare tree trunk with wiry branches. Its skeletal shape cast a frightening shadow on the glittery white carpet from the full moon. Her talons had to let go of her belongings so she could grab hold of a branch. They fell into the pristine snow below. She lunged forward precariously and had to flap her wings to right herself.

While she kept her eyes on the indistinct animal cutting a path through the snow, she hopped down to the ground and shifted back to human form. She plucked her sarong from its impact point and wrapped herself quickly. Her heart rattled away in her chest, unsure what to do now. If it was Chance, should she have misgivings for her own safety? Would he really hurt her? She thought of Lifen's story and decided to risk it.

"Chance? Is that you?" Ana called out and stumbled forward through the deep snowdrift.

The animal turned its head to the side and raced over the crest of the hill. It quickly disappeared and Ana grabbed hold of the dead tree trunk she had landed on moments earlier. Her breaths came out as gasps and she tried to hold back the urge to cry. She must have been delusional when she went flying into the night thinking she could actually find Chance with her weird telepathic ability. Now she was lost in the Canadian mountains and she wasn't even confident she'd be able to make her way back home.

Snow thumped on the ground from a grove of pines to her right. She turned and her breath caught in her throat.

A man stepped out from the shadow of the trees. His black, shaggy hair fell into his hazel eyes and the corners of his mouth curled up. A backpack hung down from his neck, covering him below his belly button.

"Chance," Ana whispered.

Tears spilled out from the corners of her eyes and her hands shook while she wiped them away. He was alive.

"You were in a fight with another shapeshifter," she said, her voice thick with emotion. "I thought you were going to die."

Ana stepped toward him, eager to feel his arms wrap her in a tight embrace. It had been too long since his lips had met hers, although the closer she got, the more wary she became. He made no move to reciprocate her feelings. She paused, waiting for some kind of response. His smile wasn't quite right. It was more of a sneer. Her focus traveled up to his cold eyes and her thoughts turned to the moments before he left her in Mexico. When his icy stare appraised her hungrily.

"You don't need to worry about that." His voice was the same, although something was different. "I can't die."

"What do you mean you can't die?" The question hung in the air and she realized something was very wrong. Besides the fact that this was going very differently than she had imagined, she started to question if the guys had been right about approaching Chance with caution. It was too late now to change her mind. It was all or nothing.

"You'll see."

His lips parted into a wide toothy grin and fur rippled down his arms and chest. A snout protruded from his face and he lowered onto all fours. In seconds, the largest wolf she'd ever seen was licking its lips only ten feet away.

Ana's heartbeat thundered in her ears and she tried to swallow the lump that had formed in her throat. Whoever this man was, he wasn't the person she'd fallen in love with. The sickness had run its course, and the only way to help him now was to get him to allow her to remove the foreign energy from him. To let her heal him. Would his love for her be strong enough so she could convince him? She wasn't sure, but her love for him *was* strong enough to hold her here and try.

Black eyes stared at Ana with a hunger that frightened her. Getting him to cooperate would be near impossible. But that would not stop her. He would give his life for her, and she was willing to do the same for him. He was her mate, her soul mate.

"Chance, I love you and I know you love me," Ana said while she eased backward, taking small steps. "I can help you if you let me. I can try to remove the voices, but you have to let me in."

The wolf mirrored her movement, following her away from the pines. He lowered his head and the hackles on his back rose all the way down to his tail.

Chills ran down Ana's spine and she narrowed her eyes. "I know you're in there. Somewhere."

She stared down the malicious beast, searching for some glimmer of the man she loved, and hoped she was right.

Chance put his weight on his hindquarters and prepared to launch. His ears flattened to his head and his lips lifted to expose his teeth. He leapt straight at Ana and collided into her body, knocking her into the snow. Perched on her chest and abdomen, he dropped his jaw to her shoulder and clamped down.

Ana's scream pierced the silence of the night. She gasped for air and began to whimper. Pain gripped her flesh. Spasms of electricity shot down her arm and into her neck. Her shock gave way to the need to do something. It wasn't in her to fight back, but she had to act. Protect herself. So she did the only thing she could think of.

The pain made it hard to focus, but she tried compartmentalizing it away from her mind. Once she beckoned to the butter-yellow energy that coursed through her body, it seemed to push against the violation of her flesh. A simple mapping came to her and she relaxed into the change. Soon, her body was falling below the snowline and Chance no longer held her between his teeth. She fluttered out from beneath him and took to the skies.

The finch's eyesight was quite different from the owl's and she couldn't see clearly where she was going, so she pointed her body upward and lifted higher. A loud screech came from behind and she knew it had to be Chance. She pumped her wings as fast as she could and tucked in one side, letting herself swoop at a sharp angle to the left. Now she was falling back down to the earth. She could feel gravity pulling her down.

She'd never had this much demanded of her and she'd never had the type of training that Chance received from Balam, but she had to survive. Without knowing how far from the ground she was, she called on the horned owl's mapping and initiated the shift. She could feel the drag of her widening wings as she held them out to slow her decent and then the adjustment in her eyes. Nearly twenty feet from the ground, she held out her wings to their full breadth and kissed the snow with her talons before lifting back into the sky. Her tiny bird heart fluttered noisily in her chest and she moved her head from side to side, searching for Chance.

She flew along the curvature of the ridgeline, a piece of land that was coated white with very few trees interrupting its rise. Ana tilted her head so she could see her shadow rippling across the ground, but then another dark smudge joined hers.

That was when the pain began again. Sharp talons dug in around her torso. She flapped her wings wildly in desperation. Her struggles caused him to loosen his grip and they sank closer to the ground. She twisted her body in an attempt to face him and pecked at his chest. Moments later, they went careening into a snowdrift.

Ana knew she couldn't overpower him, or outfight him. Plus, she didn't want to. This would only fuel his imbalance. It might be risky, but she needed to follow her instincts, so she shifted back to her human form, sat up and waited.

CHAPTER 24

Confusion clouded Chance's mind as he stared out at her from the impact crater they'd made in the snow. Ana's face glowed white in the moonlight and her cheeks flushed red. He tried to remember why he was attacking her, but couldn't.

You want her to kill you. She must kill you.

Different animal shapes flipped through his mind like a picture book, and he tried to settle on one that would frighten her into action. A tiger or lion would scare anyone.

But she would never hurt me. It's not in her nature.

His insides twisted and hatred curdled his thoughts. *Anyone will fight back given the right circumstances.*

While the internal battle waged on, he suddenly realized he was no longer a feathered eagle. He'd shifted back into his human form and was sitting waist deep in fluffy snow.

"Chance."

Ana's thin hand touched the side of his face. He couldn't fight the urge to close his eyes at her caress. *Don't let that siren weaken you. Fight back. Force her hand.* He could barely hold back the tide of aggression and hunger that clawed at the confines of his soul.

"Look at me." Her voice was so full of emotion that the words caught in her throat.

He did as she asked of him and found himself staring into her emerald eyes, transfixed with her natural beauty. It was like he was seeing her for the first time. Did she only just appear? No, he knew he'd been chasing her, but it was like he'd been watching everything happen over the last many hours from a detached vantage point, ever since Mac had helped him push aside the other personalities in his head.

"Ana." He gasped her name and placed his hand on her neck, drawing her close enough so their foreheads touched. "I've missed you."

Her warm breath billowed out and brushed against his skin. Tears welled in her eyes and poured down her quivering cheeks. After weeks of mental exhaustion and torture, he needed to feel safe and loved. Being separated from the one person that made him want to exist was reason alone for going mad, but now, his home, his soul mate, was sharing the same air as him and he wanted to savor the moment.

Chance wrapped his free arm around her bare back and his lips found hers. He tasted her salty tears and kissed her with the hunger of a man frightened of never seeing his love again. When she sputtered for air, he settled for kissing her cheeks, jaw and neck. Her rattling breaths made his heart thunder in his chest and he wanted to wrap her in his arms and never let her go.

"Chance . . . slow down." Ana sighed and the sound made his stomach twist in knots. He didn't want to slow down; he wanted to devour her—he wanted to absorb everything she was. It was his negative reaction to being told to slow down that alerted him that she was right.

"I'm having a hard time controlling myself. I'm not safe to be around—" He let go of her and knotted his hands together, trying to restrain himself from doing anything he'd regret.

"I know, Chance. I know." Her fingers traced along his temple and down to his jaw. "If you let me, I might be able to help you. I've been learning about healing."

"You have? That's great." Chance forced a grin, although inside he was bitter that he'd missed everything she'd experienced. Since he'd known her, what he'd learned just wouldn't have been as exciting without her sharing it with him. He'd been absent in her life and it was painful to think about.

"There are risks, so you have to cooperate and let me in. If you fight me, I could wind up hurting you, and I couldn't live with myself if something like that happened."

Her eyes searched his for comprehension. "Could it hurt you trying to help me?" he asked.

Ana shrugged. "Not really," she said, a little too casually. "It's more of a risk to you than it is to me, but that's why you can't fight me."

As beautiful as she was sitting in the moonlight and as long as it had been since he'd been near her, he could tell the difference between his passion for her and the hunger growing deep within his soul, like a black hole needing more matter to consume. *There's an idea. Let her help you.*

"You'd better hurry, Ana. Being near you makes it hard for me to control myself. I couldn't live with myself if I hurt you either."

Ana leaned in and kissed Chance's cool lips one last time and held his gaze. "I love you."

"I love you, too."

***

She hoped her anxiety wasn't apparent. After weeks and weeks of focusing on learning the techniques that would allow her to cure Chance, he was now here in front of her, ready and willing. Would he be as willing if he knew she'd never actually tried anything quite like it? That it was all more theoretical than practical knowledge?

He touched her cheek with tenderness and waited for her to begin. Of course he'd trust her, but would Lifen be so confident about Ana doing this without enough training? Never mind Lifen—did Ana have the confidence? She'd only just failed to heal the fox. This was so much more complicated, and she'd never had the opportunity to try it yet.

Ana slowed her breathing and began to meditate. She had no room for second-guessing herself. It was time to believe in herself and her abilities. If she didn't put all of herself into this, it wouldn't work. She knew that much.

Yellow energy awakened inside of her and it flowed like blood through every inch of her body. While she released her self-doubt and quieted her mind, focusing on the power around them, the moonlight dimmed in comparison to the glowing motes that swirled up to the sky. She settled her attention on Chance and the radiant glow that emanated from his chest and head.

Ana felt his gaze on her, but she couldn't let him distract her. She looked beyond his hazel eyes and dark features to the energy pattern around his head. Her focus was held for some time. How long, she was unsure. The strain from concentrating made her forehead dew with sweat despite the fact that she was sitting waist high in snow. Similar to when she studied the fox, a crystalline pattern began to become clear. Once it was exposed to her, she exhaled shakily.

Now she needed to find the irregularity in the pattern and light. She didn't have to search long. Almost immediately, she identified a dull shadow that wrapped around his head like a parasite trying to stay hidden. The organic algorithm of his energy moved against the flow in this section and it was obviously what she needed to remove. The only problem was she'd never pulled energy from anyone willingly. There was the first time she meditated with the guys and accidentally consumed their power without knowing it, but she hadn't been aware of what she was doing. That was why Lifen made her learn to focus and control where she absorbed energy from. Maybe it would help her now.

She reached out a fingerling of her own yellow light that extended from her chest to Chance's head. As soon as it connected, Ana became disoriented and nearly forgot what she was doing. She could hear Chance's breathing get scratchy and irregular. Chance. She was doing this for him.

With her power connected to his, she tried pulling at the foreign matter within his head. The opposite action of healing a wound. Like focusing the strong draw of power through a straw, she detached the parasitic shadow away slowly. Unwinding and detangling it was frustrating and hard. She fought the urge to grab his head in her hands because she knew it wouldn't help.

Just as she got closer to plucking away the last threads of shadow, she thought of Lifen's warning—do not absorb the energy or you will poison yourself. It was still gripped to her fingerling of power, hanging between Chance and herself. She would have to pull it free of Chance, swing it away and let go all at once so it could curl up to the sky with the energy motes that surrounded them. Easy.

Ana's concentration broke for a moment when she realized Chance was yelling at her. "Stop, you have to stop. It's too dangerous—you're what he wants."

What was he saying? It didn't make sense to her. She was almost done. All she had to do was break one last point of contact and he'd be healed.

He grabbed her shoulders and shook her violently. Just as she ripped the darkness from his mind, something dense collided into them. A burst of light ruptured the sky above them like a beautiful firework while their bodies went tumbling down the mountain face and loose snow glittered in the air.

CHAPTER 25

This whole time, while he'd battled against the personalities in his head, the dominant voice had remained clear about one thing. Return to Ana. Because his own thoughts were clouded by so many others, and he'd been constantly bombarded with gruesome memories that haunted him, he'd never been able to see clearly. Somehow, the impression of this mysterious man who'd ruined so many lives had been controlling him.

How was that possible?

His body was shaking. Hands gripped his shoulders and Chance woke to Ana's face staring down at him. Her brows were wrinkled and a tear slapped onto his cheek.

"Chance, are you okay? Chance!"

"What happened?" he mumbled.

"I don't know. I pulled away the other energy from your mind just as something crashed into us and we fell down the mountain. Chance, did I hurt you? Can you think? Are you yourself?!"

A red line of blood swept across her jaw and her hair was twisted into a jumble. He knew she was asking how he was, but all he wanted to know was if she was hurt. And most of all, if the mysterious voice in his head had done what he'd set out to accomplish.

Chance sat up and shook off his disorientation. The world flipped once and he dug into the snow with his fists until everything settled.

"I think I'm fine. I haven't heard any of the voices yet, and things are clearer than they've been in a long time. But, Ana—how are you? You don't hear any extra voices, do you?" Chance brushed his fingertips along the injury on her jaw.

Ana winced at his touch and he dropped his hand to her shoulder instead, studying her closely for her reaction to his question. She paused for a moment before she answered. "I haven't heard anything else in my head besides my own freaked-out thoughts. I'm sore from somersaulting down thirty feet, but I'll be fine after I shift."

He smiled. "Those are words I never imagined I'd hear you say."

She blushed and nodded.

Emotion overcame Chance and pain gripped his heart. After all of the agony he'd put her through, how could she ever forgive him?

"Ana, I'm so sorry . . . for everything. It wasn't me that wanted to attack you. And when I left you in Mexico, it was to protect you from myself. I . . ."

Her pale index finger rested on his lips, silencing him. "I know, Chance. I know you love me. You've risked your life for me so many times, it's second nature to you. It was my turn to save you."

"God, I love you." He pulled her into a tight embrace and began kissing her neck. Goosebumps rose on her skin and he nibbled her ear while he drank in her familiar scent. It felt like he'd been to hell and back just to hold her in his arms, but it'd been worth it.

"Ana?" A shout echoed down the mountainside.

Ana pulled away from Chance, her eyes unfocused, and muttered, "Ryan?"

"Who?" Chance asked.

"He's my friend," Ana said. "Another student of Lifen's. C'mon, I'll introduce you." She stopped suddenly and her eyes widened. Her hands fluttered over her chest and she sank further into the snowdrift. Ana called loudly, "Um, maybe we can talk once we're dressed? I'm okay, I swear. Will you follow us back to our stuff?"

His response was soft. "Yeah."

Without looking Chance in the eye, she said with flushed cheeks, "Let's fly back to our bags. I haven't gotten used to talking with naked people yet."

Chance laughed. "Sure."

It was a quick flight back to the opening in the forest where they'd reunited. The whole time, Chance kept his eye on the bird fluttering uneasily beside them.

Chance landed next to his pack and kept his back to Ana so she could slip on her sarong. He pulled on his clothes and pulled out a pair of shorts for Ryan, who stood silently next to him. His long blond hair hung limp and his blue eyes watched Chance as he moved. He was a good-looking guy and Chance couldn't help but feel a little jealous that Ana had been in such close proximity with him for so long.

Once they were both clothed, Chance stretched out his hand to him and introduced himself. "Hey, I'm Chance. You're Ana's friend?"

Ryan nodded and turned back to join Ana ten feet away. She was grinning wildly and overflowing with happiness.

"Ryan, this is my boyfriend, Chance."

"Yeah, I know. He introduced himself." Ryan crossed his arms and grimaced. "What was that back there? I thought you were in danger."

Ana seemed momentarily thrown off by the question and frowned. "Oh, no. Well, I had another dream of Chance and saw he was in a fight. I thought he was in trouble, so I left to look for him. I could see he was in a snowy area, and I hoped my weird telepathy ability would help guide me to him. I wasn't sure if he was close by or not. It turns out he wasn't very far away . . ."

Ryan interrupted her. "You know how worried I was? I was in the kitchen getting a late-night snack when I saw you go up to the driveway and fly off. I tried following you, lost you a few times. I assumed you were being stupid and when I saw your boyfriend here trying to strangle you, I acted. What kind of relationship do you guys have?"

Chance didn't like the tone of his voice or the way he was talking to Ana. She didn't deserve that kind of treatment. "Hey man, back off."

Ana touched her hand to Chance's chest and he immediately calmed down. She then turned to Ryan. "I know what it must have looked like, but he wasn't trying to hurt me. I was able to heal him from the sickness, and that's what I was doing when you saw us. Chance was only trying to protect me. I'm sorry I worried you, Ryan. You're a good friend. Thank you for coming to make sure I was okay."

A cracking branch beyond the trees drew Chance's attention. He craned his neck and modified his eyesight to see into the shadow of the forest. A broad-shouldered man moved between the trunks and Chance recognized him immediately.

Chance held his hand up to greet him and called out, "Hey, Batukhan."

When he got closer to them and emerged from the darkness of the pines, his grimace was illuminated by the moonlight. Hatred filled his eyes as he glared at Chance. Chance took a step back in surprise.

Disjointed memories from hours ago came back to him and he tried to piece everything together. They'd been at his friend Mac's campfire and he'd given Chance some drinks to help him push the voices out of his head. Then things got fuzzy.

He remembered being scorched on the fire. He'd fought Batukhan. Or more accurately, Batukhan had attacked Chance. But that didn't make sense. Based off what he knew of him, he was too similar to Niyol's peaceful nature to do something like that.

"You," Batukhan spat out at Chance.

The other two stopped talking and Chance could feel Ana tense beside him.

"Chance?" Her simple question carried all of her concerns. *Are we safe? Who is this man?*

"Hey, Batukhan," Chance said. "This is my girlfriend Ana and her friend Ryan." Chance turned to Ana. "He helped me stay out of trouble on the way north. He took me to his friend to see if he could help me with the voices. You would not believe what shape Mac took when I first met him."

Chance went from laughter to silence. A vision of Mac's sprawled body beside the fire flashed through his head.

"What did I do?" he asked aloud.

Batukhan's eyes narrowed and his thick hands clapped onto Chance's shoulders. "You have evil within you."

Ana brushed around Chance and laid her fingers on Batukhan's dark skin. The fire within his eyes dulled. "I know he had the sickness," she said with reassurance. "I have removed the dark energy from his head."

"How can you be sure?"

"I haven't heard any of the voices since she did it. I feel like myself again. Batukhan, I remember only bits and pieces from tonight. Is Mac alright? And you, did I hurt you?" A heavy weight sank in his stomach and he couldn't bring himself to meet Batukhan's gaze, afraid of the answer.

"Mac will recover, and so will I, but the world is not safe against the evil that you harbored in your soul. How can we be sure it is gone? How do we know Ana doesn't have it within her now?"

Fear struck Chance again and he worried about her safety. While she was healing him from the sickness, the voice that had grown so close to him, the one that he'd often confused for his own, had revealed its hunger for Ana. It wanted her power and her vessel. Her body.

"I haven't heard anything," Ana said beside him. "I feel fine. Batukhan? I've heard your name before. Is it common?"

Batukhan frowned and let go of Chance. "Not very common anymore."

They were so absorbed with the unfolding drama that they didn't notice the large bird that swooped down into the clearing.

A woman's voice rose above their conversation. "Ana, get away from that snake!"

**

The spite in Lifen's voice made Ana's blood go cold. She knew about the pain and hatred that had hardened her mentor's heart, but didn't want to hear any more.

"Chance is not a snake!" Ana spun around, her eyes wild. "I love him! Don't you talk about him like that! He doesn't have the sickness anymore—I removed the foreign energy. He's himself again!"

Lifen finished wrapping a cloth around her body and stared past Ana, never shifting her focus. "I do not refer to your Chance, but the snake behind you. I told you to never reveal yourself to me ever again!"

Ana sucked in her breath and turned to look at Batukhan and everything made sense. This was Lifen's Batukhan. The man who betrayed her, killed her and made her what she was.

Lifen's naturally crème-colored complexion was violet with fury. While Ana stared at her, Lifen's energy raged like a flame exposed to oxygen.

"Lifen." The expression on Batukhan's face couldn't have been more dislike Lifen's. The love and sorrow displayed there broke Ana's heart. How could a man with such apparent passion for a woman kill her? She felt Chance's fingers weave between hers and she understood. The sickness could make a person do something against their will.

**

281

Ana stood tall beside him. She'd changed so much, grown into the person he'd always seen within her. Her compassion and fortitude had always been evident to him, but now she seemed so sure of herself. The obvious power surging beneath the surface made him proud. She wasn't a weak girl he had to protect anymore. Chance took strength from her while he brushed his thumb along hers and knew he could help his poor travel companion, who looked like the embodiment of misery, standing like a scolded child in the snow. Clips and snips of memories fell into place and, teamed with the heinous voice that had echoed through the hallways of his mind, clarity came to him for the first time in a very long time. Distanced from the pernicious being, he could understand.

"Lifen, Batukhan mentioned you. He told me about the handmaiden he'd fallen in love with. He told me how you'd accepted him and kept his abilities a secret even when he used them to get further in Genghis Khan's army. How he'd changed when he absorbed another's power. He also told me how he'd believed he'd killed you on Khan's orders and then saved your life within an inch of his own. But I know for a fact that that isn't what happened."

Lifen looked at him as if he was speaking gibberish. Ana squeezed his hand and gave him a quizzical expression. The bitter anger Batukhan had aimed at Chance began to crumble, and he seemed to be holding his breath.

"Since the moment I saved Ana's life from my cousin, Markus, who really wasn't such a bad guy," he added, "I've had these voices in my head. And memories of other people's lives. I've relived murder and death. From all of it, they all have something in common and that's one person. I don't know who he was, but he killed almost everyone in my family that were born with powers and he is the one that killed you, Lifen. It wasn't Batukhan."

Lifen's face twisted and contorted. "What? What sort of lies are you making up for your friend? You men are all alike. Thinking you can play with my emotions like this."

Anger bubbled up within him. "I wouldn't make this up." The memory of tasting her blood ran through his mind and he shuddered. "You wouldn't want to see what I've seen, Lifen. None of it is a lie. I have memories of killing you. Killing my own family. I'm stuck with them, so I can imagine how hard it is for you to relive this now, but I swear on Ana's life, I am *not* lying to you!"

"Chance." Ana's warm breath brushed against his ear and she let go of his hand to wrap her arms around his chest.

His anxiety surrounding the memories made his heart race, but Ana's closeness helped to calm his nerves. She was like a security blanket that he wanted to wrap himself up in. Admitting what he'd lived through over the last many weeks was traumatizing. It had been hard to do, and now, all he wanted was to curl up with Ana and hide away.

"I cannot believe it," Lifen said, this time with far less fire and faced Batukhan. "I thought it was you who came to kill us. And I woke to find you beside me . . ."

Batukhan cast Chance a grateful look before stepping toward Lifen. His hands were open as he spoke. "It is hard for me to recall. I think when I gave you all of my power, leaving only a drop for myself, I damaged myself. I can remember being ordered to the capital to destroy the royalty and all remaining Tanguts, but I do know my thoughts fell to you. To warn you to leave. But then I relive the memory of your bloody body lying beside the princess, the agony knowing you were dead and that I would never look upon your beautiful face again. I tried to save you, but I thought I hadn't when I woke in the Mongolian camp weeks later . . . until I saw you again."

Lifen couldn't seem to look at him, her focus always falling somewhere else. Batukhan ventured to take two steps closer to her. "Since that time, I have been unable to shift completely into animal form. I saw it as my punishment for what I had done to you. I have followed your own purpose, trying to help lost shapeshifters to find their way to being good and honorable men. I have tried to make amends and put my life back in balance. Lifen, even if I did not kill you, I did make selfish choices that hurt you and countless others. I did have the imprint of another shifter, the sickness, which I struggled with and I did not fight hard enough against it—if I had, maybe things would be different. I regret every day that I did not go away with you like you pleaded. For so long I have wanted the opportunity to tell you that I am sorry that I hurt you and that I have never stopped loving you."

At that, Lifen looked into his eyes and a tear fell down her cheek. Only the sound of the forest could be heard while everyone stood in silence, waiting for Lifen's reaction.

"I have lived for hundreds of years," Lifen said, "knowing in my heart that men are deceitful and selfish beings. That they do not know true love." She paused to glance at Ana and gave a slight grin, which seemed almost painful. "Recently, I have been shown that I may have been mistaken. It will be hard for me to change after so long, but I am willing to try."

Ana let go of Chance and went to give Lifen a hug. "I'm happy for you."

"Isn't that what I am supposed to say to you?" Lifen said. "You healed Chance of the sickness? Very impressive. I have always been afraid of losing you because you are such an amazing person. It would be a great loss to the world if anything ever happened to you."

"I feel the same way," Chance said.

Ana looked away in embarrassment and then looked around in confusion. "Hey, where'd Ryan go?"

She put her hands to her mouth and called out, "Ryan!"

No answer.

"Ryan was here?" Lifen asked, surprised.

Ana walked over to a pair of shorts lying in the snow and held them up. Ana and Chance stared at each other. Chance rewound time in his mind and played back the sequence of events.

Chance swept his hair out of his eyes. "He ran into us on the mountain when Ana was healing me because he thought I was going to hurt her. There was a burst of light when we fell down the mountain. Then he followed us back here so we could get changed. Batukhan got here, but I don't know what happened to him after that."

The expression on Ana's face pained him. Clearly she cared about Ryan, or she wouldn't have so much pain reflected there.

"Maybe he went back to the house," Ana ventured, but it was obvious she was grasping at straws.

"Yeah, maybe," Chance said, not wanting to crush her hopes, but that old familiar sinking feeling settled in his stomach.

Why couldn't anything stay simple?

Over the last year he'd learned that when in doubt, it was best to assume the worst. If Ryan had absorbed the energy that had been inside Chance, then he was in for a horrific ride. The amount of torture Chance had gone through was enough to scar him for life, seeing so many deaths and being unable to suppress the urge for more power. He'd come too close to hurting innocent people, even his own mother. He didn't know Ryan, but he wouldn't wish it on anyone.

Before they prepared to leave, Chance pulled Ana aside, away from Lifen and Batukhan, who were having their own private conversation. He pulled her close to him and wrapped her in his arms. He listened close for her heartbeat like he used to do, but now she had a strong, steady rhythm. It was reassuring to him.

Ana fidgeted with her purse and lifted her arms over his head. Something cool settled on his chest. He glanced down to see his bear heartline necklace and jade jaguar.

"There," she said. "That's better."

"You kept them?" The love in his heart swelled and he felt so grateful to her.

She lifted her chin to stare into his eyes. Finding the words he wanted to say was hard. His emotions were so close to the surface, so tangible. He was certain Ana completed him and that he completed her, but he didn't know how to tell her, how to ask.

Ana lifted up and brushed her lips against his. Soon he couldn't remember what he'd been worrying about. He kissed her deeply, like this moment was their last, and felt the tip of her tongue sweep against his. The excitement of being with her again gave him butterflies, and he could barely breathe. He was certain he would never survive another separation from her.

He held her face with his hands and pulled away. She made a soft whimper, opened her bleary eyes, and stared hungrily up at him.

"What . . ."

"I want you . . ." he muttered.

She beamed and tried to kiss him again. "Me too."

Chance held her still and tenderly brushed a stray hair from her face. "No, Ana. I want you. Forever."

Ana's forehead crinkled and her green eyes pierced through him questioningly.

"Will you marry me?" Chance whispered against her lips.

The End

ABOUT THE AUTHOR

Natasha Brown lives in Colorado with her family and is busily trying to write the conclusion to The Shapeshifter Chronicles. She enjoys talking with students about the rewards of writing and strives to inspire them to follow their hearts.

To follow Natasha, you can find her here-
Twitter- @writersd3sk
Facebook-https://www.facebook.com/pages/Natasha-Brown/261525383920497
www.theshapeshifterchronicles.com
www.natashasbrown.com
Be sure to sign up for her mailing list so you can be notified of new releases!

9081702R00169

Printed in Great Britain
by Amazon.co.uk, Ltd.,
Marston Gate.